THE
BEACH
BENEATH
THE PAVEMENT

2011 Edition

Roland Denning

'Sous les paves, la plage'
(under the paving stones, the beach)
- Situationist slogan, Paris, May 1968

For Lesley, even though she wished I'd never started

ISBN 978-0-9561535-1-7

Text and cover design © Roland Denning, 2011
This version published in 2011 by Type Of Thing, London
www.TypeOfThing.com

This book is fiction. I made it up.
Any similarities to real characters or events in the world outside,
although likely, are entirely coincidental.

One

'Why all this guilt for being human? As I see it, we're the only species that gives a fuck!'

- Bernard Hawks, The Indicator - 'Notes From The Shadows'

Bernard stood on his own at the bar, a glass of warm white wine in one hand and a joint in the other. He had begun to sway slightly.

The thought struck him that he was about to face a pivotal moment in his life. Possibly the fact he was swaying made him think of pivots, but more likely it was just the drugs. Drugs always gave him the illusion he was about to experience something dramatic or, at the very least, surprising, but the tedium would persist, heartbeat after heartbeat, day after day, as it had done for all of his 42 years. Bernard was now so used to disappointment that he had begun to find it reassuring.

Above the bar, which was not so much a bar as a trestle table covered with a white cloth and massed ranks of wine glasses, was a large, convex mirror. Bernard looked up and saw his face, warped into a bleary pear-shaped balloon, and behind him, very much smaller, the last few occupants draining out of the room like the dregs of an upturned bottle. He expected he would, eventually, turn round, follow and catch the end of what he was sent here to witness. But then, behind him in the mirror, he saw a young woman's face staring at something very intently. Her eyes were improbably blue, the colour of the sea in places he would only ever see in photographs. She looked attractive, allowing for the distortion of the mirror, but the intensity of her expression disturbed him, particularly when he realised she was staring at him. He turned his gaze deep into his wine to avoid further eye contact and wondered what he had written in the past to upset her. His musings were interrupted by a shadow looming over his glass, followed by a voice that was far too close and far too loud.

'Bernard! Get your arse in gear! It's started.'

The voice and the shadow were Casper's and neither was particularly reassuring. Bernard resented Casper; he saw him as a younger, taller and more successful version of himself. It was like he was an awkward, cobbled-together prototype and Casper the simplified production model, the one that actually worked. By the slimmest of margins, Casper arrived on time, Casper got his copy in, Casper returned his calls. By equally slim margins, Bernard didn't. Whatever state Casper was in, he knew he himself would be rather worse. If Casper was a little untidy, Bernard would be totally dishevelled. If Casper had begun to slur his words, Bernard would be on the floor. But when Bernard turned round and looked up to face Casper, something immediately felt wrong: not only was Casper bright eyed and completely sober, he seemed to be wearing some sort of pyjamas.

'Didn't think you'd make it,' said Casper. 'This is just the sort of thing you hate!'

'I'm only sent to things I hate. My function is to irritate the readers.'

'Since you're here, you might as well find out what's actually going on.'

'I know enough. The Tranquility Foundation: yoga and beauty parlours to keep the rich bastards smug and healthy and oblivious to the rest of the world. Anything else?'

'You could do worse than checking into one of their Detox Retreats - look at the state you're in.'

'Since there is nothing here that warrants any further concentration there seems no point in remaining straight. Intellectually and professionally, I have retired for the evening. Possibly for ever.'

'Bollocks you have. Follow me – you need to see this.'

Casper grinned, removed the end of the joint from Bernard's mouth and stamped on it. Then he turned and marched towards the door in a manner that assumed Bernard would follow. Which Bernard did, after glancing back to where the woman in the mirror had been, but the woman had gone. Something very odd was going on tonight and there was something particularly odd about Casper. That born-again smile, the painfully healthy complexion and...

'What the fuck *are* you wearing, Casper?'

'Relaxation outfit, compliments of The Tranquility Foundation. Cross between a kimono and a shell suit. Neat, eh?' Casper pushed open a set of double doors. 'Yeah, all re-cycled fibres, ethically produced and, get this, knife-proof inner lining!'

Bernard stopped. Casper was standing in front of him grinning inanely, holding a door open with one hand, beckoning him through with the other.

'Now who in the world would want to knife you, Casper?'

'That's the genius of the TF, they're pragmatists: Serenity with Security. You can't relax when you're paranoid about being mugged now, can you?'

'They've nobbled you, haven't they?'

'Bernard my friend, the age of cynicism is over. People want something to believe in. Let's go through...'

Bernard stumbled through the doors into a large, dimly lit conference room filled with perfumed smoke and the sort of tinkly, watery music that was designed not to be listened to. Casper steered him forward. Bernard breathed in the air and coughed.

'Smells like someone's been vomiting up lilies,' said Bernard. He took in another deep breath, 'and mangoes, patchouli, cow dung?'

'*Passage to India* – one of Perdita's Scented Candles,' said Casper. 'That's how it all started....'

'Yeah, I know. And now she's going to tell us where it all ends…'

A small, silhouetted female figure moved to the microphone and spoke.

'*Just five years ago today The Tranquility Foundation started from small beginnings, helping people to develop their body and mind through natural means. We believe health and beauty are the essential keys to a better life, and a better life will create a better world…*'

The lights in the room dimmed as bright spotlights faded up on a series of large yellow banners hanging down over the stage: HEALTHY MIND - HEALTHY BODY - HEALTHY COMMUNITY - HEALTHY PLANET. The audience applauded.

'It's the Third Reich on magic mushrooms,' grunted Bernard. Casper ignored him and pointed to the edge of the stage.

'See that guy in the suit, there in the corner?'

'Where?'

'There!… Oh, he's gone. That's JJ, The Pope of PR. When he's involved you know it's going to be big.'

Casper's face was glowing in the light reflected from the banner and he had adopted a sickly, choirboy smile.

'*We have poisoned our bodies and our minds, just as we have poisoned the planet,*' boomed the voice through the PA. '*We have turned our backs on nature…*'

'Nature's brutal, it doesn't give a toss,' said Bernard. 'These people want to be nice but there's nothing nice about Nature…'

'Easy now, Bernard, you've started to rant...' said Casper, his eyes still fixed on the stage. It was actually more of a mumble than a rant but people were beginning to stare at him nevertheless. 'Your problem is that you just don't believe in anything.'

'Dead right I don't. Only mad or dangerous people believe in anything these days: vegans, football fans, suicide bombers...'

'Quiet, now, or you'll get us both thrown out. And you're not making any sense.'

The stage was filling with people, silhouetted against a golden backdrop. They formed a circle, held hands and started to hum together in a low, ominous drone.

'Casper, I don't think I can take much more of this.'

'See if this helps.'

Casper, who was now standing directly behind Bernard, grasped the back of his neck very firmly in a way that defied any struggle to escape. Bernard assumed Casper had chosen this moment to fulfil a long held desire to choke him. Then, as if that wasn't enough, Casper whispered in a voice that slithered into Bernard's ear like a wanton tongue. Bernard shivered.

'You see all this sarcastic, self-destructive stuff you write, Bernie, you degenerate twat, this 'where are we going to put the bomb today' riff, they don't want it any more. They don't think it's funny. Like that 'Ten Things I Love About Terrorists' piece…'

'Five things and it was ironic, Casper. Mostly.' Bernard felt the sweat on his cheeks bubbling under the heat of Casper's breath as he massaged his neck. 'I think you're jealous of my readers.'

'Shush now, Bernie, you know I'm just trying to help. You've had a good run, but the tide's turned. Be careful. You're obsolete…' Casper pressed his two thumbs just below the back of Bernard's neck making a loud click. 'There! That should have released some of the negative energy!'

'Fuck, that hurt!' exclaimed Bernard. He turned round to protest, or possibly to slap Casper, but Casper had his finger pressed to his lips, urging him to be quiet. Then with both hands he turned Bernard's head firmly round to face the stage.

'Look at the future, Bernie.'

From the ceiling a projection screen unfurled across the whole width of the room. The Tranquility Foundation's logo, a pastel yin-yang symbol, spun out to the corners of the screen and dissolved into aerial shots of the English countryside.

'…building on our network of local beauty and holistic therapy centres, we opened the first of our Serenity Retreats, protected by the latest advances in security technology, 24 hour community wardens…'

'Jesus Christ!' said Bernard. 'They're building fucking concentration camps!'

'Keep your voice down, there's a pair of very serious looking guys in the corner fixing you.'

Bernard looked to where Casper was nodding. Two heavy set men in padded black judo suits and wraparound sunglasses were making their way towards him.

'Let's go,' said Casper, swiftly manoeuvring Bernard through the crowd, down a corridor, through the crash bars of an emergency exit and out into the street. Bernard released a vast sigh that had been waiting in his lungs for hours.

'Thank God we're out of that. Fancy a drink?'

Bernard turned to Casper but Casper was not there. He was looking straight into the wide eyes of a woman, the one who had been staring at him in the mirror. She seemed older than she did before, thirties rather than twenties, and there was a network of tiny, wavy lines around those aquamarine eyes, like wrinkles in the sand seen from far above. It was actually quite a delicate face but her hair was thick and wild and gathered together in bunches. She wore a red linen shift dress, which sheathed a neat, almost boy-like figure.

'You're Bernard Hawks, who writes that column in *The Indicator*?'

Here we go… thought Bernard. He nodded half-heartedly, still slightly stunned by Casper's abrupt disappearance.

'You see through it all, don't you, all the crap?'

Now she looked younger again, perhaps she was really just a kid after all, but one who had lived hard in the sun. He couldn't take his eyes off her.

'Do I?'

'Oh yes, I read everything you write. You're some sort of genius… are you OK?'

'It's nothing – I was with someone, then he disappeared.'

'That tall guy - your friend?'

'Not anymore. Don't think he ever was, come to think of it.'

'He went off with the bouncers… he'll be all right.'

'Sorry - did I hear you call me a genius just then?'

'Yes! Your bomb thing, it's brilliant!'

She said this with just a little too much fervour.

'It's a metaphor,' said Bernard.

'Of course.' And then she seemed to wink at him. Or was it just a nervous tick? 'I'm Animal.'

'You're an animal?'

'It was Annabel once, but everyone calls me Animal now.' A huge grin broke like a wave across her face.

Bernard found himself grinning too. For a moment he was happy to stand there and imagine the two of them naked and entwined on some tropical lagoon, sinking back into the bluest of pools, basking in the radiant glow of this strange woman's admiration.

And that was when the bomb went off.

Bernard had never heard anything so loud, so deep. It was as if his head burst open as the blast shot through him, scooping up his body and flinging it down on to the pavement. Then more sounds: a chorus of shattering glass, the yelps and wails of alarms and, just a second or two after, the desperate cries of humans and animals: first the babies, followed by the dogs, the women and the men. He opened his eyes and saw layers of smoke - grey, then black, then brown, then orange claws of flames grasping at the sky. As dust began to rain down, he struggled to his feet. Animal was standing in front of him looking towards the end of the street. Beyond her, in the distance, people were running with arms waving, running towards them, running in all directions. He felt he had been woken suddenly out of a very deep sleep and had not the faintest idea where or who he was, followed closely by a profound feeling that the world was out of control and nothing would be the same again.

'You knew! You knew about the bomb!' screamed Animal. 'It was in your last column. It was your idea! And you actually did it!'

'You're mad! I mean, you don't seriously think I want to hurt people, do you?'

Animal had begun to look around excitedly. 'I think we should get out of here. I think we'd better hide.'

'Hide?'

'I know where to go. Help me with this.'

She ran a few steps forward to a manhole on the pavement, knelt down and took two slender, hammer-like objects out of a shoulder bag. She inserted the T-shaped head of each into slots on opposite sides of the manhole cover.

'What the hell are you doing?' said Bernard.

'Don't look so freaked. Just help me lift this.'

Bernard hesitated.

'Bernard, come on! We do this all the time!'

He knelt down and together they lifted the cover up and pulled it to one side. She threw him a torch and began to climb down into the ground. Bernard, shaking and very confused, followed.

Two

'At least no one accuses suicide bombers of lacking a purpose.'
Bernard Hawks, The Indicator - '5 Things I Love About Terrorists'

Bernard had no idea how long he had been following Animal through the cramped tunnels but it was long enough to sober him up. That and the shock of the bomb meant he was now reeling with unwelcome lucidity. And with it came that voice in his head, no longer shackled by drugs and alcohol, that questioned everything he did.

'Come on Bernard, I shouldn't think many actually died,' said Animal.

'I'm glad to see there's some compassion left in the world,' muttered Bernard.

'Anyway, who cares? It was only an ad agency - they kill people every day with their lies. They're first on the list, just like you said!'

'It was a metaphor...'

'Not any more it's not.'

'Just a sodding coincidence, all right?'

'But you knew something was going to happen tonight, didn't you? And anyway, like *everything's* a coincidence.'

She's a very disturbed woman, said the voice in Bernard's head, *and it's time to get the hell out of here.*

But Bernard had nowhere to go but follow the slim red figure in front in the torch beam. Besides, studying the shape of her hips as they touched the sides of her dress and the smooth bare legs beneath them took his mind off the bomb.

'What are these tunnels?'

'Utility tunnels. London's riddled with them. They follow all the cables and the pipes right across the city,' said Animal. 'What'ya reckon, Bernard, a good place to plant some serious bombs?'

'Look, I'm just a writer...'

'Loosen up, we're not planting any bombs tonight. We'll be home soon.'

'And where exactly are we going?'

'We're going to your place.'

'You want to go to my place?' *Definitely mad.*

'Well, there are some very good reasons for not going to mine.'

She turned round and smiled at Bernard in the light of his torch beam. Bernard shone the torch at his own face and smiled back.

A couple of hours later, Bernard found himself outside the front door of his house with Animal tapping her feet impatiently as he fumbled with the lock. A voice came out of the shadows. A slow, melancholy male voice with a slight trace of a West Country accent.

'Hello Bernard.'

'Bob - sorry mate, in a bit of a rush at the moment.'

A tall man in a well worn denim jacket stepped forward. He had a pale horse-like face, sad weary eyes, straggly yellowed-grey hair and a matching beard.

'You owe me money, Bernard. Just letting you know. Not a threat or anything like that. Just a gentle reminder.'

'Tomorrow. Come back tomorrow.'

'All right Bernard, since it's you. Tomorrow.'

The man shuffled back into the shadows.

'Who was that?' said Animal.

'Just Bob. Bob the Dealer. He's harmless, really. Just crap at his job.'

Bernard opened the front door. Once inside he pushed the round white button that dispensed a minute and a quarter of electric light. As they climbed the stairs he saw Animal's nostrils twitch in response to the ancient scents of gas, cabbage and stew long embedded in the house. The light gave up just before they reached his flat on the top floor. The door adjacent to Bernard's opened, releasing a thin shaft of light and a glimpse of a round sallow face with thick framed glasses.

'Oops! Sorry mate!' said the face, hastily shutting the door again.

'Dillwyn, my neighbour,' muttered Bernard. 'Keep out of his way. He'll deduce a whole new conspiracy from the sound of your footsteps. He's always a little distraught.'

'Why?' asked Animal.

'I don't know... he's just sort of... Welsh...'

Opening the door to Bernard's flat involved a complex series of manoeuvres of alternately pushing and pulling the door and key. When the lock eventually yielded, it took all his weight to push open the door against a substantial wedge of junk mail. He reached round to the switch and a feeble yellow light seeped out of a battered paper globe hanging from the ceiling.

Animal stood silent in the doorway, breathing in the vapours from countless abandoned take-away cartons, discarded socks and overflowing ashtrays for what seemed like a very long time.

'You live alone, don't you?'

Bernard nodded. 'I did have a cat, but she ran away.'

He was acutely aware as he watched Animal's eyes scan the room that coming back here was a very bad idea indeed. Her gaze fell on his gleaming Cydrax computer, a silver, horizontal pear-shaped pod that emanated a gently pulsating green glow, like some alien brain from a 50's sci-fi movie. She sat down on the desk next to the computer and pointed at it.

'Is this where you write?'

Bernard nodded again, rather proud of the only object in his flat that was clean, modern and working. Animal shook her head.

'You're going to get rid of it, aren't you?'

'What?' said Bernard.

'Oh, I've been there too, Bernard, but they're really just another drug. It's got to go. And all the other machines. I know you think the same, really. I read that piece you wrote the other week – *I'm going to upgrade my computer with a sledgehammer.*'

'Yeah, well…'

'And they're full of viruses. You're bound to get infected.'

'Is that a joke?'

She shook her head again and prodded the computer. 'Viruses are just information that knows how to reproduce. Some mutate into ideas. Then our brains get choked with them. Too much information.' She looked up at Bernard and laughed.

Here he was in the unprecedented position of being sober and alone in his flat with a woman who was not only attractive but who actually seemed to like him. He looked at this crazy, hippie anarchist sitting on his desk and knew the last thing he should do was to get involved but the voice in his head, not known for its consistency, had other ideas: *Don't you remember? Crazy hippie girls are spectacular in bed!*

Take it easy, don't rush. He walked over to the sofa, sat down, folded his arms and smiled. Animal moved her legs slightly apart allowing a fold of her red dress to curve gently between her thighs.

'You want to fuck me, don't you?' she said, brightly.

Bernard shuddered as a juvenile grin shot across his face.

'We will, of course,' continued Animal, 'but not tonight. It wouldn't be right tonight.'

Bernard's grin quivered. 'Sure. Fancy a glass of wine? Or a smoke? Or a line?'

'Drugs, Bernard! We don't need them any more, do we? We're past all that.'

'Yeah, right. Way past.'

'At first they help, help you cut through the noise, see things as they are, but then they just add to it, you know?' Animal jumped off the desk and sat down on the arm of the sofa. 'Come on, Bernard, we have to see beyond simple cause and effect! Once you do that the system falls apart, right?'

'I guess...'

You were right the first time, said the voice in Bernard's head, *and she's crazy enough to think you're as crazy as she is.*

'And the machines. All of them. And the Internet. We've got to let go,' said Animal, nodding at the Cydrax.

'I like my computer,' said Bernard quietly. Animal stared at him and he felt himself melting under the twin blue flames of her eyes.

'People think that computers are becoming more like us, but it's the other way round – we're becoming more like them. Machines like to control. Watch people when they're at their computers, really watch them, then you'll see the keys move under their fingers, sucking at their fingertips. The keys move and the fingers follow.'

She saw the expression on Bernard's face and leant forward until their noses almost touched.

'It's a metaphor, Bernard!'

And then she laughed. It wasn't a mad laugh, it was a sane and joyful laugh. He wanted to believe she was just a clever, eccentric, beautiful young woman with a wicked sense of humour. And just for the moment, believing wasn't really that difficult.

'The lighting in here's crap,' said Animal. 'Do you mind if I do something about it?'

Bernard shrugged.

Animal turned off the overhead light. In the darkness that followed there was a rustling sound and the click of a lighter, then a glow appeared in a glass jar on Bernard's desk.

'It's a *Perdita's Scented Candle*. I nicked it from the Tranquility gig.'

The glow got brighter and a rather sickly scent of suntan lotion, fried olive oil, fish, cheap brandy and continental cigarettes began to fill the air. Bernard peered at the label on the bottom of the candle on which were printed the words: *Spanish Holiday No.1*.

'So the stuff I write,' said Bernard watching the candle flame flicker in Animal's eyes, 'what do you like about it?'

Animal shrugged. 'I guess 'cause you know the world's fucked...'

'Yes, but...'

'... and we've got to clear all the crap, all the technologies of control, get ready for the new world. We can help each other do it!'

Easy now, Bernard.

'Look, maybe you got me wrong... I mean, do you know anything about this bomb?'

Animal looked at him very seriously. 'Do I really look like someone who wants to plant bombs?'

Bernard shook his head. She smiled gently. He examined her face very closely. Her eyes looked even bluer against the yellow glow of the candle and there was a softness, a sweetness in her face. Bernard was filled with a strange feeling of tenderness and, within that, something dark and savage. It was like he was fondling a fluffy kitten that had just eaten a bowl of Semtex.

'Well, it would be a fucking great disguise then, wouldn't it!' exclaimed Animal.

You see? Just stay well away!

'You'll help me, won't you, Bernard?' breathed Animal.

Like fuck you will.

'Yeah... of course,' replied Bernard, as he felt an involuntary smile forming on his face.

There was a knock on the door.

'I can't be seen here,' whispered Animal. 'Is there anywhere I can hide?'

'Hide? Well, only the bathroom.'

Bernard waited until she had closed the bathroom behind her. Then he turned round, put the chain on the front door and opened it an inch. There was a glint of spectacles. It was Dillwyn.

'Has she gone now, that girl?'

Bernard nodded.

'Can I come in, then?'

'No.'

'I wanted to tell you before, but I thought it'd better be private, see. There's two men been looking for you. Big blokes, they were. Do you think they might have something to do with the bomb?'

'The bomb?'

'Oh didn't you hear about the bomb? Terrible it was, miracle more didn't get hurt. All those bastards, you see.'

'Of course. Who do you mean?'

'Well, it's the government, isn't it? They're the ones that's puts the bombs down just to scare us so they can introduce more repressive measures. Everyone knows that. Anyway, just thought you'd like to know. I'll go now, then.'

Bernard pulled the door tight shut, then walked over to the bathroom and knocked gently.

'It's all right, he's gone.'

Bernard waited then knocked again vigourously. There was no reply.

She's probably dead and they'll all think you've killed her, said the voice, which had a penchant for melodrama.

Bernard turned the handle and the bathroom door swung open. He looked into the dark interior and screamed as he caught the glint of Animal's blue eyes lying in the basin, her head severed from her body.

He pulled the light cord and the bare bulb swinging from the ceiling revealed the stark truth. There was no head, no body, no Animal, just her eyes beside the taps, staring up at him. But they weren't even eyes, just two round slithers of blue glass. Contact lenses. And above them, a wide open window and a grubby plastic curtain blowing in the breeze.

'Oh fuck,' said Bernard.

Three

'When does diversity become perversity?'
- *Inspector Frank Pitmarsh, Metropolitan Police*

It was almost noon when Bernard opened the living room curtains. He closed them again immediately. He could just about cope with daylight but not the disturbingly intense sun streaming in backlighting every speck of dust in the air.

The previous day had transformed him, in a few moments, into a prophet, a terrorist or a madman. Possibly all three. Then burning in the back of his brain was the memory of a crazy blue-eyed woman in a red dress who wasn't blue-eyed at all who thought he was some sort of genius. It was a lot to handle, first thing in the afternoon. And Bernard had work to do; it was time for his readers to find out the truth about the Tranquility Foundation.

Given that Bernard was, by profession, a writer, it was astonishing what lengths he would go to not to write. When he did not write, he got depressed, and when he was depressed, he could not write. When it came to not-writing, Bernard was an un-literary giant, a genius at discovering new not-writing activities. And if ever his ability to not-write was fading, if ever he was threatened by a shimmer of inspiration, he could always rely on his gleaming Cydrax computer to delay the process indefinitely. When he did eventually write he could spend hours spell-checking, word counting, repaginating and reformatting. And that was on a good day. Today, Bernard had ground to an unassailable halt and might have stayed in his chair until he decomposed if it was not for an insistent knocking on his door. At first he ignored it, assuming it was Dillwyn desperate to share his latest glum fixation, but this knocking continued and became a hammering, and Dillwyn's always petered out after two or three minutes.

When Bernard finally opened the door he was greeted with a grinning, slightly stout figure in a cheap blazer and beige trousers. A little too formal to be a double glazing salesman, a little too casual to be flogging religion. Then he saw the shoes: well polished, black shoes with an archaic and slightly menacing solidity. It was beyond doubt - this man was a copper.

'Mr. Bernard Hawks, the journalist?'

Bernard nodded.

'An interesting piece you wrote last week about a bomb in an advertising agency.'

'I happened to write, hypothetically, that if I had a mission to destroy Western Capitalism, I'd start...'

'And just after you happened to write it, a bomb just happened to go off, exactly where you suggested. Most intriguing. May I come in?'

Bernard scowled. The policeman moved forward, very briefly flourishing an open wallet with some sort of identity card inside.

'Look, before you go any further,' said Bernard, 'you must realise it's a coincidence...'

'Of course, Mr. Hawks. You are a writer. Consequently, what you write is simply the product of your enviable powers of imagination. The force has a lot of respect for the creative community. Studies show what the public want is empathy.'

'Not less crime? Or less policemen?'

'There will always be policemen, just as there will always be crime, but we have been instructed to make the whole process, what are those dreadful phrases? *User friendly... people centred...*' He smiled, lowered his voice and moved closer. 'Strictly speaking, I probably shouldn't even really call myself a policeman, Mr. Hawks. Or may I call you Bernard? How about a Community Liaison Representative for the Quality-of-Life Monitoring Team? I'm told the term 'policeman' has too many negative connotations... Don't worry, Bernard. Just my little joke. I'm still just a humble, old-fashioned copper.' As he said this he put his thumbs in his pocket and did a swift little knees-bend, the music hall policeman's curtsy. 'May I sit down?'

Without waiting for an answer, the policeman wrenched open the curtains and sat down on one of Bernard's two kitchen chairs, his back to the window. Bernard sat down on the other, screwing up his eyes as the sunlight hit his face. For a brief moment, as the waves of sun-lit dust circled around the policeman, Bernard had the strange impression that the copper's head was belching smoke as if it was about to combust. He looked down and noticed the policeman had unusually short legs. Only the tips of his shiny black shoes were actually touching the floor.

'Of course, far be it for me to suggest you are directly linked to the event...'

'As I said, it was a coincidence. Something I made up. A satirical fantasy, if you like...'

'Inspiration! A wonderful thing, isn't it? Blowing up an advertising agency... did that come out of the dark and mysterious depths of your imagination? Plucked out of the collective unconscious? Or something you heard, somewhere, from one of your bohemian underdog friends? I am sure you have some wonderful conversations. At your dinner parties, over cocktails, at all those splendid openings and closings...'

The policeman rocked back in his chair and closed his eyes as if dreaming about the exotic world of Bernard Hawks. Then, woken abruptly from this reverie, he opened his eyes, gripped the arms of the chair and leaned forward so his feet touched the ground and the back legs of the chair raised up. With remarkable alacrity, chair still attached, he shuffled over to Bernard until their knees almost touched. He leant into Bernard and grasped his shoulder firmly with his right hand.

'Myself and my colleagues have always taken a keen interest in your career. We are, you could say, your closest followers - ever since you wrote that amusing story a year ago about putting the bomb in police headquarters. How did it begin? Something about *falling asleep to the squeals of burning piggies and waking up to the smell of crispy bacon*... You can imagine how the lads at the station loved that!'

'You're quoting me out of context. And it was a serious piece about deaths in police custody...'

Bernard became acutely aware of the tightness of the policeman's collar and the proximity of the rolls of glistening, bristly, pink flesh that oozed out of it.

'Of course, Bernard. Although, now please don't be offended, some of my more literary colleagues did wonder if the porcine metaphor has not become, well, a little bit of a cliché? Please tell me, and be honest now, can you really detect any element of the hog in my persona?'

The policeman opened the palm of his left hand with a wide-eyed expression as if to indicate he had nothing to hide. The other hand was now squeezing Bernard's shoulder very hard indeed. Bernard shook his head, despite the fact that those shiny black shoes had begun to jiggle frantically back and forth, evoking a distinct sense of trotter.

'Of course not. But we live in a free society Bernard, and let no one say we, in the force, or rather, *on the team*, lack a sense of humour!' The policeman let out a squeal of laughter and jumped out of his chair. 'Oh, I know you didn't plant the bomb. You're not the type, you're a gentleman. Yes, a man far too gentle to plant a bomb!' The policeman's small black eyes gleamed. 'Perhaps too gentle to defend his home, even when surrounded by people of every possible hue and persuasion, people dedicated to destroying everything you and I believe in! But,' he sighed, moving closer, 'I'm a professional. I do what I'm told with pride.' He tapped Bernard on the knee. 'Our policy is to support diversity!' His voice became softer again. 'But I wonder sometimes, Bernard, between you and me, is it possible to get too diverse? When does diverse become perverse? Now there's a thought! That's why I see my job as sniffing out the rotten apples, the fanatics in the woodpile... purging the weeds so a thousand flowers can bloom...'

The policeman made his way to the door. Then, as if a thought had just occurred to him, he turned round to face Bernard. 'Every heard of a group called the Primitive Front? Neo-Luddites, I think you'd call them. One of the Post-Rational cults. Nasty bunch. Very destructive. Wouldn't want a sensitive man like you to get mixed up with them.'

He stared very intently at Bernard then leaned right in to him. His breath smelt of sour tea, peppermints and decay. 'Ring no bells? Never mind. Here's my card. Call me if you remember anything. Or drop in to our drop-in centre and have a cappuccino.'

The policeman winked and left, slamming the door loudly behind him. Bernard looked at the crudely printed business card left in his hand.

```
Inspector Pitmarsh. Community Liaison.
'Your Security is our Passion'
```

There was only a brief pause before there was a knock on the door again, this time a rather more hesitant knock.

'Piss off,' said Bernard.

'It's only me,' said a thin Welsh voice.

'Still piss off.'

'But it's ree-ely important.'

Bernard opened the door an inch.

'Hello Bernard. Last night, that girl I saw you with... I'm sure I recognise her from somewhere...'

'Please, just forget you ever saw her.'

'Well, I dunno, Bernard. What if the police come round here, asking questions, you want me to lie, is it?'

'Of course I do.'

'Oh. Well, see's you're my neighbour, I'll help you out.'

'Thanks.'

Bernard began to close the door on Dillwyn's foot.

'So what are you doing now, then?' said Dillwyn, pushing against the door. 'I needs to talk to you.'

'Err no... I've got work to do. A lot of work.'

'It's about that girl.'

'You'd said you'd forget you ever saw her.'

'You see I think I knows who she is, Bernard. I think I knows where she goes. Tomorrow night I want to take you somewhere. Sort of a club, like. Somewhere she might hang out. Will you come?'

Four

'Isn't it the search for inner calm the ultimate form of one-upmanship?'
        Bernard Hawks, The Indicator - 'Notes From The Shadows'

Casper must know something, thought Bernard as he begrudgingly made his way to the gym at 8 o'clock the next morning. *Casper was there when Animal appeared, Casper was there just before the bomb went off. And Casper always knows everything. At least he thinks he does.*

The air in the gym was heavy with sweat, grunts and testosterone. Bernard had not been inside a gym since he'd left school and the atmosphere of obsessive self-improvement aggravated his nagging sense of impending doom. He was here because Casper insisted the only time he had to talk was during his early morning work-out. Already Bernard wanted to go back home to bed.

'This bomb business, Casper. I've been thinking. Maybe someone's trying to set me up. Like they planted that bomb with the sole intention of landing me in the shit.'

Casper was strapped into a heavily engineered contraption of grey steel and black leather, pulling levers back and forwards like some robotic galley slave. Bernard suspected it was designed to stretch Casper a little taller and pump up his ego at the same time. Casper grunted out his reply between thrusts.

'Now Bernard, does that seem feasible? Not that I would suggest... not that many people actually *like* you... but surely no one takes you seriously enough to... to actually go to elaborate lengths to destroy you?'

'Thanks for those reassuring words, but it's not funny. This copper came to see me. Seemed convinced I've got inside information on the bombers because I wrote about it the week before.'

'Makes sense... perhaps you've got clairvoyant powers...'

'Yeah, I knew you were going to say that. Come on Casper, this is serious. What do I do?'

'Nothing.... on the basis this is a coincidence...'

'Which it is.'

Casper stopped. He leant forward to talk allowing a generous measure of hot sweat to splash into Bernard's eyes.

'Well, if you're entirely innocent then everyone will forget about it and your few minutes of fame will be over. If, on the other hand, you're not, I suggest you find yourself a very good lawyer and someone to feed your cat for the next twenty years.'

Casper got up off the machine and began to wipe his face and arms with a small black towel.

'My cat, for your information, ran away a month ago,' said Bernard.

'I don't blame it. They're clean animals.'

'There's something else too. There was this woman I met at the Tranquility Foundation gig...'

'Red dress, blue eyes?'

'You know her?'

'No, just noticed she looked decidedly crazy. I thought she might be your type.'

'My type? I've been out with lot of very sane and attractive women.'

Casper looked Bernard up and down with an expression of feigned disbelief. 'Pity the sane ones weren't attractive and the attractive ones weren't sane.'

'She knew everything about all the bomb stuff I've been writing... and she said I was a genius.'

'Plum crazy. Sounds dangerous.'

'Know anything about her?'

'Nothing at all. Wait here. I'll be back in a minute.'

Casper threw Bernard his damp towel and disappeared behind a stainless steel door. Bernard dropped the towel on the floor with disgust. Casper reappeared moments later in a black jogging suit, his glossy dark hair immaculately combed.

'So what did this policeman who came to see you want?'

'I don't know. Muttered something about post-rational cults and the Primitive Front. Mean anything to you?'

'Well it's rumoured they were behind the bomb. These difficult times create a lot of confused people, Bernard. Some even claim that irrational violence is, in itself, an act of liberation. What did this policeman think you knew?'

'Hard to tell. He was a smarmy git - pretended to be understanding and sensitive but clearly wanted me hanged, drawn and quartered.'

Casper started towards the exit and Bernard followed. 'Well, the police are going through many changes, responding to public criticism, trying out new initiatives - they've even been doing workshops with the Tranquility Foundation.'

'Jesus Christ! Have those bastards got their fingers in everything?'

Casper strode into the street. He had substantially longer legs than Bernard, so Bernard took two and a half paces to every two of Casper's, forcing him into an awkward, lop-sided hobble.

'You don't get it, do you?' said Casper. 'The TF are a positive force for change. Unlike you, Bernie, rotting away in your stinking garret.'

'I notice you've got their logo on your sweatshirt and your towel. And you're grinning like a door-to-door evangelist.'

'And you look like shit. Did I mention that? You know what I think you should do? Check into the TF Serenity Retreat. I've got a free Press Pass I can give you – rare items at the moment – seeing they're fully booked, what with all the bombs and stuff...'

'Yeah, they must be loving it.'

'...I can't use it, far too much on. So why don't you take it! Clean yourself up, calm down, sort your head out!'

'Apart from the fact I'd rather gouge my own eyes out with a plastic fork, they wouldn't have me, would they? Not after what I just wrote about that last gig.'

'Sure, the 'concentration camp' line didn't go down too well, but they'll get over it because there's a great story here - Britain's most cynical journalist goes to a TF retreat and is transformed into a human being!'

'And what if I'm not? What if I trash it?'

'Even better. If you dump a full load of your bile on it there are thousands of readers who will think it must be good just because Bernard Hawks loathes it. You don't think you're kept in work because anybody actually agrees with you, do you? But forget it, it was just a thought. I need to start jogging now, keep up with me if you can. So what are you writing about next, Bernard?'

'I dunno. There's something going on here and I need to get to the bottom of it.'

'Do yourself a favour, write something totally innocuous for once, a cookery column or countryside notes. Forget the bombs. And think seriously about the Tranquility Foundation. You should join. Invest in the future.'

Bernard shrugged as he broke in to a reluctant trot to keep up with Casper. 'Casper, one more thing. The Primitive Front - who actually are they? You don't think that girl...'

Bernard stopped to catch his breath. Casper continued on.

'Bernard, time you did your own research, mate.'

'Casper...'

But Casper was shrinking into the horizon. Bernard sat down on the pavement, exhausted, and put his head between his knees. As he gradually regained his breath he heard a voice coming from somewhere high above him.

'Bernard, sorry to bother you, but you still owe me.'

He looked up into the sad, watery eyes of Bob the Dealer.

'Just waiting for my paycheque to clear, honest, Bob.'

Bob nodded. 'You see Bernard, these are not good times for me. My regular clients are getting healthy, giving up. Getting new lives.'

'What, all of them?'

Bob thought for a moment. 'No, about half of them.' He paused again. 'The rest are dying. You're about the only regular I got left.'

'Next week. I promise, Bob.'

Bob slowly nodded his head again then wandered away.

Five

'Paranoia is only another form of awareness and awareness is only another form of love.'

- Charles Manson

It was a mild evening but Dillwyn was wrapped tight in a battered beige raincoat with the collar turned up, a knitted woollen hat covering the top of his head. He insisted on leading the way even though they kept going back on themselves; after an hour they had progressed less than a mile.

'Do you actually know where we're going?' asked Bernard.

'I'm dodging the security cameras. Or if I can't dodge 'em, make 'em think we're going in circles. Gets them really confused,' said Dillwyn with his hand in front of his face. 'And don't let them see your mouth when you're talking. I think they've learnt to lip read. It's all about profiling, you see, Bernard. It's like there's a record of everything we buy and do, everywhere we go and everything we think, and somewhere they're building this little model of us, and when it's finished, we'll disappear, like voodoo, you see!'

'Do you actually believe all this stuff, Dillwyn?'

'Vigilance, Bernard! It's very important! Have you heard of induction, like?'

'Something they do to you when you join an organisation? Not that I've ever...'

'Exactly! That's when they put their ideas in you! But it's also what happens when you put two electrical cables together. One induces a current in another, even if they don't touch. Now, look at all the cables running under the street, and all the radio waves in the air, then think of all the little electric currents in your brain... are you with me?'

Bernard wasn't. His mind was drifting far away from Dillwyn's theories.

'Animal – that woman you saw come into my flat – you said you recognised her?'

Dillwyn stopped and looked all around before he spoke softly. 'Did she give you any clues? What she belonged to, like?'

'Err, no. She didn't like machines and she said something about seeing beyond cause and effect.'

'There you go, see! Just what I thought!' Dillwyn turned round and continued walking.

'Well, tell me then!' shouted Bernard. 'Who or what the fuck is she?'

'Keep your voice down! You'll find out when we get there. Anyway, control you see. Like with the drugs.'

'The drugs?'

'Well, by the looks of you I reckon you've done drugs and stuff - and I bet you find that your memory isn't what it used to be.'

'I suppose things I did a while ago are a little vague... even yesterday...'

'And before you did drugs?'

'Can't remember.'

'See! But it's not the drugs – it's the stuff they puts *in* the drugs to make you forget things. To keep you passive!'

'The crack heads that run up and down my street at night don't seem too passive.'

'Different tactic. They're the ones they're killing off, isn't it? They're burning them up like bluebottles under a flyspray. *Zzzzzzzz* !' In a curiously understated way Dillwyn mimed a dying fly spinning on its back as best he could without actually lying down on the pavement.

'And who exactly is *they*?'

'Oh, I don't have to tell you that, Bernard. I've read your column. I knows you understand, really. They connect, you see, all these things.'

'Look, Dillwyn, with respect, this does seem to assume there are people in control who actually know what they're doing, and, as far as I'm concerned, there's little evidence of that.'

'There's some people, some very clever people involved. Experts in manipulation. I think you should write about them! That's why we're going to this lecture, see.'

'We're going to a lecture, are we? And what gives you the idea that Animal will be there?'

Dillwyn stopped again and turned round to face Bernard. 'There are dark forces stirring underneath. There's this guy called JJ, famous a long time ago, now he's come back and he's working behind the scenes.'

'And...?'

'I think that girl's mixed up in it, somehow. Not sure what side she's on yet, to be honest... There you go, see, we're here! Wasn't too bad really, was it?'

Dillwyn pointed to a shop front where a line of people were making their way down to a basement. At the entrance was a placard which read: *Owsley's Floor - A space dedicated to Neo-Psychedelic Enquiry. Tonight: Post-Credibility Special.*

'What the hell is Post-Credibility?'

'Come on, Bernard, you should know all this. Like, no one believes adverts any more but they carry on buying the stuff and they certainly don't believe in the government, but it's still there, isn't it?'

24

'And someone's worked out why, have they?'

'We'll see, won't we! And if we get separated, I'll meet you out here at the end of the show. All right?'

Bernard and Dillwyn entered Owsley's Floor and descended into another era. In a damp, dark brown basement forty or so people were packed tight on rows of metal chairs. Mostly in their twenties, they were wearing a rather quaint notion of psychedelic fashion; the sort of clothes a mother might have bought a spoilt son in 1968, clothes destined to lie unworn at the bottom of the wardrobe. There were also a few who had actually lived through the sixties, some with long grey hair, bald crowns and multi-coloured jumpers, others dressed in black with close-cropped silver hair.

Bernard sat down as the act on stage was just finishing. In front of a tinsel curtain, two young men in purple velvet suits and a woman in a short Indian print frock bowed to polite applause. All had third eyes painted on their foreheads. A man with floppy hair and a neat tie-dyed shirt walked on to announce the final presentation: *the age of Post-Credibility - an introduction to the work of Janek James by Professor Rupert Kepler.*

A murmur of expectation passed through the audience as a small, elderly man shuffled through the tinsel onto the stage. He was wearing a battered mustard-coloured corduroy suit and a crumpled pink silk shirt, only slightly pinker than his long, leathery face. He stooped over a walking cane which he banged on the floor of the stage to get attention. Kepler had the posture of a man in his seventies but his eyes sparkled like a teenager's. Then his body slowly began to straighten, appearing to grow several inches. When he finally spoke his voice was strong and clear.

'In 1965 I was researching into the political effects of psychedelic substances. I was studying two conflicting theories; one was that drugs such as LSD were essentially subversive - once the doors of perception were opened to previously unimaginable possibilities they could not be closed. The opposing view was that such drugs were a form of social control, stultifying political action - in other words, the users would be too scared or lazy to get up and open the doors...' Kepler's voice resonated like a veteran orator, each sentence bouncing back from the corners of the room to echo beneath the next. 'As the Sixties progressed I realised I was not, in fact, studying the effect of drug intoxication as much as Theory Intoxication, which some term paranoia, a virulent growth seeded in the fertile ground of mind-expanding drugs. This is how I began my studies into the Agriculture of Belief Systems...'

Bernard turned to Dillwyn and whispered. 'What the hell is this? Some crackpot old paranoid who's done too much acid?'

'Shush, just listen... it'll get interesting soon.'

Professor Kepler continued. 'Today I would like to challenge the notion that in the age of Post-Credibility nobody believes in anything. My recent work on Atomised Belief Systems, a development of the theory of Cred Havens explains how, on the contrary, society remains permeated with belief, it's just fragmented throughout society. In fact, Post-Credibility requires a finite but transient quantity of belief that is forever shifting location. But first let us examine JJ's notion of Cred Havens - those zones where those who mistrust everything believe what they see and hear.'

'Oh no,' muttered Dillwyn under his breath, 'I've got a feeling this is all going in the wrong direction, all too academic...'

'Cred Havens have now become very volatile,' continued Kepler. 'Once they could be found everywhere, from a schoolroom to the warm tones of a familiar radio programme to the comfortable back room of a saloon bar. This is where people believed what they heard. No more. Now people need to think they've discovered Cred Havens themselves, uncovered their own source of truth, as if they were finding a far away exotic beach not yet in the guide books...'

Dillwyn suddenly rose to his feet and spoke. 'Professor Kepler, I'm very grateful for your valuable research, but don't you think the most important thing is that these theories are being used to control us? Isn't that what we should be discussing?'

Bernard had never seen Dillwyn so excited. Someone in the audience clapped tentatively.

'If you would allow me to continue...' said Kepler.

'But can you deny JJ is working for the government now, making us think what they want us to think!'

'I have no evidence of that,' replied Kepler.

'Well, of course he is!' shouted Dillwyn. 'Isn't it obvious?'

Another voice replied. A strong, familiar, female voice. 'Perhaps you don't have any evidence because JJ doesn't exist!'

Bernard turned to see Animal standing at the back of the room, pointing at Kepler.

'How can you say that, when you see his hand in all the stuff that's going on around us!' shouted Dillwyn.

'But if you had actually studied my theories...' retorted Kepler.

'We can do without those theories, can't we?' continued Animal. 'Like, JJ himself is just a myth, just another distraction. Why do you all fall for it? And do you really believe this guy is a Professor? Where did you get your qualifications from, Kepler?'

Kepler glanced nervously around the room, then froze. There was silence for a moment then laughter began to break out and a slow rhythm built up as, one by one, the previously passive audience began to clap their hands. Kepler shrank back to the stooped old man he was before and shuffled off through the tinsel curtains.

Bernard stood up and managed to catch Animal's eye across the room. She gave him a broad grin and nodded in the direction of the exit. Bernard clambered over the chairs to follow her out of the basement, but before he reached the door Dillwyn shouted out to him.

'Bernard! Can't you see what's going on here?'

'Hang on in there Dillwyn. I'll be back in a minute.'

Bernard pushed his way through the crowd out into the street. There was Animal standing alone by a bus stop, silhouetted by a yellow street light, arms akimbo. She was dressed in a lime green jump suit, her hair tied back tight behind her head. In the headlights of a passing car he caught a flash of her eyes; they were a deep chocolate brown. He hesitated for a moment before he walked up to her, his heart pounding.

'What's going on? What the fuck is this all about?'

'What do you think, Bernard? Come on, is it clever or is it crap?'

Bernard searched Animal's eyes for a clue. 'Er...'

'Yes, it's crap! All these theories, they're just more drugs, aren't they? Forms of control! At first they give you insights, and then you just get hooked on them, and then they don't mean anything...'

'Yeah, right... so why...'

She moved a little closer. 'Or is that just what Kepler's saying? Theory Intoxication! Atomised belief systems – now that's a hell of an idea! So Bernard, is he part of the problem or part of the solution?'

Bernard hesitated. 'Problem?'

She stared at him intently for several seconds then broke out into a smile.

'Yeah, you're right. That's what I think too. Something else we need to do away with.'

'So what are you doing here anyway?'

Animal hesitated for a moment. 'I was asked to come here...'

'Asked? By whom?'

'Some of my... colleagues... well, they think there's techniques we can use, turn them round, use them against the state. JJ was at the Tranquility gig - where I met you - that's why I was there.'

'But you said JJ doesn't exist...'

'That, Bernard, is the problem.'

Animal smiled, the same soft sweet smile that had reduced him to a trembling pulp in his flat.

'Oh...' Bernard stared at her, looking for a clue that this might be some sort of joke, but her smile faded away.

'Hey, by the way, that piece you wrote on the Tranquility Foundation - The Third Reich On Magic Mushrooms – brilliant! They're the next target, aren't they?'

'Target?'

She grabbed hold of his shoulder and leaned right into him. He could feel the damp warmth of her breath as she whispered into his ear. 'Do something for me, will you?'

He nodded assent.

'Write for us. Do some more on the TF. Their idea of civilisation - rip it apart! Can you do that? Then we can plant a few more virtual bombs together. And find out more about that guy Kepler, find out what he knows, OK?'

Before he could reply there was a screech of brakes and a bus pulled up beside them. Animal grasped Bernard's buttocks and pulled him tight up against her, turning slightly so her hip bone pressed into his burgeoning erection. She planted a huge, enveloping kiss over his mouth. Then she broke away, jumped on the bus and was gone.

Bernard stood there, motionless and stunned, for several minutes. He then turned back towards Owsley's Floor, vaguely aware there was something he was supposed to do. He ran to the door of the club; slumped against the wall outside was Dillwyn who looked up at Bernard and shook his head sadly.

'Oh Bernard, they don't want to hear the truth, do they? Didn't you see how that woman got them all to shout me down? Just when Kepler was going to tell us all about JJ?'

'Dillwyn, what the hell is this all about?'

'I don't think that woman's what she seems to be. I reckon she's up to no good. I'm going to have to do do a bit of research into her. Her and the people she's working for. In the meantime, if I was you, I'd stay well away.'

Six

'I hate puppets. They stare at you with their cold dead eyes trying to teach you lessons, acting out 'truths' far too banal to be put into words.'
Bernard Hawks, The Indicator - 'Notes From The Shadows'

Bernard peered out of the window into the grimy streets below his flat. It was one of those dim autumn mornings when London seemed unable to afford the sun and had switched on the economy lights; the city had the mean grey-green glow of a back street garage. He was vaguely aware his phone was ringing but he didn't answer it. It would only be from his editor pointing out, once again, he was about to miss his deadline. Besides, all his attention was fixed on what was happening below.

The surprising thing about the horses was that they made no sound. Twenty or more flowed silently into the street, no spluttering or neighing, no clattering of hooves, a rippling tidal wave of manes and tails, glossy chestnut and dappled grey coats catching the first thin streaks of sunlight breaking through the clouds. They had no riders but seemed perfectly calm and determined as they swept down the road. Then Bernard blinked and they were gone. The clouds closed in and the street began to fill again with the familiar collection of ragged characters. Normal service had been resumed.

Across the road a clutch of security cameras nesting on tall poles were recording the daily episode of life in the neighbourhood. A woman of indeterminate age, with greasy blonde hair and a skull-like face, was passing small paper packets to a line of listless people scratching their arms. She was glancing furtively across the road to where two punks with vast cockscomb Mohicans, jackets heavily studded like transgressive Pearly Kings, leaned against the wall drinking lager from cans. They, in turn, were posing for the cameras of two nervous tourists who had wandered a little too far in search of the bohemian London promised in their guidebooks. At either end of the street, two crews of road workers with pneumatic drills were working their way steadily towards each other, carving up the tarmac that had been laid down the week before. At the far end of the road he could see a group of around a dozen people with banners and megaphones marching in ritual protest, but he could neither see nor hear what they were protesting about. A small group of teenage kids in hooded jackets ambled onto the pavement opposite and, with nothing better to do, started yelling garbled insults at Bernard. He slammed the window shut. There was a loud crack as an air gun pellet made a neat hole in the glass. *Not a bad shot*, thought Bernard as he pondered, for a moment, the potential pleasure of owning a machine gun. Like one of those you saw in movies with two huge handles on the back and endless belts of bullets that shook violently as it spewed out sparks and smoke and cartridge cases. Perhaps instead of writing about bombs he should write about machine guns: *Where Shall We Spray The Bullets Today?*

Bernard sat down and started thinking again about what he was trying hard not to think about: Animal. He had to find her. She must exist; Casper had seen her, Dillwyn had seen her. Casper couldn't be trusted but Dillwyn seemed to know something about her. He had not seen Dillwyn since the night before at Owsley's Floor but the shufflings and scrapings coming from next door suggested he was in.

Bernard knocked once on Dillwyn's door and it swung open. He had never ventured into Dillwyn's flat before but had always imagined it as some sort of dank Celtic cave. The last thing he expected was a bright, airy room with bare lacquered floorboards. There was little furniture apart from metal bookshelves that lined every wall, packed with neat rows of numbered box files, all clearly labelled: *Alien Manifestations (Misc.), CIA, Disasters (natural), Disasters (man-made), FBI, Grails, JFK, Masonry, Microwaves, Mind Control, NWO, Illuminati, Religious Cults, Stone Circles, UFO's, Weather, World Leader Networks*. The shelves were spotlessly clean, perhaps related to the fact that there in the corner was a tall, skinny woman with a feather duster. She had a head rather too big for her body, thick mousey hair, beige cord trousers, a black sweater and a green disposable plastic apron. She turned round to greet him with a huge smile.

'Hi! You must be Bernard…'

Bernard nodded. 'And who the hell are you?'

'I'm Mel! An old friend of Dillwyn.'

'Dillwyn has *friends*?'

'Yeah. He had to go away. Personal, family stuff…'

'He's got friends *and* a family?'

'…so he asked me to look after his place for a bit.' When Mel wasn't smiling her face was as blank as a shop window dummy. 'Dillwyn was always very impressed with you. Said with your contacts and his knowledge you could change the world. Did he talk to you much about his theories?'

Bernard nodded. They stared at each other for a few seconds then Mel smiled again, a smile so wide that it cut her face into two segments, the bottom half of which looked perilously close to falling off. This woman seemed unnervingly pleasant and he didn't like her at all.

'What's that noise?' she asked.

'My telephone ringing?'

'Besides that - the chanting and cheering?'

'Some demo or something...'

'It must be the march! Can we watch them from your window!'

'Err - I suppose so.'

Bernard led the way back into his flat but Mel raced ahead of him, like a child running towards an ice cream van. She pulled up Bernard's window with a squeal of joy while he stood still in the middle of the room.

'It's the neighbourhood march!' cried Mel. 'Aren't you going to join them?'

'No. Just the word neighbourhood makes my flesh creep...'

'They're marching for peace!'

'...as does the word neighbour. And for that matter, hood.'

'The Tranquility Campaign! Isn't it wonderful to see people doing something positive? Making the streets safe for everyone!'

'Sounds nice. Do they sing hymns?'

Mel turned towards Bernard and leant her head on one side like a quizzical rag doll. 'Dillwyn told me you could be a bit sarcastic,' she leant her head the other way, then returned it to the vertical and recovered her smile. 'You see, I think it's very interesting, the Tranquility Campaign. They've struck a chord with so many different people. And they always look fantastic on TV. Have you seen their giant puppets?'

'Jesus, not puppets...'

'And they've got some pretty sophisticated tactics...'

'The puppets?'

'They're incredibly well organised - there's never any trouble at their demonstrations.'

'What's the point of a demonstration without trouble? I thought trouble was the whole idea. And I can't stand puppets. Dead things that stare at you and try to make you feel guilty.'

Mel furrowed her brow for a moment. Bernard thought she was going to cry. 'Dillwyn warned me you could be very negative too, but he told me not to take it too seriously.' With a little effort her smile returned. 'Oh, I forgot. He left this disc for you. I assume it was for you unless there's another Bernard.'

She breathed out a fleeting jangle of a laugh and handed him a plain silver CD with the words *For Bernard* hand-written neatly across its face. Bernard took it without comment, threw it onto his desk, and walked over to the window and looked down to the march going past in the street below.

'Aren't you going to answer that phone?' pleaded Mel.

'The answer machine will kick in soon.'

'Oh Bernard, you're so calm! Not like me – I can never let a phone ring.'

The demonstration consisted of no more than a dozen protesters but they appeared very organised, marching together in neat rows. The placards had the words *Peace In Our Street, Peace In Our World* printed over a series of photographs which, when lined up, created a panoramic rural landscape at sunrise. In the corner of each one a pastel yin-yang symbol and the letters TF and the slogan *Serenity With Security*.

'They look a bit slick for street protesters. Have they got an ad agency behind them or something?'

'They have, actually. You know, that one where they bomb went off? They're backing the Tranquility Campaign. Makes sense, really doesn't it.'

'Those Tranquility bastards. You can't get away from them.'

'That phone's been ringing for ten minutes!'

'Yeah, I know.'

'I'd better go now, Bernard. It's been so good to meet you! But there's something I have to say ...' Her face became very solemn.

'Yes?'

'The Tranquility Foundation. It's just that I went to one of their retreats once and, well - it changed my life. In a very good way. That's all.'

The smile came back with a vengeance and Mel closed the door gently behind her. Bernard walked slowly over to the phone and switched on the machine to take the call.

'Not here. Your chance to break in, or, if you really have to, leave a message,' said Bernard's recorded voice.

'Bernard Hawks? I think you'd better pick up the phone,' said the caller.

The voice sounded vaguely but unidentifiably foreign.

'I know you're there.'

Bernard glared at the machine.

'Congratulations on the bomb.'

Bernard picked up the phone. 'It's got fuck all to do with me.'

'It's your bomb all right, matey.'

'I didn't fucking plant it.'

'I know you didn't. I did.'

'You what?'

'I planted it. As a favour. Now it's your turn.'

'Who the hell are you? And my turn to do what?'

'Help me out. Then maybe they won't find the evidence.'

'What evidence?'

'The evidence that proves you were there.'

'You're out of your fucking head.'

'Sure. But supposing I'm not? I think we'd better meet, don't you? Just in case I'm totally sane and telling the truth. Anyway, you

should thank me; not many people get their bombs planted free of charge.'

'Thank you? I'd like to strangle you with my bare hands.'

'Well if that's your attitude...'

'Casper, is that you?'

The caller had hung up.

That's the last time he would write about a bomb. Perhaps Casper was right – at this delicate stage in his life he should, for once, try to write something uncontroversial, something so insipid it would upset nobody. Something even Inspector Pitmarsh could find no fault with.

He sat down at his computer and picked up Dillwyn's disc. In the hope of some inspiration he inserted it into the machine and watched his screen flood with information. He saw phrases he recognised from Owsley's Floor – *Post-Credibility, Janek James, theory intoxication, Virtual Infiltration...* More words streamed across his screen – *The Primitive Front, Neighbourhood Marchers, Post-Rational Cults...* There was probably some story there in amongst all that craziness, but he couldn't face tackling it. Not today.

Bernard leaned back in his chair and tried to think positive thoughts. It wasn't easy. In fact it was getting harder by the day. He thought about Mel's enormous smile, but that didn't help. He closed his eyes and thought about the last time he saw Animal when she pressed herself against him... *Write some more about the Tranquility Foundation* she said... and Casper... *The TF are a positive force for change...* and then Mel again...*The Tranquility Foundation changed my life.* All right! He would write about the Tranquility Foundation again but this time he would tell the world all the good things they were doing with their money and how they were helping the world to become a very nice place. That's clearly what everyone wanted to hear. Thank God the stupid are blind to irony.

The telephone rang again. He wrenched the phone cable out of the socket and sat down at the Cydrax to write.

Seven

'I'm rather touched when people believe there's some coherent plan in the universe, even if it does all come down to giant lizards or masonic satanists.'

Bernard Hawks, The Indicator - 'Notes From The Shadows'

It was sometime after lunch that Bernard got the text message. He stared at it for several minutes, pondering the plethora of possibilities contained in so few words:

Need 2 c u urgent 5pm @ bench elysium g animal

He tried to reply, after his hand had stopped shaking, but his phone simply returned the message *number unknown*. But then this was Animal: nothing to do with her was going to be simple.

Elysium Gardens was a small, triangular patch of land a few yards from Bernard's flat. Surrounded on all three sides by traffic-clogged roads and above by a railway bridge, various community projects had, in vain, attempted to transform it into a place where weary pedestrians might spend the odd minute or two contemplating council flower beds, but within days its entropy would be restored and the Gardens returned to their destined function: a patch of earth where dogs could shit, some scrubby grass where alcoholics could sleep and an archway where junkies could shoot up.

As Bernard turned the corner he could see the entrance to the Gardens was a blocked by the silhouette of a tall, stooped man. As he approached the figure began to speak in a slow, melancholy voice.

'Hello Bernard.'

'Look Bob, I'm in a bit of a rush. I'm meeting someone. Important business meeting.'

'Oh. Do you have my money?'

'Take this. It's all I've got on me.'

One of Bob's eyebrows lifted just enough to indicate surprise. Bernard handed him some crumpled notes. Bob smoothed them out carefully and counted them one by one.

'You owe me more than this, Bernard.'

'Yeah, I know. But I wasn't expecting to see you, was I. Look, here's a deal - have you got anything on you now? Add it to my bill and I'll pay you back everything, and I mean *everything*, I owe next week. Plus an extra tenner for goodwill. The paper's finally paid me. Just waiting for the cheque to clear.'

Bob shook his head in disbelief. 'You want some more gear? On *credit*?'

'Yeah, come on Bob, we've known each other for years. Too many years.'

'All I have is some crumbs of really crap soap bar. The worst bits of low grade stalk stewed up with glue, shoe polish and old rubber tyres. Would you like some of that?'

'What makes you think I'd want some of that?'

'You've been buying it off me for the last five years.'

'Give it here, then.'

'That makes two sixty you owe me. See you, Bernard.'

Bob passed him a small brown lump wrapped in cling film then wandered away.

As Bernard entered the gardens and walked towards the bench he could see someone was already there. He had little idea how Animal would present herself this time but he had not anticipated a figure in a long shabby raincoat tied up with string and a face completely obscured by a very battered straw hat. As he moved closer his admiration for Animal's aptitude for disguise was replaced by the depressing realisation that this was merely one of the local dossers, head down, drinking from a brown paper bag clutched in both hands. Bernard hesitated before he spoke, hoping to find a mode of address that was firm but not totally lacking in compassion.

'Excuse me... I was hoping to meet someone here... if I give you a fiver do you think you could piss off? Please.'

The head of the dosser slowly rose up.

'Hello Bernard. Don't get excited. It's only me. In disguise.'

'Dillwyn! With all due respect, it's nice to see that you're alive and all that, but the request stands. Would you be kind enough to piss off! I've got an important meeting. And seeing that I know you, the offer of the fiver is withdrawn.'

'Don't worry, Bernard. She's not going to turn up.'

'How do you know she's not going to turn up? I mean, how do you know it's a she?'

'Because I sent you the message, didn't I? It was about her, not from her. Anyway, this is important. Wanted to make sure you'd be here, like.'

'You bastard! You could have knocked on my door.'

'Can't go home, can I? Keeping a low profile, see. Sit down Bernard, we needs to talk.'

'You know there's a strange woman in your flat?'

'Oh, that's Mel. Go back a long way me and her. She's covering while I'm on covert operations.'

'Right. And Animal? What about Animal?'

'She's dangerous. That's what I wanted to warn you about. I think she's in with a bad crowd. The Primitive Front, perhaps. Could be a trap, see.'

'Who the hell are the Primitive Front? Do they actually exist?'

'Well, I used to think they were fictitious, before I started doing my research and that. But being fictitious is not the same as not existing, is it?'

'Well thanks for that Dillwyn. I'm going home now.'

Dillwyn let out a big sigh. 'I know, why don't you buy me a mug of tea? There's a nice caff over there. You could buy me dinner, come to think of it. It would look more authentic, with me playing the part of a down and out, like. Then I can tell you about Animal.'

*

The 'nice caff' was one of the few local establishments that would be happy to let in someone of Dillwyn's appearance. Apart from that, there was little to be said in its favour apart from an unfashionable dedication to the British tradition of frying, boiling or stewing until no trace of flavour remained.

'So, Bernard, I've been thinking about the Primitive Front.'

'You were going to tell me about Animal...'

'All part of the same story. Now the Front are supposed to be neo-Luddite strategists, dedicated to random acts of spontaneous violence, aren't they?'

'If you say so.'

'And whose interests would that actually serve?'

Bernard shrugged.

'All right, I shall put it another way. Think of it: if I was the government, what could be better for me than to create my very own anarchist terrorist group?'

Bernard was vaguely aware that that Dillwyn was fidgeting with something. He looked down and saw that Dillwyn had taken the metal tops off the salt and pepper and was obsessively twisting his little finger around inside them.

'What are you doing?'

'Checking for hidden microphones.'

'Dillwyn, you're a paranoid nut.'

Dillwyn looked up and grinned. 'Only joking, Bernard. It's just a nervous habit. Can't help it. You've not got much sense of humour, have you?'

Bernard grabbed the cruet tops and screwed them back on as a large plate of sausage, mash and unrecognisable vegetables arrived for Dillwyn.

'Go on then,' said Bernard, 'tell me why, if you were the government, which, hopefully, is unlikely for the time being, would you want your own anarchist group?'

'Well, obviously it would help with the climate, like,' said Dillwyn, as he squeezed a brown plastic tomato with both hands and smothered his food with brown sauce.

'The climate?'

'Yes, you know, *the climate of fear*. Keep the panic level up. Then it's a good test bed for the emergency services, manipulating the media and all that. Controlled experiments, see. But it gets better. It becomes like this huge spider's web, for all the dissenters and the so-called subversives. Sucks them all in so's I can keep an eye on them.'

Dillwyn paused to allow Bernard to react, but Bernard said nothing. Dillwyn then began to cut up his sausage into very small pieces and mix it into the gravy with a deliberation that suggested somehow this illustrated his thesis.

'So, now I can use them to create trouble wherever I like and distract attention from the things I really wanted to keep hidden. Or, when I felt like, I could just pump up the violence. *Es-ca-late* it.' Dillwyn started to mix vigourously all the food on his plate into one swirling brown mass.

'Now why would you want to do that?'

Dillwyn shook his head as though Bernard was a little slow on the uptake.

'It's obvious, really, Bernard. I could use them to justify *draconian measures* and lock up whoever it is I want to lock up. I can stop the bombing and say my measures are working, or start it up again and say they need to be even stricter. Can't lose either way, really,' Dillwyn paused to slurp some tea. 'If things go to plan, then I need to balance it with what appears to be a reasonable campaign group, a nice one, like those Tranquility marchers, and slip ideas to them, so the sort of people who don't believe anything the government says, which is everybody, really, could get influenced. Got everybody cornered, you see. Both the good guys and the bad guys are working for you. Brilliant, isn't it!'

Bernard watched as Dillwyn held the plate at mouth level and literally shovelled the food in at speed.

'All right Dillwyn, if I accept, for the sake of argument, that the government needs to bomb us, why did they put the bomb where I had, well, suggested it should go? I mean, that has to be a coincidence, right?'

Dillwyn dropped his plate back on to the table.

'Coincidence Bernard? Don't be naïve. They *want* you to believe it's all coincidence, don't they. No, I've been thinking about that, see, and it's very interesting. I think it strengthens their position.' Dillwyn prodded his fork at Bernard. 'Because you either planted the bomb or, what's much more likely, knew all about it in advance...'

'I didn't know about the bomb...'

'*Tech-ni-cal-ity*. Everyone thinks you did, that's all that matters. Since you knew about the bomb it backs up the idea that there's something going on, not just a one-off; some underground movement is plotting to attack.' Dillwyn sliced the air above his plate with his knife. 'So that's why they put it where you suggested. Very flexible strategy, you see, I can start a bombing campaign and then decide later who did it. You know, who it is I want a war with, like. They call it a *retrospective false flag operation*. Then as a fallback position, if they change their mind…'

'Who?'

'The Government. Or rather the forces that are running them.'

'The Lizards?'

'If you insist Bernard, metaphorically, the Lizards, they can blame it all on you. You see no one in their right mind would think you're on the side of the government…'

'Thank you for that insight.'

'…in fact, no one thinks you're on the side of anything, do they? That's why you're so useful.' Dillwyn folded his arms. The slightest suggestion of a smug smile spread across his face.

'Dillwyn, with all due respect, don't you think this is all a little fanciful?'

Dillwyn dropped his knife and fork, sat up straight and plumped out his chest. His cheeks glowed bright red. Bernard had come to realise that Dillwyn had two distinct personas. One was a mumbling, shuffling, junior clerk, the other a bumptious Presbyterian minister that took over on the rare occasions when Dillwyn got excited.

'That's nice! A little *fanciful*, is it? Well since I have very carefully outlined the obvious advantages of the government running its own anarchist group, don't you think it seems a little *fanciful* that they haven't thought of it too, and therefore *fanciful* that they haven't implemented such a scheme? For that matter, isn't it a little *fanciful* that you, coincidentally, wrote about putting a bomb in the exact place where one went off? I could say, isn't it a little *fanciful* that a lovely girl like Animal would have the slightest interest in a bloke like you in the first place?'

'Maybe she sees me as a kindred anarchic spirit. Or something,' muttered Bernard.

Dillwyn slumped back down into his chair. Bernard's irritation was aggravated by the notion, emerging from the very back of his mind that, maybe, in the midst of all his eccentric ramblings, Dillwyn had a point.

'Sorry, don't mean to be rude. Just being scientific, like.' He leaned forward and gripped Bernard's wrist. 'You've got to write about all this, Bernard. Expose it all in your column. And stay away from that woman, if you want my advice. I don't think your spirits are kindred one little bit.'

'You're not seriously trying to tell me that Animal is working for the government, are you?'

'Well, not saying she realises it yet. Most of the time none of us knows who we're working for really, do we?'

'She did say something to me about planting virtual bombs together…'

'Very interesting, that. Shall we go for a walk?'

Bernard paid the bill and followed Dillwyn through an alleyway to some steps that led down to the canal.

'Safer away from the roads, see. Less cameras.'

It was getting dark now and there was a chill in the air. Only the most desperate drug dealers still remained along the towpath, huddled up together for warmth, but even they turned their backs as Dillwyn marched along with uncharacteristic verve and determination. As Bernard followed it was becoming increasingly clear to him that Dillwyn was quite mad.

'Dillwyn, I've never seen you like this before. I think I preferred it when you were depressed. What's got into you?'

'Well, I've got something to get my teeth into now. And I know what's going on this time.'

So Dillwyn knew what was going on. But then mad people did. Mad people didn't have doubts, mad people had certainties and it was the people with the certainties who ruled the world.

'Where are we going, Dillwyn?'

'Into the park. I want to show you something.'

'Dillwyn, your theories are all very interesting. But really, I think there's a simpler explanation of what you refer to as "my" bomb.'

'Is there something you haven't told me?'

Bernard hesitated before he replied, worried that he might be sucked deeper into the mire of Dillwyn's conspiracies. But then in the context of a world ruled by mad people, Dillwyn's paranoid theories were beginning to appear as reasonable as any others.

'I've spoken to the guy who planted the bomb. Well, someone who claimed he did it. He rang me.'

'The bomber called you? That's fantastic!'

'It's not fantastic at all. He was very intimidating. Said he had evidence to prove I did it.'

'And what evidence was could that be, then?'

'I haven't the faintest idea.'

'Did you ask him?'

'No, I told him to fuck off.'

'Oh Bernard, you shouldn't have done that. We missed our opportunity there. Evidence, see, that's what we need.'

'I don't want his fucking evidence.'

'Not his evidence. Evidence of who he's working for.'

'Seems to me just a simple case of blackmail. He read my column, planted a bomb to frame me and some fake evidence. He just wants my money.'

'Have you got any money?'

'No.'

'Well, it's far too simple then, isn't it. You're going to have to meet him, Bernard, find out who he's really looking for. It's essential. All right, we go up this path here now.'

They left the towpath, crossed the road and entered a park.

'Where are we going now, Dillwyn?'

'Top of the hill.'

'This is not some Welsh Druid number you're getting me into?'

'Don't make me out to be stupid, Bernard. Druids were an invention of a 19th century opium addict. They're fantasists totally out of touch with reality.'

'Oh, I see.'

Dillwyn marched to the top with Bernard close behind. It was a clear night and the city was a shimmering mass of lights.

'Got to go away tomorrow, important research, so I might not see you for a while. I thought I'd show you this.' He gestured to the city below. 'What do you see, Bernard?'

'London?'

'It might help if you squint a little bit.'

'Blurry London?'

Dillwyn took in a few deep breaths before he spoke again.

'All that down there... what do you think this city manufactures?'

'I dunno. Gin, pop music... money?'

'Ideas, Bernard! Ideas about ideas! Speculations, fantasies, persuasions, that's what it trades in. Things you can't touch. Only the poor people trade in matter.'

Bernard looked back from the city to Dillwyn and wondered if he wasn't quite so mad at all.

'Now, look closely. I first noticed this from a plane. Coming back from holiday I was. I looked down and I saw all these twinkling lights. I realised that every glimmer was a tiny glowing bug, and all the little bugs were chasing each other, a heap of frenzied, starving creatures fighting for survival, eating each other alive. It was all madness. Very scary. Chaos. Then I started my researches. I came up here to think and you know what? It began to change. I saw that all those little lights are glints, and every glint is a jewel and the jewels

40

are set in a movement of a giant watch, a watch the size of the city, a million polished gear wheels turning in harmony, a perfect glittering machine. When you learn things, you see the world differently. Like it's all working together, manufacturing ideas!'

Bernard looked hard but all he could see through his half closed eyes was chaos. Dillwyn turned round slowly to face Bernard, reached into his pocket and passed him a handful of paper.

'Now you've seen that I think you should read these. Sort of an introduction to Post-Credibility.'

Bernard glanced at the papers. They looked like faded photocopies. 'Is this anything to do with Professor Kepler and that lecture?'

'Kepler... he wrote this, actually, but it's difficult to get hold of now. Been suppressed, like. He wrote all this stuff exposing JJ, but I now I reckon he's getting a bit scared of what he's unleashed, see. Means they're putting pressure on him.'

'Animal asked me to find out more about Kepler... what's this got to do with her? And the Primitive Front?'

'Somehow or other I think they want to use the principles of Post-Credibility to their own ends. There's new ways, Bernard. New ways of controlling us, making us think what they want us to think. You see it don't matter whether we believe what they say or not, don't matter if we don't believe anything, really. We still keep doing it. Whatever it is they want us to do.'

'But how, Dillwyn?'

'That's what you and I are going to find out. He's the one who knows. See what you can make of that.' Dillwyn stabbed his finger at the pages in Bernard's hand.

Bernard glanced at the title on the first page - *Janek James And The Theory Of Post-Credibility*, then shoved them into his jacket and looked down to the city below. And as he watched he began to see the glints of a giant crystalline mechanism, the glittering cogs turning together in harmony.

'I think I'd better go home. You're beginning to make sense to me, Dillwyn, and I'm finding that very, very worrying.'

Eight

'Being fictitious is not the same as not existing, is it?' - Dillwyn Jones

When Bernard got home he went straight to his Cydrax. Words were still pouring off Dillwyn's disc so fast he couldn't read them. He tried to make some notes but the Cydrax seemed too preoccupied with Dillwyn's theories to acknowledge a single keystroke. He turned away from the computer in disgust and picked up the paper that Dillwyn had thrust into his hand. Professor Kepler - why had Animal wanted to find out about him? He unfolded the papers and began to read.

Janek James And The Theory Of Post-Credibility

One could say the more powerful Janek James becomes, the less he is visible. Many have wondered whether he actually exists and even those who have met him often dismiss him as a figment of their imagination...

Already Bernard had the feeling this article was not going to answer any of his questions. But he read on.

The most common, contemporary description is of a tall, lean man in late middle-age with close cropped, pure white hair, cold grey eyes and an immaculate suit; an appearance suggestive of a historian or a medical consultant or perhaps an indispensable component of an obscure and stable section of the Foreign Office. You would be unlikely to associate him with the worlds of advertising, marketing or public relations, nor would, we assume, JJ wish to be associated with the commonplace applications of those trades. He could be considered, rather, as a very refined technician, gently lubricating and adjusting the machinery of supply and demand, a fine tuner of desires, an engineer of consent. If ever he did cast a distanced, professional eye over an advertising hoarding or a television commercial, it would be as a surgeon might glance at a butcher's shop window. JJ's character has been marked out by anecdote and legend. One in particular has followed him for most of his life - JJ is *The Man Who Turned Baseball Caps Round*.
In the early years of his career, so the story goes, JJ was working on a franchise for the Head - not a sports goods manufacturer or a rock band, simply that top part of the human anatomy. The rest of the body had effectively been

sold off as advertising space for the very goods that clothed it, high profit, short life products for those with slow incomes but rapid spending habits. The baseball cap was ideal - an American classic with low manufacturing costs, easy logo display and versatile enough to be appropriated with both irony and respect. JJ happened to be at a photo session for an emerging rap band who had been enlisted for some product placement. Early in to the session the photographer stopped and said - *Please take those caps off guys - they're keeping the light off your face.*

A lesser man would have fired the photographer on the spot but JJ recognised immediately this was a problem that would recur again and again. Particularly, he calculated, as you moved towards the equator where the sunlight was steeper and the contrast higher - in key emerging markets some very expensive faces would be lost in the shadows. This was not a question of the stubbornness of one rather unimaginative photographer, this could be the death knell of the whole Baseball Cap Project. Very quietly but firmly JJ made his contribution - *Turn the caps around.* The rest you know.

According to legend, in the 1980's JJ was the man who created the story about the kid in Brooklyn murdered for his sneakers. The handful of real killings that followed was handsomely compensated by the meteoric rise of a then obscure brand of shoe - Wild Fungus - to market leader. Wild Fungus became, literally, *the shoes to die for.*

For a brief period commercial joke broking became his speciality. He took a brand of clumsy East European car, the Dasgo, and set a team of writers to flood the net with jokes about just how bad this car was. People loved the jokes (sample - *What's the difference between a Dasgo and a sheep?* Answer - You feel marginally less embarrassed climbing out of the back of a sheep) and the car became famous. Not only that, people began to feel sorry for it.

A *Save the Dasgo from Ritual Humiliation* campaign started (JJ again) and the Dasgo brand was bought for next-to-nothing by a German manufacturer who relaunched it as the world's most ecological car. Those who thought they could see through and beyond the vagaries of fashion and cheap jokes (and who did not?) identified its oddball looks as functional rather than simply ugly, and assumed, despite all evidence to the contrary, that its primitive engineering bestowed reliability. A certain type of sophisticated consumer, who felt a little guilty about buying a car in the first place, rushed out to acquire what they believed was not only a solidly built and ethically commendable bargain but a design classic.

JJ's reputation had now reached the point where he was no longer identified with a particular strategy or campaign, he was out on his own, an enigmatic trouble-shooter to be employed when all else had failed. It is widely believed that it was JJ who advised the CIA how to handle a case of what is known in their trade as 'blowback' - a minor despot, who had been promoted because he was marginally more useful to their interests than the opposing despot, had now become less useful.

The details are not relevant - an oil pipeline or mineral reserves or opium fields - what is important is that a bombing raid was planned for the summer and rather too many people in the West had developed sentimental sympathies for the present incumbent. They had less than six months to reduce the appeal of the regime.

An email petition arrived in the inbox of computers across the world, purporting to come from a women's campaign group (fictional). It spoke of the appalling civil rights record of this particular regime (true), a long list of dissenters about to be executed (partly true) and a thoroughly gruesome story about a mother forced to eat her own baby (entirely fabricated). Millions across the world 'signed' this petition and its credibility was enhanced further by an official denial by the government in question that anything referred to in the petition was true. For a negligible budget they had found a Cred Haven - a point in space and time where those who mistrusted almost everything would believe. When the invasion happened the cheeks of the wet liberals remained dry. The construction and development of Cred Havens is commonly considered JJ's major achievement.

JJ has always been known for seeing slightly further than his peers. It is legendary how he studied devoutly in the seminaries of his creed, how he immersed himself in the arcane cultures of identification and resistance, the ethnographic studies of consumer empathies, the iconographic resonance of the logo, the mythic narrative of the brand. Little of that is relevant now, the public have lost faith, they no longer believe in anything. But it was JJ's great insight to realise that does not matter, there are new ways to make people buy the things you want to sell, to behave as fits your needs. They still need to consume, just as they still need to be governed.

If Cred Havens are now so elusive, it maybe because they have become irrelevant. We have entered a new era. From JJ's perspective, opinions, beliefs, attitudes are old currency - all so twentieth century. The time has come to trade in something far more radical.

Welcome to the world of Post-Credibility.

Professor Rupert Anton Kepler

London 2002

Rupert Anton Kepler, widely regarded as one of the world's leading experts in the field of Credibility Systems, has written extensively about the work of Janek James. His career encompasses academic and creative writing and performance, and he was a leading member of the seminal 1970's experimental theatre group, The Human Company.

Bernard threw the paper down. He couldn't see how any of it could help with the problems he was facing. *The Man Who Turned Baseball Caps Round...* if he was so legendary, why hadn't he heard of him before? Animal didn't think he existed - but, there again, she was following him. Had Kepler made the whole thing up?

Nine

'Of course I don't read the papers. Why should I? I write for them.'
- Bernard Hawks.

It was late morning when Bernard was finally woken by the sound of his computer cuckooing. About two weeks ago the Cydrax had learned to cuckoo. He had no idea where it had learnt it, but cuckoo it did whenever he got mail or missed an appointment or had forgotten to feed it with the latest update or bug fix. And it seemed to be getting louder. He lay in his bed for a while, wondering whether Dillwyn could be right about Animal, whether through some peculiarly devious connections that only Dillwyn could fathom, she was not so much a dangerous anarchist as an insidious agent of the state. Or could she be both? Before he could come to any conclusions the cuckooing reached a crescendo and he could stand it no more. He stumbled from his bed to the computer and slapped it hard across the screen. The cuckooing turned into hiccupping then, reluctantly, the machine released his email on to the screen in a series of gulps. In amongst the offers to extend penises and remedy ageing, there was one message that was meant for him alone and it was short and simple. His Editor wanted to see him. Immediately.

*

Bernard had never actually been inside *The Indicator* offices; he kept his communication as limited and remote as possible. He joined *The Indicator* after it had been taken over by a rising new media conglomerate which, for reasons of prestige or sentiment, decided it needed a newspaper to add to its portfolio of web portals and social networks. Ironically, all the subsidiaries had failed disastrously in the last couple of years apart from *The Indicator* itself which had been filling its pages with features and editorials gloating over the fall of their owners' empire.

Against all the odds, people continued to buy *The Indicator*, perhaps merely out of habit or, as Bernard maintained, because the weekend supplement was a perfect fit for the bottom of a cat litter tray. The marketing consultants had a simpler explanation: people bought *The Indicator* because it annoyed them. Readers could have something to complain about in the comfort of their own homes without feeling either patronised or intellectually strained. Bernard was a key element in this strategy; irreverent enough to upset everybody but sufficiently trenchant not to be entirely dismissible.

The Indicator offices had been relocated in a City office tower that had once been the hub of the corporate empire. Not much remained of their former glory other than a massive cast aluminium reception desk, placed at the end of what looked like a long, low footbridge slung over a sea of violet neon-lit pebbles. The architects' vision had been somewhat debased by the turning tides of the New Economy; washed-up on the shingle were the flotsam and jetsam of changing fortunes. Crumpled redundancy notices lay above crushed lager cans and vast molehills of exiled smokers' dog ends, and, beneath them, discarded trade show T-shirts, burst balloons and broken champagne bottles. As Bernard approached the desk a lone receptionist stared straight through him, perhaps hoping he would turn back half way.

'If you're a bike, deliveries are round the back,' said the receptionist, still staring as Bernard finally reached the desk.

'I'm not a bike. I have an appointment with the Editor.'

'Oh. I think there's somebody in. Go straight down.'

A purple fingernail indicated a staircase to the basement. Bernard descended into what he expected to be a seedy lounge full of dissolute journalists. Instead he found a long, stark room full of computers. The only human presence was a spotty, overweight youth in a heavy metal T-shirt, his hands deep in the entrails of a dissembled box of electronics. He glanced at Bernard with the disdain that those who spend their life in IT support reserve for human beings.

'The PR neural net for the LSS has gone down again. Always happens on a Monday.'

'Thank you, but that means absolutely nothing to me,' said Bernard. 'Do you know where I might find the Editor?'

The young man replied with a weariness born of countless fruitless attempts to explain to those who would never understand.

'The Press Releases addressed to the Life Style Section come into this machine. They're cross referenced with the advertisers' database. It wouldn't make much sense if, like, the readers were told to fill their rooms with white sofas if all the ads were for red ones, would it?'

'So this machine actually creates the Life Style Section on its own?' Bernard was slightly gratified; it confirmed a lot of suspicions he had about the Life Style Section.

'Course not. The copy goes to the Sub Editors.'

'And where are the Sub Editors?'

'That rack over there against the wall.'

'The Sub Editors are machines too?'

'Only for the last 10 months. Took a bit of time to tweak them. Like we had to wind the Spell Checkers down to 85%. People've got used to all the typos and get a bit miffed if they're not there.'

'I'm surprised you bother to employ any human contributors. They must be a great irritation.'

'Don't be stupid!' The youth seemed genuinely taken aback. '*The Indicator* prides itself on having the best writers in the country. Do you think you could programme a machine to, say, write like Bernard Hawks?'

A faint glow of pride spread through Bernard's body.

'Nah,' continued the youth, 'couldn't do it. That's at least, I dunno, a year, eighteen months down the line. Even then it wouldn't be cost effective.'

The glow dimmed. 'I am Bernard Hawks.'

'Yeah, I know. You came to see me, didn't you?'

'I came to see the Editor.'

'Yeah, that's me. Just for the Review Section that is. It's about that piece you wrote. About The Tranquility Foundation.'

'Go on.'

'Well the Style & Attitude Checker tagged it. You know, it didn't quite fit your profile. So I read it!' He beamed as if Bernard should be impressed. 'And I saw what it meant! It was - what's the word - I've got it here somewhere...' he scrolled down a list on one of the screens, 'yeah, *sycophantic*! That's not you, is it, *sycophantic*? We thought someone must have spoofed your mail box, you know, hacked in and pretended to be you. So we trashed it. Lucky we caught it in time, wasn't it!'

Bernard said nothing. The Editor continued.

'Anyway. That's sorted now. We've got some of your old pieces on stand-by, but we'd rather have something new. From the Bernard Hawks we know and love. That nasty, cynical sod who likes to plant bombs.'

'Is that it?'

'Yeah. And good-bye. You won't be dealing with me for much longer.'

'Don't tell me - you've been promoted?'

'Nah, you have mate! Didn't you get a phone call? In a month's time you're off to the *Glimmer* - Political Columnist! Seems you're about to get famous!'

'Jesus!'

'But I suggest you write something stronger for them. Don't go soft again. Stir up some shit, they'll like that.'

The Editor smiled again then returned to fiddling with his machine. The *Daily Glimmer* was a tabloid published by the owners of *The Indicator*. Once a stalwart Labour paper it was now largely a journal of celebrity gossip supported by adverts for telephone sex lines. But its circulation was massive and Bernard, against his better judgement, immediately felt excited by the prospect. This was his

48

opportunity to bring his penetrating insights to a mass audience, perhaps his chance to make a little money. He turned to leave and caught a glimpse of his reflection in a window; he was grinning stupidly. He stopped grinning and felt a pang of self-disgust. He wondered how many more such pangs would follow in his new appointment.

Bernard had almost reached the door when a thought struck him. He turned back to the youth who had now started to disassemble another machine.

'So all those phone calls I get from the Editor hassling me for copy. Now that wasn't you, was it?'

'Nah mate, 'course not. The Call Centre does all the phoning.'

'Of course. The Call Centre. How stupid of me. That's not in this building, is it?'

The Editor looked up from the machine and shook his head.

'Bangalore, mate. They're much better at that sort of stuff over there. Cheap, too.'

Bernard nodded slowly, turned and left the building.

*

When Bernard got home he went straight to his Cydrax. The ideas were still pouring off Dillwyn's disc on to the screen so fast he couldn't read them. Then the computer made an unearthly warbling sound and the screen went totally black, revealing nothing more than the unnerving reflection of Bernard's own face. He pressed every button, unplugged and replugged it, stroked it, slapped it, and shook it but the Cydrax would not respond. It was utterly dead.

Half an hour later Bernard was staggering down the high street clutching an his computer wrapped in a duvet. He wondered how something that was supposed to be part of a matter-less, virtual universe could be so astonishingly heavy.

Bernard and the dead Cydrax stumbled into the first electronics shop he saw. The shop window was filled with broken computers and grimy components and stuck to the glass was a large hand written sign that read:

VIC CAN FIX 'EM

The shop was stacked from floor to ceiling with boxes. The corridor carved through the mountain of equipment was so narrow that Bernard had to turn sideways to squeeze through holding his Cydrax on his head. At the end was a counter and, behind it, a middle aged man with a grey T-shirt on which was printed a single word in six inch high letters:

VIC

Vic, assuming this was his name and not a brand, had a face like crumpled cardboard, thin black hair shining with grease and tortoiseshell rimmed glasses held together with yellow insulation tape. Vic pointed to a green rubber mat on the counter and Bernard placed his computer on it.

'All right mate! What seems to be the problem?'

Bernard peeled back the corner of the duvet. Vic peered inside and grinned.

'Oh, a Cydrax. Don't work I suppose. Not a dickie bird?'

Bernard nodded. Vic lent back in his chair and folded his arms. Bernard was impressed how Vic's brown mottled fingernails exactly matched the frames of his glasses.

'What I suggest, squire, is this: you give me five hundred quid and I get one of those empty beige tin boxes, I load it with the fastest shit hot components the Chinks can weave with their nimble little fingers, give you a shed load of free software and you walk out of here with a machine that's four times as fast as this pretty little doorstop here. It won't crash and it won't do bird impressions.'

Vic grinned. Bernard scowled.

'But it won't be a Cydrax?'

'No. It will work.'

'So what do I do with the Cydrax?'

'We know a bloke who turns them into aquariums. Very nice they are too.'

Bernard hated this man. When the vet wants to put down your favourite pet at least he doesn't grin. 'But what if I want my Cydrax to work?'

Vic leant forward on the desk and said in a conspiratorial tone:

'There's always The Dark Orchard.'

Vic passed him a business card and exploded into laughter, rocking back and forwards in his chair as if this was the funniest thing he had ever heard. The card was black and printed on it in spidery silver type was an address and the words:

The Dark Orchard.
Dedicated to the Theory and Practice of the Cydrax movement.

'Now will you get out my shop, please,' said Vic.

Bernard wrapped up his computer and left.

*

The Dark Orchard turned out to be a small shop front under a railway arch. Bernard had walked passed it twice because he had assumed it to be some sort of New Age aromatherapy parlour. It was the first computer shop he had ever seen that was lit almost entirely by candlelight. A single spotlight shone down on to a small oak table. Behind it was a man with a neat goatee beard and a black roll-neck sweater. Bernard hesitated in the doorway, his nose twitching at the smell of incense that could not quite obscure the background odour of damp. The man beckoned him forward and Bernard walked up to the table and gently put his computer down into the beam of the spotlight. The man smiled and touched the corner of the duvet.

'May I?'

Bernard nodded and very gently the bearded man unwrapped the Cydrax. He chuckled when he saw it as if it was an old friend.

'Well now. A Cydrax 2000. Is she Rev.A or Rev.B ?'

'Pardon?'

'The motherboard. There are two basic revisions. Rev.A's were charming machines, they had a youthful vitality which was consistently amusing but which some found, how can I put it, a little tiresome in the evenings. Rev.B's, on the other hand, have a sort of seasoned but slightly offhand maturity. A trusty but dull old friend who sometimes just prefers his own company. But all in good time. First please tell me the symptoms.'

'Well I suppose things started going wrong, seriously wrong, when it began making bird noises.'

'Yes, of course. But the vital question is what sort? What was her final call?'

'Well, it was a sort of warble...'

'Sing it for us! Please, go ahead.'

He passed Bernard a glass of water. Bernard took a swig and then, very quietly, began to make a warbling sound from the back of his throat. The man smiled gently and nodded encouragement. Bernard's warble became louder. From the back of the shop two more men appeared. The three stood silently, nodding as they listened to Bernard's song. He stopped warbling. One of the men applauded gently. As they exchanged knowing looks Bernard realised they all shared a very peculiar distribution of facial hair.

'The wood pigeon,' whispered a man with a large moustache but no eyebrows.

The others nodded.

'It has gone into pine mode,' said a young man with a spectacular comb-over and prominent nasal hair.

The man with the goatee beckoned Bernard round to the other side of the table and pointed to the base of the Cydrax with a well sharpened pencil. With a flourish he removed a small oblong flap of metal to reveal a slot. 'There! Do you see? It's a Rev.C! Long time since I've seen one of these!'

The men with strange hair started prodding the machine and muttering under their breaths.

'It was going to be the first in a line of astonishing new computers. The concept was to join the Rev.C to another and that to another and so on... they would all work together in harmony as one massively powerful unit!'

'You see they weren't really designed to work on their own. That's why it was pining!' said the man with no eyebrows.

Bernard felt a pang of sadness for his computer, a pathetic refugee, alone in its attic, weeping for the loss of a family it never knew.

'Sadly the whole project was abandoned,' the man with the goatee continued, 'but one or two were released onto the market in this sadly emasculated mode. Poignant, but rather delightful nevertheless, don't you think?'

'So what can you do to fix it? Can you just stick a Rev.B board in or something?'

A brief but chilly silence was broken by the measured tones of the man with the goatee.

'Please. If you had a vintage Swiss watch would you want me to rip out the superb, hand-crafted movement and stick in a cheap electronic chip, just so it would keep time? The Rev.C's are eccentric machines, certainly, but they have a charisma and subtlety all of their own, an ability to constantly surprise and educate. They just hate to be alone.'

'Will it work?'

'*Will it work?* he says, as if life was as simple as that! Do you mean like an obedient servant, or a dog, or a slave? Or do you want begin to build a partnership, a relationship built on respect, a machine to work with you rather than for you?'

'Well, frankly I just...'

The man with the goatee held up his hand. 'Shush now. This is what I propose. We are fortunate that one of our colleagues is a bit of a Rev.C specialist. He will stay by its side for a day or two and try to discover where the discrepancies lie. It probably needs just a simple tune-up to release the tension built up in the chassis, a little degaussing. Just some basic care and attention.'

'And how much will it cost?'

'Think of it as a labour of love. We will only charge basic expenses which will be minimal... oh call it two fifty. Three hundred all in.'

'And then will it work?'

The man with the goatee stretched out his hands. 'If she wants to work she will work. She is a Cydrax.'

'And when do I get it back?'

'Oh give me a couple of days. No, make that a week to be safe. Or two.'

Bernard suspected he was being exploited. But Bernard was a Cydrax owner; it was his one major and very expensive concession to 21st century living and he wasn't going to give it up without a fight. For reasons even he could not quite fathom, his fondness for his computer increased as his tolerance of human beings diminished. He left the Dark Orchard with a sense of loss tempered by the belief that he owned something very special. When you own something that special there is, generally, a price to pay, and that price for Bernard was not a mere three hundred pounds but the deadening weight of the knowledge that, for the next couple of weeks, he would have to write without the aid and constant distraction of the Cydrax. Worse than that, he would have to learn, once again, how to use a pen.

Ten

'Theatre? Just two hours of self-conscious agony all in wide-shot.'
Bernard Hawks, The Indicator - 'Notes From The Shadows'

Bernard had spent most of the day rummaging through his flat for a pen. It was late afternoon and there was work to do but, having given up on the pen, he was now reduced to staring at the big oval patch in the dust on his desk where the Cydrax had sat. Beside it was Dillwyn's article on JJ and Post-Credibility that had been no help whatsoever. He was sure there were many useful and engaging tasks he could be doing; he just couldn't think of them, so he continued to stare at his desk. He was relieved when his inertia was interrupted by a hesitant knocking on the door. Until, that is, he opened the door and saw who it was.

'Any chance of the rest of the money, Bernard?'

'Bob - I said next week...'

'Yeah, I know...' Bob lowered his head slowly then raised it again. 'How about a cup of tea, then?'

Bernard moved away to let Bob shuffle in. This visit was not entirely a surprise; every month or so Bob would come in, sit in the corner of the room and spend a couple of hours drinking a cup of tea. Bernard accepted these tiresome intrusions as a necessary duty, a form of interest on his ever mounting debt to the dealer.

Bernard retreated into the murky corner that served as a kitchen to make the tea while Bob wandered around the room.

'No computer then, Bernard?'

'Apparently not.'

Bernard handed Bob a mug of tea and returned to his desk. Bob grasped the mug in both hands, lowered his head, took a slurp then looked up.

'Must be hard, writing without a computer.'

'Yes, Bob.'

'So what are you working on, then?'

'Just... got these documents to study...' He waved his hand at Dillwyn's notes. 'Nothing much... just doing some research... for this woman... for a friend... into this guy Kepler. Looks like a burnt-out old acid head, claims to be a professor...'

'Acid. Not much call for that, these days.' Bob put his tea down and ambled over to the desk. 'Not really a party drug. Now all they want to do is party, not sit around staring at patterns in the wallpaper. But if you like, Bernard, I know where I can get you some. Won't be cheap, mind you. Tabs or blotter?'

'No, Bob, please, I just want to find out...'

'Let me see...' Bob leant over Bernard's desk. 'Do you mind?' Without waiting for a reply he picked up the papers, thumbed through them and grunted. 'Hmmph!... I know that lot. Used to do a lot of business with them. Years ago...'

'You know *who*?'

'The Human Company.' He pointed at the bottom of Kepler's article. 'Sort of a theatre group. Back in the 70's. It says this guy worked for them.'

'Kepler? You know him?'

'Never heard of him... but I can put you in touch with someone who does.'

Bob sat down again and folded his arms. If Bob could have smiled, he would have done so. Instead he just nodded his head very slowly.

'Who?' shouted Bernard. 'Tell me!'

Bob nodded his head for a few seconds more before he replied. 'You should have asked me earlier, Bernard. I get around, I hear a lot of things. You don't need a computer when you've got me.'

'Go on, then!'

'Big Mikey. He was part of the Human Company. You'll find him in the pub. The Bull & Plumber. He's always there. Tell 'im I sent you.'

*

There weren't many real pubs left in Bernard's neighbourhood, most had fallen prey to the architect's eye and the wrecking ball, stripped back or knocked down to make way for the bright new world of maximum returns. But the Bull & Plumber remained, big and warm, full of dark corners and dim golden light. It was stuffed with people from another era who liked a drink and then another one, battered survivors living on the edge of the legal and the wrong side of success. Dealers in this and that, bent accountants, dodgy lawyers, bouncers, musicians, roadies, bookies, sparks, hacks. People with stories. Characters.

And that was the problem. Once you entered it was almost impossible to leave. You'd find yourself trapped within some rambling conversation or furious argument or daft bar game where any attempt to escape would be seen as an evasion of your duty to buy the next round, which was inevitably more expensive than the round that preceded it.

So when Bernard walked up to the massive oak bar of the Bull & Plumber that evening he was not feeling optimistic. His spirits were lifted slightly by a surprisingly authentic barmaid, a bleached blonde, cleaveaged Cockney girl with pump handle muscles, steel hard eyes and plump soft lips. He ordered a pint and asked if Big Mikey was in. As Bernard's gaze tilted from pupil to nipple and back she smiled and nodded across the room to a huge man in a paint-spattered canvas coat with a mass of wild ginger hair and a gypsy earring. He turned, looked straight at Bernard and gave a menacing grin.

'Don't upset 'im,' said the barmaid, 'looks like he's in a nostalgic mood.'

As Bernard approached Mikey's table he realised he'd seen him here before; he'd taken it for granted this guy was part of some heavy metal band road crew.

Mikey spoke before Bernard had a chance to introduce himself.

'I know you, don't I? You're that hack...'

Bernard nodded.

'...that hack who hates theatre?'

'Yeah, well, I wouldn't go as far as to say that... mind if I...?' Bernard gestured towards the adjacent empty place on the banquette. Mikey shrugged assent, but it was clear from the way he kept glancing at the two young women opposite that Bernard didn't have his full attention.

'*You wouldn't go as far as to say that*, would you?' Mikey turned back from the women to Bernard, narrowed his eyes, slowly pulled a newspaper cutting out of his coat pocket and began to read. '*The most obsolete and lame of all art forms... all those sweaty bodies proclaiming themselves to an audience of lard-arsed Americans, simpering old queens and tarted-up widows...*'

'You kept my piece?' said Bernard astonished, intimidated and slightly flattered.

Mikey shook his head. 'Nah. Bob the Dealer gave it to me this afternoon. Said you were coming to see me. Wanted me to be prepared.'

Bernard felt his whole body shrinking under Mikey's neolithic grimace. 'That bastard Bob... and you're quoting me out of context...'

'Don't worry, I thought it was funny...' But Mikey didn't appear to be amused. He continued to stare at Bernard for a few seconds, then guffawed and slapped him on the back. 'I'm going to have to educate you.'

'Look, there's something I need to find out... about The Human Company...'

'You're going to buy me a drink?'

'Yeah, of course...'

'It'll be a pint of export and a double whisky chaser. And two glasses of wine for these young ladies. Then I'll tell you.'

When Bernard returned with a tray of drinks Mikey was talking to the two women who seemed to be doing their hardest to avoid eye contact. Mikey slid the wine glasses across table and the women took them without acknowledgement.

'...so you're an actor then?' said one, a girl with long glossy blonde hair and a proud display of skinny midriff.

'Much more than that. An engineer of the imagination, they called me. Creating spectacles, that was my job.'

'Optician, were you?' asked her friend, who had a bright scarlet bob cut and a nose ring. The blonde tittered.

'You don't know the half of it,' Mikey turned to the blonde, pointed at Bernard and winked. 'This guy's from the papers. Doing a special feature on me and The Human Company. Very experimental, very special type of thing, we were.'

'Have I seen you on telly?' asked the blonde with a slight flicker of interest.

'Too big for TV. We'd use the streets, the sky, a forest...'

'What's wrong with theatres, then?' said the redhead.

'We used them in the early days... like you entered the theatre and found yourselves on the stage and all the actors in the stalls hurling insults at you, or there was another one where you'd be waiting outside and got assaulted by vagrants, but of course the vagrants was us and the show was over soon as you got in the theatre...'

'Doesn't sound very nice for the audience,' said the blonde, now clearly bored.

'We thought the audience *needed* to be punished, sometimes...' Mikey's voice was getting louder, 'yeah, like they should be ashamed for wanting to go to the theatre when the world's being ripped apart by greed and stuff! But, *then*, you see,' Mikey reached out and grabbed the blonde by the arm, '*then* we'd reward them, because together we could see what the world *could* be, we'd share - wot'cha call it - *a revolutionary vision of the future, a glimpse of the bliss of infinite possibility...*'

The blonde turned to Bernard and mouthed *who's he?* as she shook herself away from Mikey's clutches. Bernard shrugged and shook his head.

'Don't mean to be rude,' said the blonde, 'but we've got to go and meet some people...'

'Yeah, some people with haircuts,' said the redhead.

The two women got up and took their drinks to the other side of the pub.

'I think you put them off,' grunted Mikey. 'It was going well till you came back.'

'Yeah, well, sorry...'

Mikey leant back and sighed. 'Twenty five years ago it would have been different. Twenty five years ago they'd have been all over me...'

'Yeah, but twenty five years ago they would have been in a pram,' muttered Bernard.

'Nothing hotter than the Human Company back then... the heart of the counter culture, we were.'

'And don't say anything about *counter culture*. They'll think it means you were an accountant. Or a shopkeeper.'

Mikey glared at him. 'You think you're funny, don't you?'

Bernard felt the pint he was holding in his hand shake, then he noticed a smile work its way across Mikey's craggy face.

'Anyway, the Human Company...' continued Bernard, as soon as he was reasonably sure Mikey wasn't going to hit him.

'Yes.' Mikey picked up the scotch and downed it in one. 'How can I begin to explain... Troy - he was in charge - wanted to turn everything upside down and shake it... break down the barrier between the show and the audience, that was his thing.'

'Yeah, well, I'm sure that sounded great at the time.'

'It was fucking tremendous! You hear about the Irish one where we split the audience into Catholics and Protestants and threw real tear gas at them?'

'No, I didn't...'

'Or the slavery show, where they bid for slaves in an auction and got them shackled to them for the rest of the evening?'

'No, that must have been very amusing. Look, I really need some information... about someone who used to be part of your company. A guy called Kepler.'

'Rings no bells.'

'Are you sure ? Professor Rupert Anton Kepler?'

Mikey stared at Bernard and squinted. 'Anton? You mean Anton?'

'Lots of theories about paranoia... says he did research into acid...'

'Sounds like Anton. Must be getting on a bit now. Sort of a mad philosopher, used to go around winding people up, till Troy threw him out...'

'Why?'

'He threw him out of the Asylum Show, the one we did in an old prison hospital... back then, like, we thought there was no such thing as madness, only society decided everyone who didn't fit was mad... they'd say you could get a great trip if you shot up with a schizo's blood - you know that?'

'Sounds a bit avant-garde for my dealer.'

'Anyway, a third of the audience, right, were dressed up as warders, keeping the others in check when they were trying to get out of the padded cells... except they went a bit too far with the discipline, started *enjoying* being warders. That's how the riot started.'

'Sorry to hear that. How...'

'Wasn't meant to go that way. Later on in the show the actors are all hung up in strait jackets and beaten up and given electric shock treatment – all very heavy. And then, just before no one can take it no more, the walls around the yard come down and you're in this huge bit of waste ground lit by bonfires and strings of coloured lights going off into the distance. Then it all explodes and everyone rips off their uniforms and strait jackets and the dead come back to life and there's this huge fucking party with bands and dancing and loads of booze. A *ritual catharsis* type of thing, so I'm told.'

'Right. Catharsis. I heard that was big back then.'

'Yeah, but it didn't happen, did it? All went reels of cotton. Everyone beating seven shades of shit out of each other. Had to call in the pigs. That, for us, was the final humiliation.'

'So Kepler, Anton...'

'Anton... what'd he got to do with it, you're asking? Why did Troy chuck him out?'

'Yeah.'

'Well, there were rumours. Troy reckoned he was some sort of *agent provocatator* I think you call it, stirring it all up, making the rest of the audience think the warders were like real fascist goons working for the state.'

'And was he?'

'Anton on the other side? God knows. He was out of his head most of the time. So was everybody. We had our enemies, you see. Or we thought we did...'

'That's all you know?'

'That's the last I heard of him. Must have been 30 years ago, now...'

'Great. This isn't very helpful.'

Mikey shrugged. 'It's the best I can do. So you're going to buy me another drink and write about our next show?'

'You're still doing shows?'

'Not for 25 years we haven't, but I can let you into a secret. Troy's come back from America. To do his final show. The big one. On Great Britain Day! You've heard about that?'

'Yeah, vaguely...'

'Oh course it's all bollocks, but it's government-backed big time bollocks. They're not going to know what hit 'em. Maybe you could help us. You know people who plant bombs, don't you? Bob reckons that's your thing.'

'Not any more it's not. In fact it never was.'

'Pity. We might need some explosions. That's my job - all the effects. And I'm the only one who doesn't have a script - I can do whatever the hell I like!'

'So what's the show about?'

'Not sure yet, to be honest... Troy, you see, starts with the Elements...'

'Which are?'

'Stuff he sees around. Like, what are people worried about these days?'

'House prices, asylum seekers, public transport, terrorists, what's the best surround sound home cinema system...'

'Yeah, stuff like that. Then he applies the Strategy...'

'Which is?'

'Well, the Strategy turns the Elements into the Show.'

'How?'

'Don't know, mate. He never told me that. I think it's your round, Bernard. Do you reckon we should have another shot at those girls?'

*

The next morning, his head cloudy and throbbing after a long night in the Bull & Plumber, Bernard continued his search for a pen. Finally, at the back of the bottom drawer of his wardrobe, he found it. It was a very special fountain pen, one he had been awarded at school when he was ten for a thoughtful essay entitled *'Will Robots Build Us A Better Future?'* (conclusion - not if Bernard has anything to do with it). The pen at the time had been considered positively futuristic: it was bright turquoise with a clear plastic barrel and a piston that sucked up the ink. It looked like a hypodermic syringe custom built for a wealthy, literary junkie. Bernard even managed to find an old bottle of ink, a weird reddish brown ink that reminded him of dried blood, and a spiral bound notebook.

He sat down at his desk and slowly wrote the heading *'Bombs And Puppets – Who's Lighting The Fuse And Pulling The Strings?'* He spent several minutes watching closely as the ink made its way through the veins of the nib on to the page, resting his head on the desk so he could scrutinise each globule of ink as it was sucked into the fibres of the paper. There was something faintly depressing about the transformation of the liquid ink into indelible marks as three dimensions sunk into two, as if his free flowing thoughts congealed into clumsy banalities as soon as they touched the page.

The evil of technology - perhaps the neo-Luddites have a point... Bernard had only written the first sentence when he found he could not get up; his back seemed to have set permanently in the huddled-up posture of Dickensian clerk. Very slowly, his pen and writing pad still in his hands, he rose and stepped a couple of paces into the middle of the room. He knew the thing to do would be to lie down flat on the floor; that was what his back was begging for. He gently lowered himself down, feeling he had been dipped in plaster that had just set; one tap in the right place and his body would surely snap into neat segments like a chocolate orange. Eventually he was flat on the ground. It was not quite the relief he anticipated but at least there was some improvement. He raised his writing pad above his head and began to write. He was vaguely aware that gravity had a part to play in the process but he hoped the paper might be absorbent enough to suck out a little ink. But no, it was not to be. He thought for a moment then pulled the back of the pen off with his teeth to reveal the plunger inside. Perhaps he could compensate for lack of gravity by applying a little pressure to the plunger with his forehead; then, with his other hand, he could move the note pad around and, in principle at any rate, write.

Bernard had only written one more sentence when the inherent weakness of the technique was revealed. Too much pressure of forehead on plunger resulted in a reddish brown spurt that managed not only to cover the writing pad but to ricochet back on to his face and body. Bernard slowly put the pen and pad down by his side and lay there, ink-soaked and very depressed.

It was at this point that Mel chose to enter. All that Bernard could see out of the corner of his eye was a vast bunch of yellow chrysanthemums followed closely by an enormous, blank smile.

'Bernard? I heard some screaming noises... my God, what happened?'

'I'm just in pain. It's my back.'

'You look like a big ugly new born baby!' She burst out laughing.

'It's really not very funny. The pain is quite bad.'

'Oh don't worry, we'll get that seen to! I have this friend who'll put you back together again in no time!'

She had a friend, did she? Who put people back together again? The thought was terrifying.

'He's fantastic. He works in a Serenity Centre. Part of the Tranquility Foundation.'

'Oh God,' said Bernard, letting out a long moan.

'Just remember, in these situations it is very important to try and stay positive.'

Bernard's moan got longer and louder.

Eleven

'I don't expect everyone to appreciate my work, but, unfortunately, the ones I want to like it, hate it, and the ones who love it, I despise.' - *Bernard Hawks.*

'By the way, Bernard. I've got some good news...'

'Tell me later. When I'm not in pain.'

Bernard was slumped on the bony leatherette back seat of Mel's car; the previous night his back pain had got so intense that he no longer had the strength to fight Mel's insistence that he see her 'specialist'. To his surprise, her car was the one aberration in her relentless campaign of cleanliness: it was old, round and filthy; a rusty, homely sort of British car that smelled of cough sweets and steered like a tractor. Surrounded by old sweet wrappers and discarded tissues and rocked from side to side by the creaking suspension, Bernard had the disturbing feeling of being shrunk down and transported in the bottom of her handbag.

'No, listen... You're invited over to dinner at Sarah's tomorrow night. She's a lovely woman, Sarah, isn't she!'

'What, Sarah? My ex? How the hell do you know her?'

'Oh, I bumped into her a while ago, on the stairs, she was bringing you your mail and I was coming to see Dillwyn. We got chatting... you know how it is... one thing led to another... then I invited her to do The Retreat.'

'The Retreat?'

'Yes, The Tranquility Foundation Retreat. It changed her life too.'

Bernard let out an ear-splitting banshee wail as the car hit a series of speed bumps in the road, each one sending seismic tremors rippling through his spine.

*

Mel helped Bernard up the stairs of the Serenity Centre and left him outside the consulting room. As he opened the door it only took a second or two to realise this was all a huge mistake. The tinkling music, the scented candles, the preponderance of unpainted wood and natural fibres - Bernard expected medical practitioners to operate from rooms with shiny walls and polished lino that reeked of disinfectant. What proper doctor would wear a hand knitted pullover?

'So our approach, Bernard, is holistic - we want to get to the root cause of the condition, how it relates to the rest of your life. We don't believe in just treating the symptoms in isolation.'

'The problem is my back. That's what I want to get sorted.'

'But of course. But let's put it into context. Tell me about your life. Do you find your life particularly stressful?'

'Of course it's stressful. I'd be an idiot not to find it stressful.'

'Very good. What, in particular, are your sources of stress?'

'Well I find this stressful for a start...'

'Go on.'

'And I find the 21st century stressful in particular.'

'Excellent. Can you be more specific?'

'All right. I'm 42 years old and I live on my own in a ludicrously expensive shit-hole surrounded by drunks. The country is run by patronising morons who would send us to war at the drop of a hat, the health service doesn't work, the trains don't work, traffic doesn't move, I get mugged by fourteen year old drug barons when I go to the corner shop to buy a packet of fags, I'm employed by a bank of computers to write prose whose sole purpose is to annoy people, I go to sleep depressed and wake up confused in places I don't recognise. I've become both an enemy and agent of the state, depending on which you find the most abhorrent, so now everyone hates me. The world's fucked and I'm fucked, except I haven't been fucked in any meaningful sense for the last 10 months. I met a beautiful girl who turned out to be a deranged anarchist and promptly disappeared, our hopes for social change hinge on a bunch of hippie puppeteers whose own strings are pulled by some evil conglomerate of which I believe you are part, and my computer has turned into an aviary. Yes, please sort all that out and I'm sure my back pain will go away. Personally I think it would be much simpler to deal with the back pain out of context, on its own, un-holistically. Very strong opiates would be an excellent start.'

'Very good indeed.'

'Could you stop congratulating me? I'm not used to it.'

'We try to encourage a positive attitude.'

'I guess that's why you call it complimentary medicine.'

The therapist switched his ingratiating smile for one that was a little more serious. 'Do you have a drug problem?' he said softly.

'The only drug problem I have is that I owe my dealer three hundred quid and I suspect that, at this very moment, he is planning to take out a contract that will result in yours truly being ground up into a fine white powder to cut with the rest of the noxious crap he flogs to other poor bastards like me.'

The therapist made a whole page of notes on his pad in intricate handwriting. Finally he looked up and smiled again. 'Good. Anything else?'

'I seem to be having occasional lapses of memory... and sometimes I have premonitions...' said Bernard quietly.

'Can you be a little more specific?'

'I keeping losing the odd hour or two here and there. Sometimes a whole day. Then every so often I think of something, or dream of it, and then it happens...'

Where did that come from? thought Bernard. It was true; up to that moment he hadn't really confronted the problem, assuming it to be an inevitable side effect of his aberrant life style. But something very disturbing had been happening; his brain seemed to losing bits of the present and replacing them with the future.

'Before we go any further I suggest you should go on a programme of detoxification. I would like you to take this homeopathic remedy that has proved to be very effective in these circumstances.' He passed Bernard a small brown bottle.

'And what exactly is in it?'

'A very, very dilute solution of the toxins that have induced your condition.'

'Does it have to be that dilute? My body is more used to the concentrated kind.'

'Strange as it may seem, the weaker it is, the more effective the remedy.' The therapist once again smiled pleasantly.

Bernard felt his mouth open. A torrent of observations and rational deductions rushed towards his lips but, exerting enormous self-control, he managed to shut his jaw just in time. This was not the moment to start an argument and delay his escape from the clutches of this home-knitted quack. 'Fine. Can I go now?'

'I would like to end this session with a little gentle manipulation. Is that all right?'

'Great. Being manipulated is part of my lifestyle. Go ahead, enjoy yourself.'

Bernard wanted to get this all over with as quickly as possible so he could go home and get drunk. He lay face down on the couch, his head stuck in to a face-shaped hole lined with leather. His initial impression of being trapped in a medieval torture device was confirmed by the events that followed: somewhere in the room he heard a snapping sound, like someone was breaking up cheap furniture for firewood. Simultaneously a pain shot through his body and he realised he was listening to the sound of his own bones being reordered. He was infused with hate for this sadistic little torturer and the bunch of gangsters who employed him. But then there was quiet followed by a strange feeling of calm.

'You can get up now please Mr. Hawks.'

'I doubt it.'

But he did get up. In fact Bernard rose surprisingly easily and, to his great astonishment, found the pain in his back had disappeared.

Through some miracle he had been given a body transplant; he wondered what poor bastard had been given his old one.

'And Mr. Hawks...'

'Yes?' said Bernard as he rushed towards the door.

'You may find that a more positive attitude to the world will have a very beneficial effect on your overall well being.'

He smiled again. Bernard glared back and slammed the door behind him.

*

Bernard walked back home; it was raining hard and it would take an hour but it was worth it just to get the feel of his new body. There was a spring in his step, not just because of the sudden release from pain but because waiting for him at home was a large package that had been delivered just before he left. In that package was the Cydrax, back from convalescence at the Dark Orchard. For once Bernard felt surprisingly positive, but that feeling did not last for long for, as he turned the corner, blocking his path was the looming figure of Casper.

'God Bernard, you really do look like shit.'

'Thanks Casper. I actually feel great.'

Bernard carried on, walking as fast as he could. Casper, with long leisurely strides, strolled along beside him.

'You've been getting yourself into trouble, haven't you Bernard? Upsetting everybody.'

'People deserve to be upset. It's good for them.'

'That's as may be, but you're going way off the scale now. They're calling you a fascist, do you realise that?'

'Yeah, sure. Makes a change from being called a degenerate anarchist.'

'All that stuff about machine gunning down all the dope dealers and yobs. Was that a joke or what?'

Bernard stopped. 'What the hell are you talking about? I might have thought... occasionally... but I never wrote anything...'

'It's in the *Daily Glimmer* and they're lapping it up.'

'Bollocks. I haven't even had a computer for the last couple of weeks. Have you actually seen it in print?'

'Not exactly in print. It's in their on-line edition. Middle England fights back.'

'Middle England?'

'Maybe you think you're being ironic, but I'm not sure if anyone else does. You even had a go at the Neighbourhood Peace marchers.'

'Yeah, well, protest is fine, but how can anyone take them seriously when they're backed by that bunch of Tranquility shysters...'

'I told you, Bernard, your cynicism is out of date. If you want change, it's going to come from people like the TF.'

'Jesus, Casper!'

'They're harnessing the power of consumer choice, they've left people like you far behind. Anyway, I don't know why you're getting so uptight. They've always been your audience.'

'Who?'

'Middle aged, middle class, middle England. You know the average age of your readership is 57? They're the ones who share your bomb fantasies.'

'Piss off!'

'Yeah, I know you think of yourself as some sort of revolutionary, but the rest of the world thinks of you as a curmudgeonly old fart who's got old twenty years before his time. By the way, here's that pass to the TF Serenity Retreat I promised – looks like you'll need it more than ever now.'

Casper passed him what looked like a credit card. Bernard glanced at it suspiciously before putting it in the back pocket of his jeans. Casper stopped on the next corner, laughing, and Bernard carried on home, convinced that Casper had finally lost it altogether.

Or did Casper have a point? Had Bernard become, to use his own phrase, a media twat, a twat beyond redemption? In his teenage years he had been a revolutionary; he had campaigned and protested, marched and picketed, walked out and sat in. Disillusionment had come with age; as lines appeared around Bernard's eyes his anger grew slack, his fighting muscles began to ache, his revolutionary vision blurred in low light. He found that those with the right ideas were no better people than the those with the wrong ideas. If he questioned other people's certainties he was judged disloyal, if he argued his case he was a traitor. He got weary of doing and saying the right thing and found being difficult kept boredom at bay. By the time he had reached his thirties the rest of the world had come to regard him as a cynic but, from where Bernard was standing, all he wanted was to work things out in a disintegrating world distinguished only by its mediocrity. He had grown to expect disappointment. He had tasted the fruit of the tree of knowledge of good and evil and found it to be a Golden Delicious.

*

Bernard gingerly lifted the Cydrax out of a box lined with apple-scented black polystyrene chips. It had clearly been very well looked after. It was wrapped in a black towelling robe and came with two complementary sachets of Cydrax Cream Case Cleanser and Cydrax

Screen Mousse, a helpful order form to replenish the supplies, and an informative note warning against the dangers of unauthorised cleaning agents. It was as if the gleaming Cydrax had returned from a well earned holiday at a luxury hotel; Bernard would do his best to make it feel at home.

He switched the computer on and it chimed and purred into life. This was a whole new Cydrax. It was fresh and vital, it responded to Bernard's mouse and keyboard swiftly as if it could anticipate his every move. It was like falling in love all over again. Now he could go back into the archive and tie together all those loose connections between The Tranquility Foundation, the Primitive Front, the mysterious JJ and the world of Post Credibility. He moved his cursor across the screen to click on the archive folder - but there was no archive folder. In fact, there were no email files, no notes, no database, no documents and no sign of Dillwyn's disc. The computer had come back to him born again, but it had not just been cleansed and rejuvenated - the Cydrax had been brainwashed.

Twelve

'Watch people when they're at their computers, really watch them, then you'll see the keys move under their fingers, sucking at their fingertips. The keys move and the fingers follow.'

Animal

Bernard woke up and was shocked to find his back was still free from pain. He decided to exploit this reprieve and make a new start. Now he was as a columnist for the *Daily Glimmer* and he was reaching out to a wide audience, there were vitally important things to say, important enough for forces unknown to wipe his computer clean. He had responsibilities; no more writing about planting bombs, no more chasing crazy anarchist girls. But where to begin? He decided to get out of the house; a quick morning stroll would clear his head. It seemed like a good idea but for one oversight - he had not bargained on New Weather.

Bernard had fond memories of the time when Old Weather ruled, performing its repertoire with reassuring predictability: it would be cold in the winter, wet in the autumn, warm in the summer. Now that the whole universe was open to offers, New Weather had taken over. It was auditioning for the elements franchise with an aggressive demonstration of its work experience and flexibility. One day tropical sunshine, the next day snow; floods on Monday, drought on Tuesday.

It was mild and dry when he left his flat but seconds later the sleet came. Sleet, for Christ's sake, buckets of the filthy cold stuff sinking down under his collar and creeping into his pockets. Was sleet a peculiarly British phenomenon, did any other nation feel the need for it? It was impossible to experience joy in sleet; there would never be a great musical called Singing In The Sleet, no Hollywood dreams of a Sleety Grey Christmas. It was the most depressing and depressed of all precipitation; snow that had lost the will to live.

He had just reached the end of his road when he made the decision to go back. As he turned to face home, his damp reverie was brutally interrupted by a screech of brakes directly in front of him. A car had driven up on the pavement, blocking his path, and out of it leapt the small, rounded figure of Inspector Pitmarsh. He ran up to Bernard, reached up and shook him by the shoulders.

'Oh Bernard, good to see you. Nice to be in civilised company again. You wouldn't believe some of the people I have to spend my time with. Criminals, Bernard! Thieves, thugs, animals... a young woman called Animal – does that name mean anything to you?'

'No.'

'Give it some thought,' Pitmarsh paused, then leant forward and spoke softly as if he had a great and painful secret to share. 'You know, you're very lucky you've got me as a friend. Colleagues of mine have told me these stories you write, the ones about the bombs – and I don't mean to be funny – might actually be illegal. Our lawmakers have made you some sort of criminal.' Pitmarsh drew back and threw his hands in the air. 'Yes, I know, absurd! You go to bed an innocent man and wake up a traitor! They want you arrested! They want you banged up, Bernie! But I said no, leave him be. We'll have a chat in private, head to head, man to man, and he'll tell me things ordinary people don't know...' With a sudden gesture Pitmarsh gripped Bernard's shoulder hard. It was still sore from their last encounter and the gap between his collar and his neck was beginning to fill with cold, wet sludge. Pitmarsh moved so close Bernard could feel his spit. 'Like who those bastard bombers are... the Primitive Front, perhaps... friends of yours?'

'I don't know anything about the Primitive Front, I don't know anything about bombs and I don't write about them any more. And even if I did, a journalist never reveals his sources.'

Pitmarsh pinched tighter. 'Of course Bernard, I forgot. How foolish of me. But, sadly, we have to compromise some of our principles in these troubled times.'

'Let me guess. You're, like, the Good Cop, next I get the Bad Cop who's going to kick me down the stairs...'

'Oh no, Bernard. There are only Good Cops now! We have to treat everyone with dignity and courtesy, even freaks like that...'

Pitmarsh wheeled Bernard round until he faced a vaguely familiar group of hooded youths in the distance walking fast towards them. Then he let go of his shoulder, jumped back into his car, slammed the door and wound down the window.

'Good luck Bernard. I'd love to stay and help, but you don't know how much paperwork that would mean, and if it came to court it would be dismissed as youthful enthusiasm, some sort of tribal celebration, a cultural event - courts are very understanding towards kids who use violence as a means of self-expression. Still, if you'd really like to arrange police protection, just give me a call.'

'What the hell are you talking about?'

Inspector Pitmarsh winked, reversed back off the pavement and sped away into the distance. Bernard turned back to find the youths were now only a few yards away from him. There must have been about six of them, limbs threshing around fat bodies like badly strung marionettes. Their bloated hands clutched paper bags from a fast food takeaway and, as they drew closer, Bernard could see beneath the hoods misshapen heads with small eyes, thin lips and skin like freshly plucked chicken. They formed a circle around him and began to pelt him half-heartedly with morsels of battered fat.

'Look who it is – Bernard Fucking Hawks, the Bomber Lover!'

'Where shall we put the bomb today, Bernie? Up your fucking arse?'

They sniggered in unison.

'You read my column?' asked Bernard meekly.

'Oh you don't have to read to know who you are.'

One by one they began to prod Bernard with their fingers.

'We know all about your bomb.'

'There's evidence!'

'There can't be,' said Bernard. 'It's got fuck all to do with me. It never had anything to do with me.'

'Ooh, he doesn't believe us! Calling us liars, are you?'

'You don't believe in anything, do you Bernie?'

'He don't deserve to be white!'

'Scum like you make me sick...'

At which point the lad who made this last remark threw up adroitly over Bernard's chest, causing a great outburst of laughter among the other youths.

Bernard's mind was not surprised when the first kick hit him in the stomach but his body took it badly, winded and outraged by this bewildering action. Bernard fought back in the only way he knew, which was to curl up into a ball and pray the attackers would get rapidly bored. Which indeed they did, but not before they had delivered a series of hearty blows, and not before Bernard had passed into well-earned oblivion.

*

Bernard opened his eyes long enough to glimpse a large figure blocking out the sky. Sleet filled up his eyes and he half closed them again. He could just detect the shape move as it crouched down to talk to him.

'Hello Bernard. I suppose this wouldn't be a good time to ask for some money?'

'Bob. Even if I had any, I couldn't give it to you. I'm cold, wet and in pain. I can't move. I can't do anything.'

'I suppose not, Bernard. This weather. It's the end of the world. Or maybe just the beginning of the end. It will get a lot worse.' He emitted a long, deep sound somewhere between a grunt and a sigh. 'I'll see you soon.' Bob's shadow moved away and Bernard closed his eyes completely.

The next thing he was aware of was someone shaking him vigourously.

'Hey, Bernard, take it easy... didn't think it would be long before the police got to you...'

It was a very familiar female voice. Bernard squeezed one eye open again.

'Animal... they weren't police... they were just thugs... kids...'

'Oh they were police all right. Plain clothes juniors. New recruits. Given the choice of probation or joining the force. Don't worry, we'll get our own back.'

'Don't want to get anything back... just want to go home... I've given all this up,' mumbled Bernard. He looked up and found himself staring directly into Animal's face. She looked different again; she was wearing what looked like army surplus combat gear with some sort of knitted hat. Her eyes were olive green. 'He was asking after you - that copper Pitmarsh...'

'And what did you tell him?'

'I said I'd never heard of you and, anyway, a journalist never reveals his sources.'

'Oh Bernard, you're so quaint!'

'Thank you.'

'But you needn't have done that. We want them to think we're the Primitive Front.'

'You what?'

'Come on, let's get you home.' Animal grasped his upper arms, someone else grabbed his ankles and Bernard found himself being loaded into the back of a van. The doors closed and Bernard became dimly aware of the presence of Animal sitting beside him, some old sacks beneath his head and a distinct smell of rotting vegetables. As the world became a little clearer, so did the pain.

'I thought you didn't believe in technology and machines?'

'It's just a van, Bernard. Don't be daft.'

The van reversed with a jolt then accelerated forward. Bernard let out a yelp of pain.

'Hey, Bernard don't sound so negative,' shouted the driver, 'you're doing great! Even better now you're a criminal!'

'Who's he?' wheezed Bernard.

'Oh that's Gabby. Another fan of yours.'

'I don't need any more fans. I just want to hide. You know someone rang me? Said he planted my bomb. Said he had evidence that I did it.'

'You're lucky. Most people don't get their bombs planted for free,' said Gabby.

'That's what he said.' Bernard pulled himself up to a half-sitting position. 'So – was the bomber one of your lot? The Primitive

Front? That's what Pitmarsh thinks you are, but then the Front are supposed to be a government invention. So was he? Are you? Is it?'

Animal looked at Bernard and gave the very slightest shake of her head. 'Just keep Pitmarsh thinking we're the Primitive Front and everything will be fine.'

'Kepler - you asked me to find out about Kepler... I tried...'

'Forget Kepler. There's more important things happening now.'

'But... just someone please tell me what the fuck's going on.'

'Relax, Bernard. Give him some of this, Ani,' said Gabby, passing to Animal an elaborate looking glass pipe. Animal handed it to Bernard. As he took it he noticed his hands were red with blood, presumably his own.

'I thought you didn't believe in drugs,' said Bernard.

'Did I say that?' said Animal with a shrug, 'Oh yeah, well you were getting a bit frisky that night. And I was on duty.'

She winked at Bernard – or was it just a nervous tic again?

'Like, inconsistency is a great tactic,' shouted Gabby. 'You know, an inaccurate missile is a better weapon than one that always lands in the right place. Scares more people, does more damage.'

'Is he one of them too?' murmured Bernard.

Animal shook her head and put her fingers to her lips. Bernard inhaled from the pipe. As the acrid fumes hit the back of his throat the whole world, him included, suddenly got vastly bigger.

'What the fuck is that?'

'Just some roots and leaves. Shaman stuff. Should help with the pain and shift your perspective a bit.'

'Helps decrease the options,' cried Gabby.

'The what?'

'You have to give up choice, Bernard! So our lives can be ruled by accident and necessity, the only way to be free...'

'What the fuck's he on about?' murmured Bernard.

'Like they control us by giving us what we want,' continued Gabby with increasing enthusiasm, 'so we have to stop wanting things. They want us to think life's a supermarket, and the longer shelves are, the more free we are, right Bernard?'

'Well I don't feel free, I just feel used.'

'Don't worry about Gabby,' whispered Animal, 'even he doesn't know what's he talking about half the time. Just stay cool. We've got work to do together.'

'Look,' said Bernard, 'I've had enough of being a revolutionary. I want to go back to being a hack. I'm not going to write about planting bombs any more. It just gets me into trouble.'

Animal's eyes narrowed very slightly. He had the distinct sense that she was disappointed in him. 'Maybe it's not so easy to stop now.

You're part of a process. We couldn't control it if we wanted to. And of course we don't.'

Bernard realised he was now lying flat on the floor of the van with his eyes closed, his arms stretched out wide hoping to stabilise himself against the spinning universe. He sensed something warm and human coming towards him. He opened his eyes and saw two green pupils far too close for him to focus. A nanosecond later a pair of warm moist lips touched his own and two strong hands clutched his head. It felt unbelievably good. Then she drew away and spoke to Gabby. He could hear their voices clearly but they seemed strangely distant.

'What's he talking about, wanting to pull out?' said Gabby. 'I thought you said he was going to be useful. Pond won't be pleased with that.'

'He wrote about the bombs before we even knew they were going to happen,' Animal replied. 'That was good enough for me.'

'Yeah? I don't know what Pond is playing at with this one. '

'New strategies, Gabby. Got to be subtle now. Anyway, I want to give Bernie another chance.'

Animal climbed into the back of the van and moved close to Bernard.

'There's just one more thing you need to do for us,' said Animal. And then she smiled. It was a smile that was so deep and warm that Bernard felt they were conspirators sharing a great secret together, a secret that would make all the bad things fade into insignificance. 'Look, Bernard, I know you fucked up on that TF exposé you were going to write for us...'

'I wrote it...' muttered Bernard, 'but it got pulled for being too nice.'

'Doesn't matter now. There's plenty more targets.'

'We got to smash the mechanisms, Bernie!' shouted Gabby.

'Break up a few machines? Is that what you want to do?'

Animal moved closer to Bernard so her lips just touched his ear and whispered very softly, 'It's not just about machines any more. You know that, don't you? Well, not machines you can see and touch...'

She was interrupted by Gabby's shouts. 'Hey, Ani, Pitmarsh is still behind us. We'll have to chuck Bernie out. Feed him to the pig.'

'It's me they want, not him. Just drop him at his house for Christ's sake – it's just here!'

'OK, but still not stopping. Bomb doors ready!'

'Slow down at least!' cried Animal, 'Bernard, I'm sorry, but there's no gentle way of doing this. We'll finish this one later. I'll be in touch very, very soon...'

She opened the back doors of the van and, with both hands, rolled Bernard out.

There was a moment, a very brief moment but one that seemed eternal, when Bernard felt immensely optimistic about the world. In that fraction of a second, when his body had left the van but not yet hit the curb, all pain had gone and his head was filled with a curious image that bubbled up from the depths of his childhood. It was the very first advertising poster that had ever grabbed his attention: a small woolly-hatted boy and girl, dressed in red and green, were walking hand-in-hand down a long straight avenue lined with blue-green fir trees and white picket fences, stretching to the horizon. Despite the fact the journey was infinitely daunting and the children hopelessly vulnerable, an optimistic glow radiated from the picture. The children possessed an irrepressible jauntiness, perhaps emanating from their shiny new sandals, that assured they were ready to face anything on the long road ahead.

Then the road, yellow and bright, rose up from the ground and wrapped itself hard around Bernard's head, pulling tight until he could see and hear no more.

Thirteen

'The natural world! So what's that then, some bucolic fantasy about going back to the days when we hunted and gathered and lived in the trees and all loved each other and pulled the bugs out of each other's fur?'
                                      - Bernard Hawks, The Indicator - 'Notes From The Shadows'

For not the first time in his life, Bernard woke up in a place he did not recognise. It had an air of familiarity about it which was at odds with the scents of bleach and synthetic pine, the distant sounds of scrubbing and the stark quality of the light. He had been to war and woken up in a hospital; he must have been in a coma for - God knows – weeks? Months? His suffering had been long and hard but now, by the grace of medical science and the care of that smiling nurse with the big head, he was returning slowly to the world.

Within the second or two it took his eyes to adjust to the light he knew something was not right. No hospital had a carpet with red and orange spirals or bookcases lined with old magazines and neat rows of shoe boxes. He sat up abruptly and had an odd feeling that he might be at home. But everything was wrong: it was like a cheap sci-fi fantasy where aliens on another planet, with not entirely convincing results, had done their best to reconstruct a human environment.

Bernard felt an urgent need for a very strong cup of coffee. He put his feet on the ground and stood up with unexpected success, then found himself falling towards the ground. By flinging an arm out against the nearest wall, he managed to remain on his feet. Very slowly he stood up straight and began to explore.

It soon became clear that this was, indeed, his flat; it was just that it was terrifyingly clean. The carpet with the red and orange spirals was the same one he had known as dark brown. A window which he had always assumed to be smoked glass was now crystal clear and his ebony bathroom suite had been restored to its original, disturbing, avocado. On his bookshelf there were three shoe boxes: one was filled to the brim with anonymous keys, another with rubber bands, a third with not quite empty disposable cigarette lighters. The large hole in the plaster on the living room wall was now covered by a brand new, wood-framed, cork notice board. And on the board was a note in large, childish handwriting:

```
Looks like you needed a bit of a rest so
I thought I'd let you sleep. Did a bit
of tidying up - hope you don't mind.
I'll pop in later to see how you are.
All the best    Mel xx
```

It took all of thirty minutes to find the necessary items to make a cup of coffee. After lengthy research he found coffee in a jar labelled 'coffee', sugar in a jar labelled 'sugar' and, finally, a mug on a pine wood mug tree. Jesus Christ, a *mug tree!* Did it mean there had been a previously undiscovered mug tree in his flat or had that woman actually gone out and bought one? The implications of either were too distressing to contemplate: he had befriended a woman who bought, or at the very least unearthed, *mug trees.*

Bernard sat down with his cup of coffee. Before he could even begin to come to terms with what had actually happened to him there was a loud knock on the door. Without waiting for a reply the door opened and there, in all her beaming splendour, was Mel. Bernard did not beam back.

'Hi there!' said Mel. 'Good to see you've come back to life.'

'Why?'

'Sorry?'

'Who did this? Was it you? I can't pay you, you know.'

'Don't be silly, I don't expect to be paid.'

'If this is some sort of penance you must have done something very, very bad.'

'It's nothing - since I was cleaning up Dillwyn's place, I thought I might as well do yours too. He said to look after you if I could, besides, your place was getting a bit depressing. I always think when you wake up somewhere fresh and sparkling the world feels so much better, don't you?'

'No. How did I get here?'

'You were on the doorstep – don't you remember?'

'Well, it was a long time ago...'

'Yesterday afternoon. It's 10 o'clock in the morning now.'

'Oh. And you put me to bed?'

'Well, I helped a bit. No bones broken – I checked. How's your back?'

'I hate to say it, but it seems fine. It's just everything else that's fucked.'

Her huge, face-splitting smile got even bigger. Bernard knew he should be grateful but instead he found himself thinking about his fantasy machine gun.

'Thanks.'

'I'm going to go now, to the march, but I'll check back later, just to make sure you're OK. By the way, there was a message from your editor. You missed your deadline, but don't worry - they're going to re-run one of your old stories.'

'Yeah, they do that... you're going to what march?'

'The Tranquility Campaign marchers - they're protesting about the police.'

Bernard stood up and felt a twinge of guilt where his back pain had been. 'Oh.... I guess I should join you. I mean, I would if I wasn't still bruised from my last encounter with the fuckers. Well, good luck. Sorry I can't come along.' He sat down again.

'Yes. Well, marching isn't your style, is it Bernard? I'm not sure if walking is actually, either. Anyway, must dash. Don't forget Sarah's expecting you for dinner tonight.'

*

Sarah. Animal. They couldn't be further apart. It was only when he found himself rifling through his wardrobe looking for the least crumpled shirt that Bernard admitted he was actually looking forward to going to Sarah's. This was a shocking revelation. He sat down, poured himself a large whisky and started pondering the implications. Was he just getting old or simply coming to terms with the responsibilities of being a mature, committed journalist? Or was the appeal simply that it was easier to pursue his radical insights in a comfortable middle class dining room rather than out in the streets where policemen attacked him and anarchists threw him out of vans?

He and Sarah had parted just over two years ago. He had got the sense that all was not right when he came home one evening to find all his possessions on the pavement stuffed into black bin bags. This was followed by three hours of shouting and mutual incomprehension, some ritual destruction of photographs and soft toys and a small amount of bloodshed. Bernard retreated to 'temporary' accommodation, where he still lived. It was only in the course of the last year that they had re-established contact, agreeing to meet once every two months through some dim obligation to remain friends and be 'grown-up', to retrieve his mail from their former address, and more than anything else, to reassure himself of the total absurdity of the idea they could have ever successfully lived together or, in fact, even liked each other. That and the remote, never realised but still feasible possibility of a momentary reconciliation, just long enough for a night of furious, uncomplicated sex.

His fears that Sarah had invited him over to show off her latest, pitiful boyfriend were put to rest when he realised there were just the four of them – Bernard, Sarah and a neatly dressed but curiously bland young couple called Simon and Miranda, who, like all of Sarah's friends, seemed to have been chosen to match her furnishings. Miranda did something in (or possibly on) television and Simon claimed to be 'changing the system from the inside', which turned out to mean managing an 'ethical' investment fund.

Since splitting up Sarah's life had flourished. Or so she assured Bernard. She had begun training to be some sort of therapist or

77

counsellor, a career he had inadvertently driven her towards and in which she found solace, revenge and justification for her patronising disapproval of Bernard. Or so it seemed to him.

He had to admit to himself that Sarah looked extremely well. Her hair, now a dark and glossy auburn had been reengineered into a style that reminded Bernard of one of his favourite 1960's *nouvelle vague* movie heroines. She wore a silky black trouser suit that radiated a feminine authority combined with a slightly oriental hint of sensuality. To his surprise, he found her irksomely attractive. The thought struck him that, despite everything they had been through, there might be something to be said for being with a grown-up, sensible woman like Sarah. Perhaps he had learnt something over the last couple of weeks; perhaps it was time to put aside their differences.

Sarah's creamy beige flat, a monument to life post-Bernard was bright and soullessly clean. It occurred to him that he had been invited as a counterpoint so the flat would appear even more tasteful, or perhaps as a sort of novelty sideshow for Simon and Miranda. Then there was the third, intriguing possibility that Sarah had began to realise how much she missed having Bernard in her life. Whatever, his chosen strategy was to say nothing at all through the first course. He smiled and nodded in what he assumed were the right places until he made his excuses and retired to the lavatory.

On returning to the dining room Bernard had suddenly summoned the nerves to engage in conversation, and indeed, had begun to look forward to it, despite the fact his nostrils were burning ferociously from the two long lines of amphetamine sulphate he had just snorted off the lid of the cistern.

'So Bernard!' said Simon. 'That column in *The Indicato*r… causes quite a stir, doesn't it!'

'Actually I'm working for *The Daily Glimmer* now.'

Bernard grinned and leant back in his chair. He carried on leaning back until the sudden realisation the chair was on the point of toppling over, then, not a moment too soon, grabbed the edge of the table and pulled himself back upright again.

'Oh fantastic,' said Sarah, dryly, as she began to hand out the main course, 'so now you can encourage even more people to plant bombs!'

'I've stopped doing the bomb stuff. I've turned over a new leaf. And all I ever said was, *if* terrorists want to undermine our so-called civilisation they should get their priorities right. You know - advertising agencies, TV chat shows, cappuccino chains, celebrity gossip magazines, church youth clubs, bingo parlours, garden centres, financial consultants…'

'Blowing people up isn't funny, Bernard,' said Sarah.

'Sorry, I should have put a warning at the bottom: *remember, killing people is wrong, please don't try this at home.*'

'You could, perhaps, try writing something positive,' ventured Simon, 'just to see how people react?'

'What, like, *cheer up, it might never happen*?'

Bernard poured himself a second large glass of red wine.

'But Bernard, I'm afraid I don't actually see the point,' said Miranda.

'What is the point of any of us here?' Bernard grinned, Sarah frowned. 'Aren't we all in the amusement industry now? Isn't that our primary function? To produce an endless tawdry circus of entertainment and distraction, while on the other side of the world ragged half-starved children sew our clothes and pick our food and religious maniacs plot our destruction?'

'So you mean... what you write is all just... a sort of a joke?' asked Miranda.

'In a way. All right, I do like to think I can make people question things. Not just accept the crap they're given on a plate...' as he said this Sarah deposited a large white plate of carefully arranged limp vegetables in front of him, '... no offence.'

'None taken,' said Sarah. 'It's all organic, of course.'

'I'm sure it will be delicious!' said Miranda.

'Well you can't be sure, can you,' said Bernard, with what he hoped was relaxed good humour as he placed a friendly hand on Sarah's waist. 'Not with Sarah's cooking!' Sarah moved rapidly round to the other side of the table. 'And because it's organic doesn't mean it's going to taste any good, does it?'

'Now you don't have any objections to organic food do you, Bernard?' asked Simon.

'No, it's fine...' Bernard breathed in.

'Thank God for that,' said Sarah.

Bernard breathed out again. '...if you're part of a privileged elite who can afford to purge their guilt by paying twice as much for their food grown in animal shit rather than chemical shit, why not do it, that's what I say!' Bernard laughed, but nobody else joined in.

'I think confronting our ecological crisis a little more than purging guilt, Bernard,' said Simon, smiling pleasantly.

'All right then, I could object to it on political and ecological grounds,' Bernard continued. 'Ecological because you use twice as much land to grow half as much and political because it's that same old *get back to nature and everything will be all right* reactionary bourgeois schtick.'

'What does he mean, Sarah?' said Miranda, looking rather puzzled but trying to hang on to her smile.

Sarah shook her head very slowly. 'Bernard was a Marxist in his youth.'

Miranda still looked puzzled.

'You know,' continued Bernard, his voice gaining pace, 'the God-Given Natural Order: trees, animals, the monarchy, the class and the caste systems, the rich and the poor, all in their place, not to be disturbed... anyway, what have you got against chemicals? They've been responsible for some of my most memorable experiences.'

'It seems you don't take the fate of the planet very seriously,' said Simon.

'I take it extremely seriously. I just don't like token gestures, and cynical marketing ploys dressed up as good deeds. In fact, I've actually got a lot of empathy with the planet. Like I feel particularly finite at the moment since my own stocks of non-renewal energy are running pretty low. That's why I recycle as many of my ideas as possible. And I've been polluted and pillaged and no doubt I'm doomed too... I've had enough of all this guilt for being human. As I see it, we're the only species that gives a fuck. That's right! The planet has fucked us up with droughts and floods and tornadoes. Yes! This planet has fucked us over good and proper and what's it going to do about it? When's it going to start worrying about conserving us?' Bernard stopped midstream as he realised he was rushing headlong down a one-way street in the wrong direction and he wasn't even sure why he started on the journey in the first place. Miranda and Simon still wore smiles, but wore them like last season's fashions that they would drop off at Oxfam any minute now.

'Tell us, Bernard,' said Simon, diplomatically shifting topics, 'seriously now, who do you think was behind that bomb in the advertising agency? They keep talking about some bunch of delinquent neo-Luddites called The Primitive Front. Apparently they want to do away with all technology.'

'Oh they're absurd!' added Miranda, 'I know we're all very concerned with our carbon shoe size, or whatever you call it, but they seem to want to drag us back to the Dark Ages.'

'Yeah, well, the Dark Ages have always had a bit of a bad press,' said Bernard, 'Unfairly, in my view. But I wouldn't worry about the Primitive Front. They probably don't exist.'

'I'm sorry?'

'Well they could be a government invention. To cover up their own bombs. Or maybe they do exist and the government is planting bombs in order to trash them. That's why they wiped my computer!'

'Oh Bernard...' said Sarah in despair.

'On the other hand,' Bernard continued, oblivious to the fact he had just knocked over a full glass of organic claret, 'the Primitive Front might have created the whole idea that they are a government creation to cover up its own activities. Or maybe the Front are planting bombs, but they're doing it to make it seem the government are planting bombs to discredit them.'

'Shut up, Bernard. You're beginning to sound like that mad Welsh neighbour of yours,' said Sarah.

Bernard froze for a moment, then sank his head into his hands. Rivulets of red wine poured across the table cloth on to Bernard's lap. 'Dillwyn. Fuck, you're right. I'm turning into Dillwyn... it wasn't supposed to go this way.'

Bernard whimpered quietly as he contemplated this prospect, then joined the silence that had now descended on the dinner table, a silence that was broken a few minutes later by the door opening and a large head and a vast smile.

'Surprise!' cried the bearer of the smile, throwing out her arms.

'So glad that you could make it,' said Sarah. 'You know Miranda and Simon. And, of course, Bernard.'

'Hello Bernard.'

'Hello Mel.'

'So how did the march go?' said Sarah to Mel.

'It felt really good. You should have been there. You would have loved it.'

Mel gave Sarah a kiss and a big hug. Then carried on hugging her for what seemed to Bernard like an inappropriate length of time.

'So you gave the cops a good hammering, then?' said Bernard.

All four turned to stare at him.

'You know, put a stop to police brutality!'

'Not quite that, Bernard. It was the Neighbourhood March...'

'Yeah, I know...'

'They're campaigning for more Bobbies On The Beat. Part of the Peace in the Neighbourhood campaign I was telling you about.'

'More of the bastards...'

'And more cameras in the street. Cameras to watch over us and keep us safe!'

'Oh yes!' added Miranda. 'We're pressing for one of the new designs - they look so much more discreet - just like Victorian lampposts!'

At that point Bernard's mobile phone rang. Generally speaking, in these circumstances he would not dreamt of answering it – not through any sense of etiquette, but because he preferred listening to his calls as messages rather than risk engaging in conversation. But now it gave him a perfect excuse to leave the room.

'Excuse me. I'd better take this. Business, you know.' Bernard ran out into the hall, slammed the door and answered his phone. He was greeted by a disturbingly familiar voice.

'Hello Bernard. Long time no hear.'

Bernard said nothing.

'Bernard, do you like animals?'

'Who is this?'

'Oh you know who this is all right. Last time I was trying to help you with your bombing campaign and you were very rude to me – out of your fucking head, you said, wanted to strangle me, you did. Not nice. But there's something we need to discuss...'

'You know where Animal is?'

'Of course I do, Bernard.'

'Well, I don't want to see her. I've left all that stuff behind.'

'I'm sure you haven't, but first there's something much more important on my mind. And it should be on yours too. Like what happens when your next bomb goes off? I think we need to talk.'

Bernard attempted to stay calm. Was this, perhaps, a journalistic opportunity he couldn't overlook? 'Yeah, well maybe we should meet.'

'Now that's better. I thought you'd come to your senses sooner or later.'

'But I've stopped writing about bombs now...'

'You have, have you?'

'...so maybe just an informal chat. Over a drink.'

'Oh Bernard, I don't think you're taking this matter seriously enough. You see my expenses are building up. It costs money to plant these bombs - you've got to pay your bills. We need to come to an arrangement. So how about this: why don't you write something. Something to help my business...'

'I can't believe I'm hearing this.'

'It wouldn't be hard. A little bit of PR. Like a piece discussing the effectiveness of violence. You and I both know how crap that "no negotiating with terrorists" stance is...'

'You want me to give you a mention...'

'Yeah, just put in a good word. You know, you scratch my back...'

'Go fuck yourself.'

'Charming. Have it your own way. But don't say I didn't try to help.'

'Hey, you said you knew where Animal was...'

But the bomber had hung up. Bernard flung his phone across the hall with such violence that a spasm of sharp pain rippled through his arm. And then, as if in sympathy, his back echoed and amplified the pain until he found himself flat on the floor screaming in agony. The door to the dining room opened to reveal Mel and Sarah staring at him in horror.

'Oh Bernard. What are you up to now?' said Sarah.

'It's my back!' shouted Bernard. 'It's totally fucked again! I'm in agony!'

'I took him to my specialist,' said Mel, 'and he did some wonderful work. But Bernard's attitude is so negative...'

'Why should I trust him? He's one of those Tranquility bastards,' shouted Bernard between screams.

'Ah, The Tranquility Foundation!' said Simon, as if he had just woken up. 'They're offering some very interesting investment opportunities. Peace Derivatives!'

'You shouldn't knock the Foundation, Bernard,' shouted Sarah, 'and you should appreciate what Mel is trying to do for you. She's a wonderful person!'

Mel's face became one vast smile again. She turned to face Sarah and they kissed. A long, warm and very passionate kiss. Bernard's screams mutated into a series of deep, painful sobs.

Fourteen

'Hasn't the porcine metaphor become a little bit of a cliché?'
                    - Inspector Frank Pitmarsh, Metropolitan Police

Bernard lay on his bed contemplating the rare pleasure of the full night's sleep that had just passed. The pain in his back had receded to a barely acknowledgeable twinge, which he attributed to the fact he hadn't seen Mel for a couple of days. The ageing but powerful pain killers he found in the back of his kitchen cupboard probably helped too.

So now his back was free of pain, his flat free of clutter, his computer free of data. But Bernard didn't feel free, he just felt empty. He sat up and looked out of the window but there was nothing to see; the sky was a flat dishcloth grey, no wind to move the skeleton branches of the trees or blow the litter down the pavement. He lay back down again and may well have stayed there all day until he realised this was Friday, and Friday was a special day for Bernard: it was the day he bought the newspaper.

Half an hour later Bernard entered the newsagents at the end of the street. As he walked towards the counter the proprietor swiftly folded a newspaper and offered it to him.

'I expect you want your *Indicator*, Mr. Hawks. End of an era, I have been told. A swan song, is it not?'

'Thank you, Mr. Patel.'

'Rather unusually quiet today. Perhaps there's going to be a storm. The calm before the storm, as they say.'

'Yeah, great.'

'I haven't seen your neighbour Mr. Dillwyn. Nor that lady Mel who helps him. Are they not in town currently?'

'No idea. I haven't seen them or anyone else, to be honest. Nor any phone calls for that matter.'

'That is a pity. But you must look on the bright side. People have been talking about your column today. It seems to be causing quite a commotion. And some of those large cigarettes papers you favour?'

'No, not today. Thanks.'

'And your back, Mr. Hawks? How is your back?'

'My back is fine, thank you. Everything is fine. Everything is great. So everybody tells me and who am I to argue.'

As Bernard left the newsagent and turned the corner he found himself facing a familiar tall figure in a crusted denim jacket, shuffling his feet as he stared at the ground. The man looked up and spoke in a slow, mournful voice.

'Hello Bernard. Don't suppose you've got some money for me?'

'Bob, look, I'm not trying to be funny, but I've got a new job now. On a tabloid. I'll be solvent again very soon. Even moderately well off. Maybe.'

'A new job. I heard about that.' Bob thought for a moment. 'Guess you'll be able to buy lots more gear off me now.'

'No Bob, I'll settle all my debts then everything's going to be different. No drugs, no conspiracy theories, no mad anarchist girls. I'm trying to lead a normal life.'

'A normal life.' Bob nodded his head for what seemed like a very long time then looked straight at Bernard with his wet animal eyes. 'So how's that going then?'

'Crap, actually.'

Bob almost smiled. 'Tell you what I'll do Bernard, to help keep you off the straight and narrow. A free sample.' He handed Bernard a small, dark lump. 'Burmese black. Hand pressed by orphans in prison camps.'

'You're giving it to me for free? And I owe you money?' Bernard rolled the lump between his fingers suspiciously.

'I think you'll like it. You're sure to come back for some more. It's a marketing strategy, you see, Bernard. Loss leader, they call it. The Job Centre put me on a course. You learn about that sort of thing.'

'I don't...'

'Yes, Bernard?'

'Nothing. Thank you.' Bernard put the lump in his pocket.

'I suppose you've got *The Indicator* there. I heard it's the last time you'll be in it. Heard they reprinted one of your old favourites.'

'How do you know about that?'

'Oh, I get around. Hear a lot of things. Ear to the ground, eyes to the heavens, that's me.' Bob sighed and shuffled off into the distance.

Bernard walked back to his flat. Mr. Patel was right, it was peculiarly quiet, apart from the siren of a distant police car or, perhaps, a fire engine.

It was only when Bernard got back into his room that he realised that the street was no longer quiet, and the siren he heard was the first of many. He went over to the window and saw that the street was filling up with cars. In the distance there was some black smoke curling into the air. Probably some local lads had set fire to a car again; it was becoming an increasingly popular local pastime, and he had begun to suspect it was part of another council strategy to reduce congestion.

He went back to *The Indicator* and flipped through the pages until he found his photograph and his column. Printed above it in large, bold type, were these words:

'Falling asleep to the squeals of burning piggies and waking up to the smell of crispy bacon…'

The bastards reprinted it! He heard two more sirens in the street outside. He ran back over to the window, opened it and leaned out. He realised the smoke, now a thick black cloud, was coming from the vicinity of the police station. He looked down to the pavement and saw a policeman with a loud hailer pointing straight at him.

'Mr. Bernard Hawks. Please give yourself up or we will have no choice but to make a forced entry.'

The house began to shake as if something very heavy was ramming repeatedly against the front door. Crashing noises and a cheer from the ground floor were followed by the sound of a dozen booted feet running up the stairs and a further pounding on the door of his flat.

'Bernard? Are you there? This is your friend Inspector Pitmarsh. Fancy a little stroll down to the station?'

Bernard instinctively searched his pockets for possible incriminating substances.

'Are you going to open the door, Bernard? I'd rather not break it down…'

But Pitmarsh's voice was drowned by the sound of splintering wood as a battering ram broke through the door. Bernard found he was holding the small lump of hash that Bob had given him. He swallowed it. The ram struck again and the entire door disintegrated.

'I do apologise, Bernard. Patience is not a virtue shared by my colleagues.'

Four young officers in combat gear ran in and grabbed Bernard from either side. A fifth pulled his hands behind his back and clamped a pair of handcuffs on his wrists. Pitmarsh stood in the remains of the door frame, stubby hands on hips, grinning.

'You've disappointed me, Bernard. Here was I giving you the benefit of the doubt, thinking maybe the poor lad got in with a bad crowd. But no, you're right in the thick of it, aren't you! The Primitive Front! They took the cue from you to burn down my station!'

'This is all totally and utterly wrong. I…'

'Bernard Hawks,' shouted Pitmarsh, 'you're not obliged to say anything, and anything you do say… well, probably wouldn't help much, would it?'

'You could have rung the door bell,' muttered Bernard.

'All right gentlemen, take him down.'

Bernard was pummelled and dragged down five flights of stairs to the ground floor while Pitmarsh ambled leisurely behind. His captors pinned him against the wall until Pitmarsh caught up with them.

'Anyone got a blanket to cover this ugly bastard to shield him from his fellow hacks? No? All right Bernard, we'll do the best we can.'

Pitmarsh grabbed Bernard's leather jacket by the collar and wrenched it over his head until his face was completely covered. Bernard felt something hit him hard on the skull several times as he was bundled out into the street.

In the dark world of his jacket lining Bernard could see nothing, but he heard a multitude of things. There were murmurings and sirens and the shouts of reporters asking him why he had done it and who he was working for. There were distant sounds of motorbikes and helicopters and, getting louder by the second, horses' hooves.

'Last time I saw them but didn't hear them,' shouted Bernard from inside his coat. 'Perhaps these are yours. The only animals with cunts on their backs.'

'What are the fuck are you talking about?'

'Police horses. Just for me? Bit over the top, isn't it?'

'Hit him again someone, please. You might knock some sense back into the bastard.'

As the truncheon smacked against the thin leather of his jacket the sound of the horses seemed very close indeed. He could even smell them. Bernard felt himself passed from one person to another on his way to what he presumed was the police van. He heard a series of loud bangs followed by shouting, then a thick, oily vapour hit his nostrils. He coughed violently then, over the fumes, he caught a whiff of a flowery feminine cologne as a firm hand pressed his back and a genteel female voice whispered in his ear.

'Don't worry Bernard, you're among friends. You don't have to hide anymore.'

He felt his jacket being pulled off his head but to his horror he was still in the dark. He had been struck blind – no, not quite, he could just make out the trace of something or someone moving in front of him. He realised he was in the middle of a thick cloud of black smoke. He coughed again.

'Put your foot in there…' said the voice, as his shoe was guided into what felt like a small metal hoop, 'put your hand on my shoulder and Gerald will lift you up.'

Bernard found himself being pulled up into the air and onto what could only have been the back of a horse. There was whinnying and shrieking and an odd sort of chortling laughter. He felt himself being strapped on to someone in front of him, then heard the rallying notes of a hunting horn, very loud and very close to his ear. Bernard and whoever it was he was attached to galloped away through the smoke, jumping high over the row of vehicles and people that were blocking the end of his street.

Bernard's hands were still handcuffed behind his back and he was strapped so tightly to the rider in front of him he could only look sideways. He could hear the sounds of another horse the other side of him and the female voice that had aided his escape. Before long they had cleared his neighbourhood and came to rest in an industrial estate. As the horse turned round Bernard caught a glimpse of a steel shutter rolling up at the back of a large truck and a ramp being lowered. Bernard's steed trotted up the ramp, then he heard the shutter roll back behind him.

When Bernard's eyes adjusted to the light he found he was being unstrapped from a man clothed in full hunting pink. A similarly dressed woman pushed a small step ladder up to him and together they helped him down off the horse. The horse snorted and stamped its feet on the floor of the truck.

'Easy now, Oswald, you too Di,' said the woman as she fitted nosebags on to the horses' heads.

'Mr. Hawks! Time for some introductions. I'm Penelope and this is Gerald. We've been looking forward to this for a long time!'

'Awfully glad to meet you, Bernard!' Gerald thrust out a welcoming hand then realised Bernard's were still cuffed behind his back. 'Silly me! Do your stuff, Penny!'

Penelope picked up a large pair of bolt cutters from the side of the van and cut through the chain that was that was holding Bernard's wrists together.

'Don't worry, the smithy will take the rest off,' said Penelope.

'Right now, Bernard,' said Gerald. 'We mustn't dally around or you'll miss the party! Major can't wait to meet you!'

'We're taking you to the country, Bernard, isn't that wonderful?'

'Please, not the country...'

'Get you away from all this squalor. We're going to Major's farm!'

'Tally Ho!' shouted Gerald, hammering his fists on the driving cab.

The truck moved off and Penelope, Gerald and Bernard fell down on to the straw covered floor. Penelope, Gerald and the horses seemed to find this exceedingly funny. Bernard didn't; Bernard had a very bad feeling about this whole affair.

Fifteen

'The city's not always pleasant, but at least you can *live* in the city. The country's for people who have stopped wanting things, who have given up and gone there to die.'

- Bernard Hawks, The Indicator - 'Notes From The Shadows'

'Gin and tonic?' asked Penelope, cheerily.

Bernard hesitated before he replied; he was struggling to come to terms with two unsettling observations. Firstly, if this was how the hunting class lived it was nothing like he imagined it, for the Major lived not in a mansion or even a farmhouse but a modest home counties bungalow. Secondly, it was becoming increasingly clear that the very small lump of hash he had swallowed an hour ago when Pitmarsh hammered on his door was not such a small lump after all.

Bernard was standing with his back to the wall of the lounge. Glaring at him from the opposite wall was a wrought iron coal-effect electric fire surrounded by glittering horse brasses and copper scuttles, and they all seemed to be pulsating. Thirty or so people were crammed in along with two overstuffed sofas, a vast cocktail cabinet, three standard lamps and a television hidden in a mock-Regency mahogany cabinet. The majority of the guests, who were all laughing in a deafening mix of chortles, whoops and screams, were mostly in their thirties or younger, but, confusingly, dressed in the clothes of a previous generation. Even Gerald and Penelope had swapped their hunting pink for beige.

He was struck by a sudden revelation: these people were in disguise. This was some sort of bizarre fancy dress party, or perhaps, more intriguingly, a small band of Bernard's dedicated followers dressed for covert operations behind enemy lines. Accepting the ingenuity of those around him, Bernard began to relax, and he stopped worrying that the walls of the room seemed to be bulging. He realised he actually felt rather good.

'Bernard? Gin and tonic?' asked Penelope again.

'Perfect!' replied Bernard, and burst out laughing. Penelope laughed too.

'Double? Triple?'

'Make it two!' They all laughed again.

'Drink while you can, that's what I say,' said Gerald as he poured the drinks. 'It'll be banned before you know it.'

Penelope passed the drinks to Bernard.

'I have to say, you saved my skin today,' said Bernard, a crystal tumbler in each hand.

'Excellent training opportunity – preparations for the struggle ahead!' said Gerald.

'Don't think I would have lasted long in the police van,' said Bernard.

'World's falling to pieces, Bernard. You can't even rely on the police any more.'

'Of course – they're complete bastards.'

'Absolutely!'

'You know I've been getting a lot of hassle from them lately…'

'All this stuff and nonsense about civil rights and diversity - they've gone mad!'

'Sure. I've got the bruises on my head to prove it.'

'It's them against us, Bernard my man!'

There was a loud clink of glass against glass as Bernard found he had raised both gin and tonics to his mouth at once. He was aware of a certain heaviness in his hands, then noticed the severed handcuffs still clinging to his wrists. He lowered his arms and paused to allow a pang of anxiety to pass through his body.

'Am I one of them or one of us?'

Gerald and Penelope screeched with laughter. Bernard joined in, but with rather less enthusiasm. His brief phase of euphoria was fading fast and there was a tightness in his chest and a familiar, nagging feeling in his brain which he knew heralded the onset of paranoia.

'By Jove, you're a funny man!' said Gerald with a nudge. 'Don't know how you get away with it!'

'Are you all right?' asked Penelope. 'You look a little pale.'

'I just feel… confused…' mumbled Bernard.

'Of course, dear boy,' said Gerald, 'these are dark times. That's why people like us have to stick together!'

He slapped Bernard heartily on the back. Bernard spluttered.

'Come on Gerald, let's leave him to mingle. Oh Annabel,' shouted Penelope to a woman in a sage twin-set and an olive tweed skirt, 'there's someone I'd like you to meet – I'm sure you'll get on like a house on fire.'

Gerald and Penelope walked away leaving Bernard standing alone. He realised his heart was pounding very fast and he did his best not to panic as the voices in the room merged and rose together into a single roar. A wave of paranoia broke over him. Everyone was throwing him glances. And laughing. *They're taking the piss*, thought Bernard, *they're all taking the piss and sooner or later they're going to come clean. And shoot me.* The person called Annabel was staring at him suspiciously. He glared back, doing his best to look cool. She was a slim woman with long permed brown hair, thick oval framed glasses that matched the colour of her skirt and an orange suede shoulder bag. She smiled and wandered over to him. He froze.

'Hello Bernard.'

Bernard shuddered. There was a rattling sound which he realised was the chain of one his handcuffs hitting the side of a crystal tumbler. He looked at the green eyes behind the green framed glasses.

'Animal... what the fuck are you doing here?'

'Looking after you. I heard that story of yours was being reprinted so I tipped off these guys. Pulled a favour. Shame about the police station, wasn't it!'

'That wasn't... I didn't... and how did you know? Did you do it?'

'They think it was you. Don't worry, they're very sympathetic. They've had a few run-ins themselves with the cops lately.'

'Well, thanks for saving me, anyway.'

'No problem. We haven't finished with you yet.'

She winked. Bernard stared back, struggling with the fact that although she was dressed like a 1960's librarian, he found her insufferably sexy. He wasn't quite sure why. At least it gave him something to concentrate on, a green horizon in a choppy brown and beige sea.

'Animal?'

'Yes?'

'Get me out of here. At first I thought it was all some sort of joke but they're just a bunch of deranged Tories.'

It was the skirt. It was tighter and shorter than it should have been. And there was something about the roughness of the tweed and the smoothness of the slender bare legs beneath it.

'You're staring at my legs, Bernard.'

'Sorry, just trying to focus'. He looked up. 'Who are these people? You know them?'

'Major is my uncle, or second cousin or something. Haven't seen this lot for twenty years. They think I'm the prodigal daughter.'

'The Major. Where is the Major?'

'Major – not 'the'. That old guy over there in the blue velvet jacket.' She pointed to a scrawny man of around sixty with long dyed black hair, an emaciated, craggy face and a cigarette holder clasped between thin stained fingers. He was shaking everybody's hand and laughing manically. 'Look familiar?'

'Vaguely.'

Bernard was beginning to feel a little steadier. Another feeling was creeping up over the paranoia. An edgy, hungry feeling.

'Sixties rock star – Major Ursa and The Constellations – OD'd in the seventies, married a penniless deb he met in rehab, decided to be a country squire, bought a mansion, lost it in the eighties, bought this instead, been here ever since. Still thinks he's Lord of the manor.'

'And the others?'

'Mixed bunch - farmers, haulage operators, the odd toff fallen on hard times.'

'And Gerald and Penelope?'

'They run a B & B. And before you ask, yes, the hunting stuff's for real. Except they have to import the foxes from the city now – the indigenous population got the hell out when the Rottweilers arrived.'

'Right!' said Bernard. He felt a grin beginning to form on his face.

'Pull yourself together - Major's coming over to talk to you...'

With great effort Bernard pulled his eyes away from Animal and turned to see Major bounding towards him.

'Bernard Hawks! We've been waiting a while for someone like you to come along.' Major's eyes were small, black and glazed and his voice cracked and slurred, with a trace of a Birmingham accent. 'We knew things were getting heavy then we got the word they were going to bust you. Don't worry, won't blow your cover. No one else here knows.' He winked conspiratorially at the separated handcuffs.

'Err - what can I say?' said Bernard.

'Take it easy, Bernard, you've said it all already. No one believes in anything any more. That's why we have to take the lead. Return to traditional British values, solid principles. This, Bernard, is where it's at! Here! The red-blooded heart of England!' He leant forward so his forehead almost touched Bernard's. 'I trust you'll be riding with us on Great Britain Day?'

Before Bernard could think of anything to say a gong sounded followed by a shrill voice from the other side of the room and the smell of burning fat.

'Dinner everyone! Time to go through!'

'I'll let you go now, Bernard – and don't worry about Annabel – you can trust her. By the way,' Major whispered, '*Third Reich on Magic Mushrooms* – far out!' He winked again and staggered off to the dining room. The rest of the party followed.

Bernard reached out to Animal and pulled her closer to him. 'I don't think I can handle dinner with this bunch.'

'You're right, their cooking's disgusting.'

'I think they all want to kill me. Soak me in fox piss and throw me to the dogs.'

'But they love you! You're their hero!'

'That's even worse. Much worse.'

'Bernard? You're looking very pale. Are you stoned?'

'Very. I think I'm going to die.'

'We're all going to die, Bernard. Let's go out into the farm. I want to show you something.'

Bernard followed Animal through the back door of the bungalow into a large yard which backed onto a half dozen long, corrugated-iron sheds. Bernard felt huge relief in being outside even though it was overcast, cold and beginning to rain. His anxieties had begun to fade but a void was opening up within his head. A void that only Animal could fill.

'So where's the farm then?'

'This is the farm.'

'Have they got one of those hayloft places? I always liked the idea of those. Rolling around...'

She grabbed Bernard's arm and shook him, 'Come over here. I want to show you something.'

She led him to a wire fence that marked the edge of Major Ursa's property. In front of the fence was an old oak tree which she proceeded to climb. She gestured to Bernard to follow, which he did with surprising ease as he found the tree had deep footholds cut into its trunk. He looked up at Animal above him. Her tight green skirt seemed on the point of splitting along the seam and he was struck by a sudden urge to run his tongue up the back of her legs.

'Bernard – what are you doing? We haven't got much time.'

Animal had stopped at a platform half way up the tree and was pointing into the distance. Bernard wrenched his concentration away from Animal for a minute or two and stared out into the landscape. Below the bungalow, the land dipped down into a small valley. It was the sort of tamed, weary countryside where nature had got in the way of an otherwise straightforward suburban development. A double white-lined road made a detour around a hillock of ancient trees then forded a stream by means of a defiantly ugly concrete bridge. Beyond the road a procession of electricity pylons headed triumphantly towards the horizon. Just before the stream a lane led off into ring of trees, behind which Bernard could just make out a series of small huts, each with its own wooden veranda.

'That was my grandparents' place. The Colony.'

'What was it? It looks like a holiday camp.'

'It was in a way. A naturist resort. One of the first. It was hilarious – they thought if we just took all our clothes off it would sort out all the world's problems.'

'I suppose it would fuck up the fashion industry...'

As Animal turned round to face him, Bernard watched the tips of her breasts press against the thin fabric of her cardigan. At that moment he felt he could empathise completely, in a rather profound way, with the fundamental principles of naturism.

'My parents were born there. And so was I. Grew up there, in fact. But by then they had ditched all the naturist stuff. Since the Sixties it had been The Hive. Bernard, are you listening?'

'Yeah – go on.'

'The Hive was a sort of a hippie research lab. A commune with lots of acid and sex with a bit of tantric Buddhism and psychotherapy thrown in. They had a fantastic time for a while...'

'Those hippies. They got it so right.'

'...but they were doing serious stuff as well. Cartographers of the inner space, they said they were. Made some real breakthroughs. Major was there too but he fell out early on – tried to sell some crap photos of sex rituals to the Sunday papers. My side of the family wouldn't have anything to do with him but they ended up giving him this bit of land a few years ago to get him off their backs.' She laughed, but it was a distant laugh, not the gloriously infectious one Bernard had heard before. 'Now I've got some work to do. Follow me to the barn.'

They climbed down. Animal led Bernard back across the yard to the largest of the sheds and pulled open a small side door. He followed her inside.

It was dark and Bernard was deafened by the high pitch screeching of machinery that ran the length of the building. It stank like a cesspit in the height of summer. As his eyes adjusted to the light he realised that what he thought were rows of machines were, in fact, cages and in the cages were thousands of chickens squawking as loud as their lungs could manage.

'For old times' sake, you understand,' said Animal, shouting above the noise and pulling a small drum of cable and some wire cutters out of her shoulder bag. She began to thread the thin cable carefully through each of the cage doors. The birds in the cage she was working on went strangely quiet until she moved on to the next one.

'I get it, you're part of that Animal Liberation bunch...'

'Once, years ago. Then some of us got to realise that we're animals too... like, maybe that's the best way to think of ourselves. Except our heads get fucked up because we think we're more than that, we think we're in control. Well you know all this, don't you, Bernard. So these days my work is with the humans. You know, blowing open our own cages...' She carried on threading the cable through the cages, clipping the sides of the cage doors and sticking a small amount of a putty-like substance on each one. 'Like the trick is to leave just one hinge, bend the door a little to get the tension right, then it will sort of spring open... oh, you'll see... you don't need very much, mustn't hurt them...'

Bernard watched her, totally involved in her work. There was something strangely compelling in her concentration and the delicate

94

but firm way her fingers pulled the cable. He walked towards the cages and immediately a thousand beakless chickens turned and stared at him and started squawking even louder. It was like they knew him.

'Bernard Fucking Hawks! Where are you going to put the bomb today?' screeched the chickens.

He backed away. An egg dropped down from one of the cages into a long metal trough and rolled away out of sight. He turned back to Animal. 'So what did you mean by that - blowing open our own cages?'

'Like we think we're free because we can buy all the shit we want, but really, we're just the same as these chickens here, all part of the production line, all doing what we have to do. But what's worse is we've let them build the cages inside our heads, right Bernard?'

'The smell in here is really, really bad. I think I'm going to throw up.'

She looked up and grinned.

'Nearly done now, Bernard. We'll save the rest for the front.'

'The Front?'

'Front of the barn.'

She applied the remaining large lump of explosive to the main barn door, then threaded the cable through it. She attached the end of the wires to a small black box with a dial on the front, studied a digital watch clipped to the inside of her jacket and carefully adjusted the device.

'Timing is everything - finding the rhythms - that's what we have to do.' She looked at Bernard and laughed. 'Oh – I nearly forgot...'

She reached into her bag and withdrew what looked like a large hatpin. She inserted it in turn into the handcuffs on Bernard's wrists, and, with a deft twist, released them. The cuffs fell to the ground and Animal went back out into the yard. Bernard followed. It was raining hard now and the skies were as dark as mud.

'I need to get out of here. Very soon,' said Bernard, shivering as he pulled his jacket over his head to keep the rain off. Animal moved very close and pulled the edge of the jacket so it partly covered her too. There was a strange look in her eye that he could not quite decipher.

'I want you to go to the Tranquility Foundation retreat. It's the only safe place for you now. Guaranteed anonymity to protect the celebrity scum who go there. Trouble is, not quite sure how we're going to smuggle you in. The more bombs go off, the busier they get.'

'I've got a pass.'

'Bernard! I said you were a genius. How did you get it? People kill for those!'

'Casper gave it to me. There must be a catch...'

95

'That's sorted, then. Let's go back inside – they'll be doing the film show now.'

The went back into the bungalow and, as Animal had predicted, a film projector had been set up in the dining room. The guests, seated around a long table, were still finishing their trifles when the lights dimmed. There was just one chair free at the corner.

'Go on, sit down,' whispered Animal.

Bernard sat down and Animal stood behind the chair. She put her hands on his shoulders and the show began. Major started playing the chords to "Jerusalem" on a synthesiser as the brown velvet dining room curtains were pulled open to reveal a screen. He flicked a switch and a drum machine kicked in with an early 80's hip-hop beat. The projector clattered into action and Major raised a fist into the air.

'Yeah everybody!'

The audience applauded and Major began to rap to the beat.

'Look out of the window and you'll see the bright green
Of our glor-i-ous country is 'coming obscene
Blackened by the dirt of a million foreign scum
If they don't like our country, why do they come?
The dope heads and the perverts and the filthy hippie tree huggers
chavs pikeys wogs and all the state supported muggers...'

'This...' muttered Bernard, 'I mean, this is seriously fucked up...'

'Yeah pretty intense, isn't it,' said Animal, 'Major always was crap. I'm going to sit down.'

Animal slid round to the front of the chair and sat down on Bernard's lap.

'Hang on tight, Bernard, this could be a bumpy ride.'

Bernard put his arms around her slim warm waist and moved his head to the side so he could watch the screen. He became very aware of her weight pressing down on him and another pressure rising up to meet her.

The film seemed to have been spliced together from old British movies and public information films. There were idyllic images of sunlit corn fields, thatched cottages, cows grazing in green pastures, smiling milk maids and happy ploughmen crudely intercut with shots of factories, street demonstrations, riots and black and Asian faces looking pained or angry.

'The city's lost its way and the country soon will rise
To those who know the truth, it will come as no surprise
That hard work, good breeding keeps our spirit pure
The City is the past and the Country is the fut-ure!

The audience cheered and, loudly and discordantly, shouted out the chorus.

So let's all cull the weak and feed up the strong!
Stand up for the right and shoot down the wrong!'

Now there was a sequence of huntsmen blowing their horns on hilltops at dawn followed by a frantic montage of rifles, pitchforks and marching feet. The audience became very excited, clapping in time to the beat, and Animal joined in, rocking back and forth on Bernard's lap.

'I don't think you should do that,' whispered Bernard, 'this is all getting too much.'

Animal simply laughed, looked at her watch, lifted herself up then thrust her hand underneath her. For a brief moment Bernard wasn't sure what was happening, but then he was very sure indeed. She had unzipped his flies and grabbed hold of him. Bernard gasped as Animal, naked beneath her green tweed skirt, lowered herself down on to his resolutely erect penis. Bernard entered another universe. He let go and clutched the back of the chair. For a moment he was an astronaut stepping out of his claustrophobic capsule onto a wondrous new planet; instead of being confined to a small dark room with a bunch of deranged neo-fascist farmers, he was released into the shocking bliss of Animal's body.

On the outer edges of his consciousness Bernard was dimly aware the film was drawing to an end. Major was playing a climatic chorus of 'Land of Hope and Glory' and the guests around the dinner table were singing along with great abandon, banging their spoons on the table. Animal was rising and falling to the music and shouting out obscenities that only Bernard seemed to hear, alternately gripping and releasing him with impressive control. As he continued to cling desperately to his chair, his desire for this moment to go on forever was as intense as the certainty that it was all going to end horribly soon.

The film finished, there was a round of applause, and then a moment of eerie silence, broken only by an explosive sound, somewhere between a scream and a grunt, from Bernard as he reached his own conclusion. Animal got up and Bernard tumbled off his chair on to the floor. At that moment the entire house shook to a real explosion, the blast taking with it all the windows of the bungalow and the electricity supply. The room went black and people began to scream. The first explosion was followed immediately by a battery of smaller ones like a long string of firecrackers. Bernard looked up from the floor to see Animal, her arms raised triumphantly, silhouetted against smoke and fire. She looked magnificent. He watched as she ripped the digital watch off her wrist and threw it into the flames. Then she turned to him and spoke.

'Time to go Bernard. Don't forget to do your trousers up.'

'Jesus,' said Bernard, picking himself up off the floor.

They ran outside into the yard. The rain was pouring down and with it were burning fragments of timber. Something wet fell onto Bernard's arm which had the look and texture of scrambled egg.

'Up the tree!' said Animal. Bernard followed her as she climbed back up to the platform on the old oak.

In the yard below chickens, dazed and bedraggled, were wandering from the barn into the dining room. Bernard heard gun shots and saw a rifle poking out of one of the shattered windows of the lounge.

'They're firing at the chickens,' said Bernard in disbelief.

'They'd say it was self-defence, but really, they can't help it. It's just what they do. But don't worry, they won't hit any – they're crap shots.'

'Shouldn't we run away somewhere?'

'No rush, the animal tranquilliser will kick in soon - I spiked their Brown Windsor.'

Bernard looked down and saw that the guests had emerged from the house and, rather than running about madly, seemed to have gone into slow motion, wandering around in circles among the chickens. One or two had even begun to lie down in the yard, oblivious to the rain.

'And anyway,' continued Animal, 'I want to see the other charge go off. I set it before you arrived.' As she said this there was a huge explosion from one of the other sheds behind the barn. Animal's eyes gleamed in the orange-red light of the blaze that crackled across the roofs.

'What the fuck was that?'

'Their munitions dump. They've been stockpiling for the big day.'

'The big day?'

'Yeah, well, that's something we don't have to worry about now. And we can't have them taking any more credit for the explosions.'

'What do you mean?'

'Never mind. We've got to head off for the TF retreat now.'

'How do we get there?'

Animal looked at Bernard as though he had just said something very stupid.

'We walk – I showed you, it's just down there.'

'What, The Colony or the Hive or whatever?'

'Yes, Bernard. It's part of the TF now, like everything else. They hijacked all the ideas and used them to build up their empire. You can tell me what's going on in there.'

'Ahh...' said Bernard, as if, for once, something was beginning to make a little sense. He turned to put his arm round Animal to comfort her but she had gone. She was already climbing back down the tree.

'Come on Bernard, time to move on. Before the fire gets to us.'

Sixteen

'Serenity with Security'

They had been walking for about ten minutes down the hill towards the Retreat when Bernard realised that the drugs were beginning to wear off. The paranoia of the last couple of hours had now been displaced by a more everyday anxiety and a vague feeling of excitement.

'Hey, Animal…'

'Yeah?'

She stopped and turned round to face him. It was the first word she had said since they left the farm.

He didn't know whether she was tired or just deep in thought. He looked for some trace of emotion in her face but all he could see were the flames of the burning barn reflected in her green eyes. In the distance, behind her head, there was a misty yellow glow in the trees from the lights of the Retreat.

'I've just thought of something. A couple of years ago I wrote a piece once about how the countryside didn't exist. It was just like shit, blood, diesel and slave wages on the one hand, and some sort of warped suburban fantasy on the other. Fucked off labourers and rich city bastards pretending to be country squires. Said if I had my way, I'd…'

'Burn it to the ground?'

'Yeah, well, I think I said *burn it to the ground or give it to the hippies*. But it was never published. No one ever read it. Weird, isn't it?'

Animal shrugged. Bernard continued.

'So, you can tell me now - was it them? Did they plant my bomb?'

'Are you crazy, Bernard? They're just moronic throwbacks. An aberration. They couldn't plant a potato, let alone a bomb. They can be useful, though. Like today.'

She turned and carried on towards the Retreat. Bernard followed.

'So why did you blow up their barn? Not that I'm complaining or anything…'

'For old times sake, just like I said. And one less factory farm can't be a bad thing.'

'So, you do blow up things for the Primitive Front, right? You burnt down the police station, didn't you?'

100

'No, Bernard. I didn't have to - it was burning already when I got there. You should be glad - it kept you in the news.'

'Yeah, terrific. Now just explain what you actually want with me...'

'Your time will come soon. But no more explaining now - we're there.'

The entrance to the Retreat was uninviting; two floodlit solid heavy steel doors, each with a discreet TF logo painted on them, set between high old brick walls.

'I don't feel good about this,' said Bernard.

'You'll be safe in there. Things will quieten down soon. Try your pass on that.' She pointed to an illuminated, blue convex disc, about a foot in diameter, set into the wall.

'After this...,' said Bernard, 'when I get out of this place, it would be great to go away somewhere...'

'Go away? You are away.'

'No, I mean far away. Like together. Have some fun. Fuck it, I've been through a lot. I've put up with enough crap.... where do people run off to? Paris? Berlin? Bali?'

'Travel's part of the old world, Bernard. There's nowhere to escape to any more. Anyway, my work is here.'

Bernard reached out and grabbed Animal's arm. 'Work? I thought you were supposed to be some sort of anarchist. Who gives a fuck about work? I tried being straight and it was a disaster. You and I – we see through the crap, don't we – isn't that what you said? Fuck the lot of them!'

She shook free of his hand. 'Yeah well, there's a few things I've got to do right now...'

'Well, that's all right. I mean, blow something up if you want to, I don't care. If that turns you on, it's fine with me. Just try not to kill anyone if possible. Then just let's fuck off some place... I don't know, a beach hut somewhere hot? Like on an island...'

'So you like beaches?'

'No, hate'em, but I don't mean the ice cream and donkeys sort... more like getting stoned together beneath palm trees as the sun sets, waking up to the sound of waves breaking on the shore, just you and me in a little hut that smells of pineapples and mangoes... no bombs and fat greasy policemen and hooded kids and traffic... no machines, no computers... you'd like that, wouldn't you?'

'*Sous les pavés la plage*?'

'You what?'

'Never mind.'

They stared at each other for a few moments then Bernard shrugged and walked towards the gates. Animal stayed where she was. He hesitated for a second then turned round.

'One more thing - what happened in the dining room – you and me – do you think we might do it again? Like, in a bed or something?'

For the first time in half an hour she laughed. 'Oh Bernard, you're hilarious sometimes! Don't ask me – you're the one who sees the future.'

'Hey - do you have a phone number or anything like that. When I get out...'

'No phones, Bernard. I'll keep an eye on you, don't you worry.'

She raised a hand to wave a vague good-bye then turned and walked away. Bernard went up to the gate, took the pass that Casper had given him out of his back pocket and pressed it against the glowing disc. The gates opened slowly and silently revealing a long, straight driveway lined with conical bushes. The drive, which was lit on either side by rows of small yellow lights set flush into the ground, led to an imposing Victorian house. It could have been a respectable country hotel or a golf club. Bernard looked back to see if Animal was still there but she had gone. He sighed and walked on as the gates closed behind him. It was eerily quiet apart from the sound of his own feet crunching on the gravel.

He was half way down the drive when something grabbed his arm very tightly. He turned and saw, half concealed by a bush, a ghostly, bespectacled face lit from below by a shaft of yellow light.

'Psst – Bernard – it's only me!'

'Dillwyn – what the fuck...'

'Saw you coming in, just then. I happened to be on guard duty tonight. There's lucky, isn't it?'

'What the hell are you doing here?'

'Been here for a week now, doing research, like... there's so much to tell you...'

'Calm down Dillwyn, just try to explain.'

In the distance Bernard heard a dog bark. Then several dogs barking.

'But I gotta go now... I'll come and find you... whatever you do, look out for the strings...'

'Dillwyn, what the hell are you talking about?'

But Dillwyn had gone. Bernard heard a rustle in the bushes, but beyond the yellow lights of the driveway there was nothing to be seen but dark, shadowy trees.

He's finally cracked, thought Bernard.

He walked on towards the house. The front door was open and it led straight into a large, brightly lit reception area. Behind the desk was a slight, smiling, oriental woman.

'Welcome to the Tranquility Foundation Serenity Retreat.' She placed her palms together in front of her face and bowed.

'So,' said Bernard, 'have you, err... got a room? For a couple of nights?'

'I do assume you have an invitation, sir?'

Bernard handed over the plastic card. She inserted it into a computer, scrutinised the screen, took the card out and handed it back to him.

'Very good. Welcome Bilberry...'

'Bill Berry?'

'Bilberry. It is a fruit. We assign everyone a name taken from nature. Our guests like to keep their identity to themselves. You're here for cosmetic surgery, is that correct?'

'Give us a break. Do I look like someone who wants plastic surgery? Don't answer that. Anyway, I thought this place was all about being natural.'

'Inner and outer beauty, sir. And our surgery process is strictly organic. Ah... I do beg your pardon, it was my mistake. You are booked into Premium Body and Mind Serenity Refreshment. That is excellent. Come this way, please...'

The woman led Bernard out into the grounds and to small chalet with a wooden veranda. Inside was a bed, a basin and small shower room. A pile of folded clothing and a pair of slippers were laid out neatly on a table.

'This is your cottage, sir. Please put on the relaxation suit and slippers and leave everything you have with you in the box in the corner. I will wait outside for you and take you to your Assessment Session.'

'Do I have to do it now? I've had a hell of a day.'

'It is required, sir. It will be brief. After that I will meet you and return you to your cottage.'

'Yeah, all right,' said Bernard. At least it might give him something to write about.

The woman waited outside for Bernard to put on the pyjama-like garment, similar to the outfit he had seen Casper in at the TF anniversary event. When he came out she smiled, bowed then led him across a lawn to what might have once been a barn. In the background he could hear a low, rhythmic hum of machinery. She opened the door for him, bowed again, and Bernard stepped inside.

'Welcome to your Assessment Session, Bilberry.'

The words were spoken by a bearded man with a slightly pock marked face wearing a silkier, darker, version of the standard relaxation suit. The room was humid and dark, lit only by a purple glow that seemed to radiate from piles of pebbles that lined the edges of the room.

'My name is Rodger.'

'How come you're not named after a fruit?'

'Guests are anonymous, we are not. Make yourself comfortable.'

Rodger pointed to something that looked like a cross between a wooden dentist's chair and a couch. Bernard climbed onto it and Rodger adjusted the back rest into a semi-reclining position. Then Rodger sat down on a complex adjustable stool in front of him. What sounded like an electronic xylophone was playing a circular melody in the background, accompanied by the soft babble of running water and the occasional hissing of steam.

'Look, I've been through this before,' said Bernard. 'One of your lot did some stuff on my back.'

'And was the treatment a success?'

'Yeah, it seems all right. I'm fine at the moment. So I don't need any of this. Can I go?'

'You will find the approach at the Retreat is very different from our local Serenity centres. Here we go a little deeper. Our aim is to get to the root of your problems.'

'Deeper? What's deeper? My problems are the shit that's happening all around me. Right here on the surface.'

'Much of what we are, Bilberry, is formed very early on. Let us go back to your childhood. Your relationship with your parents, what was it like?'

'Very ordinary. They were your average suburban parents.'

'Just think back, think through the fears and anxieties of growing up... what feelings come in to your mind?'

'Well, I suppose...'

'Yes?'

'Dullness. Preternatural dullness.'

'You seem to be resisting this exercise, Bilberry. If there are any difficulties there, you should let them rise to the surface. What are your earliest memories of fear?'

Rodger stared at Bernard. Bernard decided that the sooner he came up with something, the sooner he'd get out. He began to trawl through distant memories.

'All right, then. I've got one. I must have been 10. I was at a funfair.'

'Excellent. Were you left on your own?'

'Can't remember. I was just hanging out in the side shows with all the freaks and the monsters and all the things that I wasn't supposed to see.'

'And they frightened you? You saw something you wish you hadn't seen?

'No. They were an incredible disappointment. Every time. I'd hand over my pocket money, hoping to be shocked or astounded only to see grimy jars of sewn-together giblets or disintegrating waxworks or just old faded photos.'

'Nothing in the fairground was real – and that disturbed you?'

'Oh God, no. The real ones were the worst. Like the Tallest Man In The World or the Fattest Woman, they were real but infinitely depressing. The poor sick fucks. I'll never forget them - terminally sad creatures selling postcards of themselves. I could never look them in the eye.'

'They terrified you?'

'No, not really.' Bernard thought for a moment. 'With hindsight you could say I identified with them. A freak selling souvenirs of himself in the tackiest of side shows. That's just what I do for a living, right? I'm a squalid novelty act who upsets everybody. How about that?'

'Let us focus on your fears. What was it you found so traumatic on this visit to the funfair?'

'All right, I'm getting to that. I'd paid my fifty pence to see the Terrifying Creature From The Black Lagoon. In this tent were all these horror movie dummies - I was fascinated by the tackiness, even though it was sort of depressing.' Bernard began to get a little excited. 'There was a Hunchback of Notre Dame with the stuffing coming out, a lopsided Frankenstein, and a moth eaten Dracula... finally I got to the Creature himself, a scaly body made from strips of plastic dustbins with a Guy Fawkes mask for a face. Fifty pence to see a pathetic pile of junk and rags. I was outraged. Then the junk and rags jumped up and attacked me, howling and spitting, grabbing me by the throat with its claws. I struggled for a second or two and then ran away fast as I could. There I was, running away from a man dressed as a pile of junk. I felt a complete moron. I can still hear him laughing at me.'

'That is, I believe, a traditional fairground technique. Just why do you think it caused you so much anguish? Tell me what this man actually did to you.'

'Do to me? Nothing really.'

'And where did he touch you?'

'I told you – he put his hands round my throat. Like, he didn't really hurt me or feel me up or anything. But looking back now - it was a moment of realisation...'

'Carry on.'

Bernard paused for a moment. 'Yeah, I've got it. I realised how freak shows actually work. They're not about persuading you some grotesque fake is real, they are about convincing you that everything is fake. And when your expectations are at their lowest, when you know the whole world is a cheap facade - bam! They catch you!' He paused again. 'You see! That's my job! Trying to tell people how it's all a charade so when something real hits them, they'll wake up, because it

105

is the real things that are actually frightening.' Bernard felt quite pleased with himself.

'Is that the most disturbing experience you can remember from your childhood?

'Seems like it. Have I failed, then?'

'I think we have a lot more work to do, Bilberry. But I would like to move on to the next stage of the session.'

'There's more?'

'You should find the next stage very pleasant. Our aim is to get you to relax, to unwind, and release some of your deeper feelings, the ones you may be hiding from yourself. I'd like to introduce you to Serena.'

Serena, a slim woman with long black hair tied tightly behind her head, stepped forward. Bernard was not sure whether she had just quietly entered the room or whether she had been standing in the shadows all along. Serena adjusted Bernard's chair until it was horizontal and he was flat on his back. Rodger wheeled his stool forward in front of Bernard and raised it so he was looking down directly into his eyes. Behind Rodger's head on the ceiling was a large video screen displaying the TF logo, slowly spinning and mutating into throbbing, paisley-like patterns.

'So tell us,' said Rodger, 'what made you want to come to a Serenity Retreat?'

'Just a rest. To get away.'

'Now, you see, your answer immediately opens up another question. To get away from what?'

Bernard shrugged.

'Please lay back, Bilberry,' said Serena. She began to massage his neck and shoulders.

'One of the things we find very helpful to our clients is reframing,' said Rodger. 'We take a problem and make it dissolve by seeing it differently, replacing the negative with the positive. Allow you to look at your life and yourself in a fresh way.'

'I have looked at myself, and yes, I'm a little fucked up. But that's OK, that's normal. I just need a break. As I said, get away from it all for a couple of days.'

'So let's talk about what it is you are getting away from,' said Rodger gently.

'Do we have to?'

'Please Bilberry. We're here to help you.'

'All right,' said Bernard heaving a huge sigh. 'It's just that things happen and people think they're something to do with me. And they're not'.

'Disconnection syndrome,' said Rodger as he scribbled something down on his clipboard. 'Can you be a little more specific?'

106

'I don't know how much you know about the history of the Retreat,' added Serena as she gently turned Bernard over and began to knead the stringy muscles of his back, 'but there's a long established tradition of expressing ourselves in any way we feel. Don't be afraid to say whatever comes into your head. We're not here to judge you.'

'I write stuff and then it seems to happen. Like I wrote about a bomb going off. Then one did just where I said it would. But I knew nothing about it. Now everyone's after me.'

'Everyone?' asked Rodger.

'Well, the police for a start. And probably a bunch of deranged fascist farmers. And I doubt whether your bosses like me very much.'

'You are clearly experiencing a lot of stress. I can feel it in your shoulders,' said Serena as she pummelled his back as if it was a thick rubber bag full of small rocks that needed to be crumbled into powder.

'Let's look at the issue from another perspective,' said Rodger. 'Let's start from the premise the police aren't really after you at all.'

'They put handcuffs on me and beat me up. It felt real enough to me.'

'Perhaps a case of confused identity.'

'Are you confused, Bilberry?' asked Serena.

'Frequently. Isn't everyone?'

'What if you did know all about the bomb,' said Rodger, 'but your mind has shut it away? We often suppress the memory of things that are painful to us. Just as an exercise, why not accept you knew all about those events before you wrote about them. Perhaps you even enacted them yourself.'

'Right. So in this exercise I spend the rest of my life in jail for something I didn't do?'

'Let's concentrate on the psychological issues, not the legal or penal,' said Rodger. 'There seems to be a struggle going on here. Two competing elements: A, someone who actually plants bombs, and B, who merely fantasises and writes about them. Imagine them as two belligerent children fighting for attention. Our task is to either separate these two characters or to reconcile them. It seems they share the same desires, but one acts on them and one does not. Perhaps A, the one who acts, is more at ease with himself than B, who merely thinks about it but stays at home. Taking a holistic view, A is, psychologically and physically, the healthier personality. Legally, it might seem that B has the advantage, but that is a moot point given the recent changes in the law. Perhaps we should work together to let A come to the fore.'

Serena started to massage his head so firmly it felt that her fingers were pressing directly into his brain. He found it oddly calming.

'What exactly are you trying to tell me?' said Bernard.

'Embrace the fact that you are a man who plants bombs. Purely as an exercise,' said Rodger, gently.

'No, no. I can't. I'm not. I didn't. This is mad.'

'*Mad* is not a word we use here. The term we prefer is *inappropriate*. Which of course this isn't, since this entire session is tailored to your specific needs.'

'I need to go back to my room now and go to bed. Can you tailor that in please?'

'On a superficial level your resistance is understandable, but I would like you to examine my proposal on a deeper emotional and spiritual level. There is a conflict within you. That conflict is the source of your stress and that stress is tensing every muscle in your body. Accept the deeper truth and all will fall into place.'

'But I've talked to the guy who planted the bombs.'

'Really? In your sleep?'

'On the phone.'

'And what did you say to him?'

The massage, the heady scent of the oil, the music and the warmth had all conspired to engender an unexpected drowsiness. Bernard had to concentrate hard to remember what he had said.

'I told him to fuck off.'

'That is a classic case of denial, symptomatic of an immature mind. What did this 'man' want from you?'

'He wanted a mention. In my column.'

'A mention. Interesting. You see the suppressed side of your persona is struggling for recognition.'

'But he was trying to blackmail me.'

'Blackmailers exploit guilt, isn't that so, Bilberry?'

'Yeah, I suppose.'

'Very good. Since there is no blackmail without guilt it would suggest that you are guilty.'

Bernard struggled for a moment for the logic of this notion. 'Wait a minute - do you mean feeling guilty or being guilty?'

'From the therapeutic perspective there is little difference.'

'No difference? But I didn't plant any bombs...'

'Are you certain? You have already said that you have suffered confusion about your identity. We also have record of you admitting that you experience occasional memory lapses.'

'I don't remember saying that... oh.'

'It is in your notes, Bilberry.'

'Notes? So you know who I am?'

Bernard had the feeling he was sinking deeper and deeper into a warm, syrupy pool.

'We do not need to know your real name, Bilberry. Only the information relevant to your stay: your medical history, anything that might illuminate your general well-being and stress level is very helpful to us. Work patterns, drug use, domestic environment, hobbies, all this is essential to determine the appropriate course. It seems you have denied writing certain articles that have appeared under your name – let me see – machine gunning people in the street, burning down police stations…'

'No, I didn't write any of that, well, didn't mean to… but… but you said this is all going to be completely anonymous…'

'Let us assure you, if we discover your name, it is purely by accident, Bilberry,' said Serena, very softly. 'And please don't be defensive. We make no moral judgements here. We are just trying to help.'

'But, of course, we do have certain security obligations,' added Rodger. 'The law now requires us to screen for damaged personalities who could be considered a security risk, and thus we have access, when required, to the national database.'

'Sometimes it is helpful to think of our nation as one rich and complex personality. And like any personality, there are negative elements that need to be identified and treated. So we can be at peace with ourselves.'

'Serenity with security,' whispered Rodger.

'And there's me thinking you were just a bunch of hippies…' said Bernard as scented fumes filled his eyes.

Serena turned Bernard again so he lay on his back and covered him in hot thick towels. The sound of splashing water became louder and the room filled with steam. Bernard could now see nothing but a faint purple glow that barely penetrated the mist. He opened his mouth to protest but a strange heaviness had set into his body. The vapours of scented oil and steam and the hot towels were inducing a hypnotic calm. Before he had a chance to say another word, Bernard's mouth closed, followed by his eyes. He sank into a deep sleep loaded with bewildering dreams.

Seventeen

*'I pray for social unrest. In the fissures in the smooth surfaces of society
I can drive my tiny wedges of discontent.' - Janek James*

'I couldn't agree more. Do you mind if I join you?'

When Bernard heard these words he was sitting on a bench outside his chalet drinking his first morning coffee. So far, he had not uttered a single word. He looked up and saw a tall man with short white hair wearing a finely tailored business suit striding towards him.

'You what?' asked Bernard shakily, still struggling with the memories of the night before. He was willing to accept it had all been an intense, troubled dream, if it were not for the strange aches in his muscles and the thin layer of scented oil on his back and shoulders. A mild sense of pride that he had survived some sort of brain washing attempt was tempered by the fear that the worst was yet to come. And now strangers seemed to think they could read his mind.

'Only mad and dangerous people believe in anything these days! Couldn't agree more!' said the man as he sat down beside him.

Bernard began to wonder just how many of his thoughts he had spoken out loud. The notion was terrifying. Was he actually saying what he was thinking now? He touched his lips and was relieved to find that they were not moving. He smiled weakly and nodded, still keeping a finger on his mouth to ensure no further loose phrases spilled out.

'As you must know, I am a regular reader of your columns...' the man hesitated. 'I must apologise. You clearly don't recall meeting me... the Tranquility Foundation anniversary event?'

The man held out his hand and flashed a smile loaded with perfect teeth. Bernard relaxed a little; not that he remembered him, but then there was a lot he could not remember about that afternoon when the bomb went off. Bernard shook the hand limply.

'You are Mr. Bernard Hawks, are you not? The journalist famous for not believing in anything?'

'Yeah, well certainly no one believes anything I write. I suppose that evens it all out.'

He found himself staring at this man's suit. Bernard had little interest in sartorial standards but he could not fail to notice that the suit was made of the lightest, softest material possible yet maintained a perfect form, as if an army of invisible tailors were constantly blowing and smoothing it into shape.

'The truth, Mr. Hawks, is that it's really immaterial whether anyone believes you or not. That's not how we work today. Does anyone believe the government? Does that stop them being in power?'

'I guess not.'

'And you are writing about this intriguing institution?'

'Not if I can help it. I came to get away.'

'Of course. All of us must get away.'

'And yourself?'

The man emitted a self-satisfied sound that was half grunt, half chuckle. 'I'm here in a professional capacity. You could call me a consultant. I've done some work with the owners of the Foundation.'

'So maybe you can give me some idea of what's actually going on here?'

'Very simple, really. Contrary to what we have just been saying, this establishment is full of people who believe in something: they believe they are the ones that matter, the ones in control.'

'These people are in control? The inmates - I mean, clients?'

'That's what they think. Whether they actually are is not our concern. They've come here to enhance their sense of themselves. They're the last bastions of belief, and, if they think they're going to be in charge, the least we can do is make sure they're fit for the task they believe they've been encumbered with: to set an example of peace and order in a chaotic world.'

'That sounds...'

'Insidious? Sinister? I am sure you will be amused to learn that my current assignment is on behalf of Her Majesty's Government. I am helping them with their day of celebration, Great Britain Day, which they hope may raise national spirits.'

'Why does the government keep planning celebrations for us? What have we got to celebrate? As far as I'm concerned the whole thing...'

'Is naive? Absurd? Asinine? But of course. That's what makes my task so fascinating. I suggested that if they wish to present what they describe as our traditional quality of resilience, perhaps it might be necessary to evoke an element of peril, a threat without appearing either weak or incompetent, and then control the fear with the panacea of caring government. How does that sound to you, Mr. Hawks?'

Bernard was speechless for a second or two. Was this guy simply taking the piss, or was he some sort of embodiment of Dillwyn's paranoid theories? Perhaps this man was as mad as Dillwyn. Perhaps they were all mad, himself included, and The Retreat was simply a moderately benign asylum.

'Are you sure you should be telling me all this? Suppose I write it up?'

'Mr. Hawks, it really doesn't matter what you write, does it? As you've suggested yourself, it's unlikely that anyone will believe a word of it. This is, after all, as so many have pointed out, the era of Post-Credibility.' The man rose to his feet, and as he did so, Bernard caught a glimpse of gold cufflinks glinting in the morning sun. They appeared to be made up of two entwined initials, and Bernard was almost certain that they were the two letters *JJ*. 'You must excuse me, but I must take my leave now. Delightful to have met you, but I mustn't keep you from your Refreshment Session. I believe you may already be late.'

He flashed Bernard a curiously cold smile and walked away. As he watched him cross the lawn Bernard had the strange impression that the suit was moving under its own power, maintaining its perfect form independent of the human presence inside.

Well fuck me... thought Bernard, *I've met JJ.*

*

At around 11 a.m. Bernard finally wandered into the Great Hall which was, in fact, a large, undistinguished room with about 30 very weary looking people sitting on wooden chairs. They were being lectured to, or rather shouted at, by a short, stocky man with a messianic gleam in his eye.

'... as I have said, the future is in your hands! You are the ones with the courage, the knowledge, the determination to lead us forward! But does anyone deny that something is holding you back, stopping you reach your full potential?'

Bernard crept in and sat down on a chair as far away from the lecturer as possible.

'The way we live is based on an illusion we ourselves construct; it's a performance, a play. We tell ourselves stories about the things that happen in our lives to make us feel OK, and come up with a puppet play that has nothing to do with reality. If we don't free ourselves of the puppet, it will appear again and again, controlling our lives...'

The speaker stopped and turned to glare at Bernard. The rest of the class turned and stared at him too.

'Sorry I'm late. I'm afraid, I – err - overslept...'

'Afraid...' said the lecturer. 'An interesting choice of words. What is your name?'

'Err – Bilberry.'

'Welcome Bilberry,' chimed the class.

'I'm Justin, your Session Leader.' Justin continued to glare at Bernard for a few more seconds then raised his eyes to the ceiling and addressed the class. 'As Bilberry has pointed out to us, he was late for the class and he was *afraid. He blames his fear.*'

'Yeah, well, I didn't mean afraid in that sense, I was just saying sorry. Sorry I was late.'

'We all have a lot to be sorry for, don't we Bilberry? And we always have excuses, someone else to blame for the things we do...'

'Well, maybe sometimes it *is* their fault. Like, I'm always being blamed for the things I haven't done, so *someone* must have done them.'

'Oh no, Bilberry, it's never your fault...' The eyes of the class followed Justin's pointing finger and glared at Bernard. 'Bilberry may be in denial, but I'm sure if he looks deep into himself he will find many things that he is afraid of. Fear holds us back, but we make up that fear, it's all part of the script we have written for our puppets, we blame the fear but it's an illusion. This is a crucial lesson. I want you to close your eyes and picture all the people in this room. Imagine you're frightened of every single one of them. That's because each and every one of them hates you.'

Bernard found this very easy.

'Now I want you to imagine that you're frightened of everyone in this village...'

No problem with that either.

'... and everyone in the next town.'

Bernard had no idea what the next town was but it wasn't difficult to imagine that everybody there hated him too. He was actually beginning to enjoy this, although a few people around him had started to whimper.

'You're terrified of everyone in the country, not just this country, but every single country in the world. Examine that notion. That's a lot of people to be frightened of.'

There were gasps all around. Several people were sobbing. Justin allowed this mood of despair to continue for a minute or two.

'Now keep your eyes shut tight. I want you to think about all those people – in this room, in the village, in the world... now picture as many of them as you can. Can you see them? Now listen. Every single one of them is frightened of you!'

There was a moment of stunned silence then a shriek of joy from the other side of the room.

'And now you can open your eyes. Just feel your own power!'

A wave of murmuring rippled through the room followed by laughter. And then they all began to hug each other. Bernard fought the clinging arms that were reaching out to grab him from either side and stood up.

'But they're not, are they.'

'I beg your pardon, Bilberry?' said Justin.

'They're not frightened of me. None of them are.'

'Bilberry, are you trying to undermine the group?'

'No, it's just patently not true. No one's frightened of me. No one I've met, anyway.'

Justin stared at Bernard for a very long time.

'Come on, Bilberry, sit down!' shouted someone.

'Perhaps, Bilberry,' said Justin still staring unblinkingly into Bernard's eyes, 'you're frightened of yourself?'

Arms reached out to Bernard again.

'Bilberry, we all love you!' cried someone.

'You're frightened of what you would do if you realised your full potential, if you stopped playing games with yourself, if you just let go?'

Bernard and Justin continued to stare at each other.

'I've had enough,' said Bernard.

'You're breaking your commitment to learn, Bilberry. You're falling back into old familiar patterns. If you leave the room you're just running away from yourself. More than that, you're running away from your future, the future where everything you want to achieve can be achieved.'

'Bilberry, you must stay! We're all on your side.'

'Oh bollocks,' said Bernard. He sat down again.

There was a little round of applause. A woman in a business suit sitting next to Bernard tried to hug him again but he shook her away. Justin started to pace the room while continuing to point at Bernard.

'Bilberry enjoys being clever. He's frightened of change. He clings to his old familiar ways. He thinks *we're* the enemy!' Laughter rippled through the room. 'Why? Because we want him to make his life work. Which is why he came here. So who is the real enemy, Bilberry?'

Bernard shrugged.

'Would anyone like to tell him?'

'It's the puppet!' yelled out the class.

'Yes, it's the puppet Bilberry that dangles in front of him. It's the puppet Bilberry that gets in the way. It's the puppet Bilberry that has learned all the tricks. It's the puppet Bilberry that can't achieve. It's the puppet that Bilberry has constructed. But now Bilberry is not controlling the puppet – the puppet is controlling Bilberry! What must we do if we want to be free?'

'Cut the strings! Throw away the puppet!' shouted the class.

'Bilberry?'

'Yeah, I guess.'

'We would all like to hear you say it. What must you do?'

'Throw it away. The puppet,' mumbled Bernard, 'and the strings and stuff.'

'Very good.'

The whole class whooped and cheered and stamped their feet.

114

'Let us help Bilberry cut himself free of his strings. But first he must discover them for himself. Come here, Bilberry.' Justin beckoned him forward. Someone behind starting kicking the back of Bernard's legs until he stood up. The class applauded and, with grim resignation, he walked forward until he was face to face with Justin.

'Tell us who you think you are.'

'What do you mean? I'm just a bloke. A bloke who lives on his own and writes stuff.'

'Just a bloke who writes stuff,' said Justin quietly. He nodded, smiled, then paused before he turned to the class. He waited a moment longer then threw out his arms and shouted. 'For Bilberry the writer, bring me a string!'

The class applauded again. An assistant appeared carrying a bunch of long ropes, each with a leather wrist strap attached to it. Justin attached the first strap to Bernard's right wrist and tightened it until Bernard winced.

'What else are you, Bilberry?'

Bernard shrugged. 'I don't know. Can we stop playing this game, please. It's very stupid.'

'Bilberry says we're stupid!' shouted Justin. 'Tell me why!'

'It's because he's a smart arse. He thinks he's too clever for the group,' said a shrill voice from the back of the room.

'For Bilberry the smart arse, bring me a string!'

'And a cynic!' said another voice. 'He can't believe we're only here to help him.'

'For Bilberry the cynic, bring me a string!'

'A misfit! A layabout! A loner! A loser!'

Within a couple of minutes there were ropes attached tightly to Bernard's wrists, thighs, ankles and upper arms. Justin raised his hands and everyone went quiet. There was a creaking sound from above and Bernard looked up to see the ropes were being pulled through a series of pulleys set into the ceiling. The ropes tightened and Justin stood face to face with Bernard, holding on to his shoulders as the ropes attached to Bernard's ankles raised them up to head height. Justin let go and Bernard horizontal, face down and yelling loudly, ascended to the ceiling.

'You miserable fuckers! Get me down from here!'

'We can't hear you, Bilberry,' shouted Justin as he marched around the room, 'we can only hear your puppet speaking. Look at that pathetic piece of shit swinging from the roof! The misanthropic, dope-addled, irritable, arrogant, uncouth, dirty, cynical, egotistical, foul mouthed ape who walked in here today thinking he was better than everyone else.'

'Disgrace! Leave him to rot!'

'But that's not Bilberry we're talking about,' Justin's voice softened. 'Our love goes out to the real Bilberry...'

'We love you, Bilberry!'

'...it's the puppet Bilberry that swings from the ceiling. The puppet Bilberry with all its schemes and rackets that prevents the real Bilberry from achieving his potential. And free from his puppet, what can Bilberry do?'

'Anything!' chorused the room.

'If you want me to do something, why did you put me up here?' yelled Bernard.

'You see, he hasn't got it yet. He still thinks *we're* holding him up there!' shouted Justin.

The class laughed and shouted some more.

'Shame on you, Bilberry! Let go of your puppet! Your puppet put you there!'

Justin gestured for the class to stand up and guided them until they all stood beneath Bernard with their arms outstretched.

'We're here for you Bilberry! Just cut your strings and fall into our arms!'

Justin raised his hands again and the class went silent.

'All right, that's enough for today. Clearly, Bilberry is not ready yet to confront his puppet. He must learn that the Bilberry he has constructed, the puppet Bilberry hanging from the ceiling doesn't exist. Only then will he be free. Only then can he join us. See you all in the morning.'

'You're all a bunch of cunts,' shouted Bernard as the room emptied.

'We still love you, Bilberry,' cried the last woman to leave the room, blowing him a kiss.

Bernard hung there, swinging gently from side to side. He was desperate for a drink, he was desperate for a piss, he was desperate to go home.

'God, I hate the world,' he shouted to the empty room.

After twenty minutes his bladder could hold out for no longer and he felt a warm, wet sensation in the crutch of his trousers then heard a gentle trickling as a stream of urine splashed on to the floor. There were no other sounds other than Bernard's breathing and the creaking of the ropes until, another twenty minutes later, he heard a tapping on the window and a muffled voice.

'Pssst Bernard! It's me! Over by 'ere!'

Bernard turned and saw a very familiar face pressing up against the window.

'Dillwyn!'

'Hang on a minute – see if I can get the key.'

After a couple of minutes and series of shuffling and banging noises, Dillwyn appeared in the room and stood directly underneath Bernard. He looked at the pool of liquid on the floor and took two steps back.

'Hello Bernard.'

'Well I never thought I'd hear myself say it, but it's very good to see you.'

'How's it been, then? Been messing with your head, have they? Telling you you're shit, is it?'

'Yeah, something like that. Are you going to stand there staring at me or are you going to let me down?'

'All right Bernard, don't get touchy now.'

Dillwyn went to the back of the room, played around with some pulleys and lowered Bernard down. He helped him out of the straps then stood in front of him, grinning. Bernard looked Dillwyn up and down. In other circumstances he would have laughed out loud but all he could manage was a snigger. Dillwyn's head was completely shaved and he was wearing what looked like a Boy Scout's outfit.

'So what have they done to you?' asked Bernard as he rubbed his aching arms vigourously.

'They made me a Steward, didn't they. Got a reduction on the course fee. They think I'm working for them. Not going to be happy when they find I've cut you down.'

'I've got to get home, Dillwyn. Soon as I get some feeling back into my limbs. Are you going to help me?'

'The police are after you, aren't they? I heard you're a wanted man, like.'

'I don't care. I'd rather have Pitmarsh beating me up than this bunch of evil shysters.'

'You better follow me, then. Got somewhere you can hide. Which is a good thing, really. They can get a bit angry, this lot. And I got you your clothes – thought you might want them.'

Dillwyn threw Bernard his jacket, trousers and shoes. Bernard changed and stumbled after Dillwyn who lead him out into the woods to a small hut half hidden in the bushes. He opened the door and beckoned Bernard inside. It was about the size of a small garden shed and there was just room for a table with a kettle on it, a rudimentary sink and a small folding steel and canvas chair.

'Let's have a nice cup of tea. And a biscuit.'

Dillwyn switched on a kettle and put a tea bag into a tin mug. Bernard sat down on the chair.

'How did you end up in this place anyway?' asked Bernard.

'Mel booked me in. Said I needed a bit of a rest, like.'

Bernard nodded as he took in this information. Somehow it didn't make him feel any better. 'They've been trying to brainwash me, Dillwyn.'

'Probably, Bernard. It's sort'a what they do, you see.'

Dillwyn poured water into the mug.

'So what's actually going on here?'

'One thing at a time, let's have a nice cup of tea first...' Dillwyn carefully poured the milk into the tea. 'Sometimes it needs a bit of a clean, don't it, the brain? Gets clogged up. Too many ideas, see,' he began to slowly stir the tea. 'But you've just had the one day. Gets harder after that, and then the fourth day, when you really feel like dying, you're in this big black pit... so when you open your eyes you're surrounded by all these things the Tranquility people make...then everyone throws their puppets on a big fire... you feel you're part of them. It's all clever stuff.'

There was something not right about Dillwyn. He seemed oddly calm.

'Dillwyn, did you end up doing the course?'

'Yeah, I completed. Just the first one. Cut the strings, like. Threw away my puppet. Feel better now.'

'You haven't fallen for it, have you?'

'Oh no, Bernard, still doing my research, like, but I think I'll stay on for the advanced course, next week it is. You find out where we all came from. Beans from another planet, I think it is...'

Bernard grabbed Dillwyn's arm.

'Dillwyn! This is all madness. You've got to pull yourself together. Let's make a run for it - you and me. Now!'

Very gradually and subtly, Dillwyn's eyes began to light up.

'Yeah, I know... been thinking about escaping myself...'

Bernard got up to leave the hut but Dillwyn stayed where he was, still stirring the tea and staring into the distance.

'But the thing is, Bernard, everyone who does it says it changed their life. For the better, like. I'm torn, you see...'

Bernard went back over to Dillwyn and shook him hard.

'We've got to get out of here!'

'Perhaps it's your puppet, see, it's your puppet that wants to escape, not you really...'

Bernard hadn't noticed it before, but on the wall of the hut was an old telephone. Dillwyn stopped stirring the tea and lifted up the handset.

'And they don't like it if you run away. They got dogs and that. Gets a bit nasty...' Dillwyn turned and spoke slowly into the phone, 'Yeah, I got him 'ere. I think he'll be all right. Shall I take him to the South Gate? All right. Be nice to him, will you? I used to know him, see...'

'Dillwyn, you released me so you could turn me in?'

'Well, got responsibilities now, since they gave me this job. Security, like.'

'You slimy Welsh bastard!'

'Don't worry, Bernard. We're going to the North Gate, aren't we. We got about four minutes. And no need to be nasty.' Dillwyn's face broke into a fractured grin. 'Got you fooled for a minute, didn't I!'

Eighteen

'Cities are alive with the stories people bring to them, the stories we tell ourselves to make sense of our lives, that against all the evidence there is some point, within all the madness there is a sliver of sanity. The country tells itself stories too, but they're few and old and dull.'

- Bernard Hawks, The Indicator - 'Notes From The Shadows'

True to his word, Dillwyn led Bernard to the North Gate of the Retreat without hindrance from any guards or officials. The gate led straight to a small tarmac road that wound downhill with no signs of civilisation other than a wooden bus shelter a few yards ahead.

'So which way do we go, Bernard?'

'God knows. Given the choice, I'd go for downhill.'

As they ran towards the bus shelter they heard the sound of a bus coming up behind. The bus overtook them and stopped. Bernard glanced at Dillwyn and shrugged, then they both jumped on board. Bernard threw a handful of coins into the driver's tray and followed Dillwyn, who was speeding upstairs towards the top front seat.

'That was lucky! So where are we going? Sort of a mystery tour, is it, Bernard?'

'Don't ask me...' Bernard looked around; there was no one else on the top of the bus and all he could see outside was greenery. 'Dillwyn, the Retreat, what do you think was really going on there?'

'Well, I reckon it's a combination of security and control, isn't it? Sorting out the types they don't want, making the rest into docile citizens who actually think they've got power.'

'So they filter out the dangerous ones and brainwash the rest into smug bastards who do what they're told?'

'If you like. Per'aps.'

Bernard was about to mention the mysterious man with the gold cufflinks who may have been JJ, but he decided against it. It would be more fuel for Dillwyn's conspiracy theories which were already racing ahead far too fast for comfort.

'Problem is, see, you might say it was simply brainwashing,' continued Dillwyn, 'but you and I haven't been brainwashed, have we? Or we wouldn't be having this conversation if we were, like. Or maybe we all are, anyway. Like one man's brainwashing is another man's education, if you know what I mean...'

'Yeah, I guess,' said Bernard, but he was only half listening as his attention had begun to shift to the scenery sliding past the window. The road was lined on both sides by tall trees whose branches met above to form a dark green tunnel. Bernard had the distinct feeling he had been down this road before.

'...but then maybe that's the clever thing about it, see. We've been brainwashed to think we haven't been brainwashed. Per'aps they deliberately let us escape - could all be part of the plan. Maybe they planted a post-hypnotic suggestion – sort of like we've been programmed to do something on cue. So we better keep a close eye on each other, then.'

Bernard nodded and continued to stare out of the window. The dark green became light green then turned to grey as the spectre of the countryside faded before the presence of the town. In turn a large mock Tudor pub, a petrol station, a garden centre, a cash-and-carry warehouse and a DIY superstore paraded past.

'The thing about post-hypnotic suggestion, Bernard, is that people always explain away what they've been programmed to do, sort of instantly. As if it all makes perfect sense, like. So I ask myself, what if everything we do is like that, we're just sort of rationalisation machines...'

Dillwyn was still theorising when the bus arrived at its terminus but Bernard was no longer listening. He had realised why everything looked so familiar.

'So what we do now?' said Dillwyn as they stepped off the bus.

'We get on another bus. That one over there will do. Then we walk.'

'You know where we are, don't you?'

Bernard nodded. 'What's more, I know a place where we can hang out for a day or so.'

'Well, don't look so glum about it, then.'

*

It was just as he remembered it: a small, semi-detached house with a stained glass rainbow set above the door. The same crack in the terracotta tiles on the doorstep, the same plastic disc with a dial to indicate how many pints the milkman should leave, as always set to '1'. Above it was the same worn white button, faintly engraved with the word 'Bell', recessed into a faded wooden mount. Bernard's thumb moved towards the button, then he hesitated and turned to Dillwyn.

'Look, this is all a bit delicate. They don't really approve of me. You know, what I write - it horrifies them. They might not even let me in – I probably represent everything they hate in the world.'

'Right you are, then. I'll be discreet.'

Bernard pressed the button and heard a muffled two-tone chime somewhere deep within the house. A minute or so later there were some scurrying sounds and the door opened to reveal an elderly couple: a tall, amiable looking man in a mustard yellow cardigan and grey flannel trousers and a small, round woman in a turquoise floral dress.

'Hello, Bernie. Long time no see,' said the man, in a slow, cheery voice that denoted he was no stranger to bemusement. He turned to the woman beside him. 'Did you know he was coming?'

'No, but it's a lovely surprise,' said the woman, smiling very warmly. 'Pity you didn't have time to get a haircut, Bernie.'

'This is Dillwyn,' said Bernard. 'He's a friend. Dillwyn – this is my mum and dad.'

'Hello Dillwyn,' said Bernard's mother. 'Hope he's been looking after you. He can be a bit thoughtless at times. Come in and I'll make some tea.'

They entered the house. Bernard was expecting to be reunited with the familiar dark brown hall, the wood-grained painted banisters, the faded velvet curtains and the shiny, caramel coloured embossed wall paper. But everything had changed: the house had been infected by a rash of pastel pinks and greens and a frenzy of floral borders and runners. Little china bowls of potpourri nestled on the windowsill and sprigs of dried up flowers sprouted from every corner.

'What the hell happened?' asked Bernard.

'We had a makeover. Country Cottage. Your sister helped us. Isn't it lovely?'

'No, it's evil.'

'Never mind, Bernie,' said his father with a wink. 'Have a look at this, boys.'

He pushed them into the front parlour, the parlour Bernard remembered anointed with lavender scented furniture polish, the parlour that was seldom used except to entertain visitors too important or too unpleasant to be taken into the kitchen. But now, to Bernard's horror, the very same sacred room was filled with some of the largest and ugliest items of computer equipment he had ever seen. A mass of flickering green and grey screens had taken over the dining table, the sideboard and two rickety coffee tables.

'What's this, Dad? Since when were you into computers?'

'It's a wonderful thing, Bernie. All of us are linked up now…'

'All of who?'

'All of the neighbours. The Watch. Webcams, you see. We can keep an eye on all the goings-on in the street.'

'What do you watch for? What goings-on?'

'Well, it's not like down in the city where you live. Not so many, you know, foreign types. No offence, Dillwyn. No gangs of hoodlums or anything like that. In fact not much goes on here at all.'

'So you don't really need the surveillance systems, do you?'

'Oh no, that just shows that it all works, you see. Keeps us all safe. I can sit here all day and watch these screens. In fact I often do. But the clever thing is, I don't really have to look at it at all, because it's all fed back to some little chap in India who watches over us day and night.'

'Very impressive, Mr. Hawks,' said Dillwyn.

'Dillwyn,' called out Bernard's mother from the kitchen, 'would you like to come in here and help me with the sandwiches?'

'With pleasure, Mrs. Hawks.' Dillwyn left the room.

'This is all very scary, Dad.'

'It's a scary world out there, Bernie, as well you know. But what's really splendid is that we're all joined up now. All the little neighbourhoods like us, all over the country, we're all connecting together. We can all watch over each other!'

'Beats twitching the curtains, I guess... I'm worried about you, Dad. I think you've got in with a bad crowd...' Bernard turned away from the screens to look out into the garden where he had comforting memories of playing on the lawn with the family dog, snogging with a girl with teeth braces whose name he had long forgotten and smoking his first joint. But as he looked through the window he gasped. 'What's happened to the garden? Someone's covered it with planks of wood!'

'They call it decking, Bernard. Everyone has it now.'

'Over the whole garden?'

'I suppose once we started it was difficult to stop.'

'But what was wrong with the lawn? I liked the lawn.'

'We thought you'd be impressed. It's very good for barbecues.'

'You have barbecues?'

'No, but you never know, we might some day.'

Bernard could hear his mother and Dillwyn laughing loudly together. He left his father engrossed in the screens and wandered into the kitchen where his mother, with Dillwyn's messy assistance, was putting together a vast pile of sandwiches. He sat down at the table and his mother poured out some tea from a large brown pot.

'Dillwyn seems very impressed with your Dad's system. Do you have the hoodlums where you live, Bernie?'

'It's the cops I'm scared of more than the kids. You know I got beaten up by police recruits the other day?'

'Oh Bernie, I'm sure it couldn't have been the police. You can't believe everything people tell you,' she turned to Dillwyn and touched his arm affectionately. 'Oh the stories he used to come home from school with. He believed everything people told him! And he was quite a little fibber himself!'

'This is serious. The police are out to get me.'

'Of course they're not. Help yourself to a cup cake, Dillwyn. Have you done something wrong, Bernie?'

'Well that's it - nothing. Not really.'

'Well there's nothing to worry about then, is there.'

'I think per'aps, Mrs. Hawks,' said Dillwyn, his mouth full of white bread and fish paste, 'some people may have taken offence, see, with some of the things he writes...'

'Oh, we stopped reading his stuff years ago. Not quite our thing. And it always brought on his dad's asthma. So you've been upsetting people again, Bernie, have you?'

'*Me* upsetting people? It's the world that's been upsetting me! I've been blatantly framed! Haven't you seen the papers? A fire in a police station yesterday morning and *they're blaming it on me!* Look – you'll see I'm not making it up!' Bernard got up and grabbed a newspaper that was lying on the sideboard. He thumbed through it furiously until he found what he wanted.

'There! Have a look at that!' He opened the paper wide and held it right up to his mother's face. She jumped back then leaned forward again to scrutinise the text.

'Just says there was a fire in a police station. *The police refused to comment on reports that the incident was linked to a known terrorist organisation...*'

Bernard grabbed the paper back. 'It doesn't mention me or anything I've written?'

'Why on earth it should it mention you?'

Bernard read the next line: *The similarity previously reported to an event described in a satirical newspaper column has now been dismissed as coincidence.* He flung the paper back on to the sideboard. 'No reason...'

'You can't always be the centre of attention, Bernie.'

'This means I can go home...'

'This is your home.'

'No, *really* I can go home.'

'Do you mind if I go and talk to Mr. Hawks for a bit?' said Dillwyn. 'All that stuff is very interesting to me, see.'

'Of course, Dillwyn.' When he left the room she turned back to Bernard with a big smile and lowered her voice. 'He seems very nice but I do wish he'd clean his fingernails. He does have some strange ideas, though. He thinks your dad works for the government but I told him, he retired eight years ago and, anyway, it was the council, not the government. Never mind. Oh, you can both sleep in your room tonight. I've made up the bunks.'

*

124

It was twenty-five years since Bernard had slept in the bedroom that his mother had referred to as 'his', but at least there little had changed. A bunk bed, a wind-up tin alarm clock with animated space rockets, curtains printed with images of palm trees and desert islands and a series of tattered posters taped to the wall – a red racing car, the mushroom cloud of the first atomic bomb and a 1950's poster advertising children's shoes. Bernard assumed his right to take the top bunk and Dillwyn crawled into the bed below.

'I think there's something you ought to tell, me, isn't there, Bernard?'

'What do you mean?'

'Well, I 'eard about another fire. On a farm not far from the Retreat. Got a feeling you might have been there. With that girl Animal, was it?'

'Yes, as it happens. But it had nothing to do with me. And I doubt whether I'll ever see her again.'

'Not so sure about that, Bernard. But it's funny that whenever there's a suspicious fire or an explosion, you happen to be around, isn't it?'

'Dillwyn, you're not...'

'Course I'm not saying it's you, just handy for someone that you're there at the time. And that fire... bit of a big fire, wasn't it? For a farm, like?'

'It was just this bunch of deranged fascist farmers with a stockpile of arms. Waiting for their fucked up little white power revolution.'

'Quite handy, then, for the government that they all got blown up, isn't it?'

'Don't give me that *Animal is working for the Primitive Front and they're working for the government* line again. You even thought my dad was working for the government.'

'It's not like he knows he is – more that he's *internalised the system*, see. It's what we *end up doing*, not what we *think* we're doing, isn't it? That's the thing. *The silent copper in the head*, Bernard, policing us from within.'

'It doesn't seem I'm being policed as much as I thought. It said in the paper it was just a coincidence I wrote about the police station burning down. So that means Pitmarsh got it wrong and they've got nothing on me. I'm free.'

'Well, I wouldn't go as far as to say that. Per'aps it's a trap, like. Per'aps they're lulling you into a false sense of security...'

'Do I seem lulled to you?'

'I'm just saying, per'aps you should keep a little alert, like. The bomb, these fires - does all seem to connect with that girl Animal, doesn't it?'

'And you're saying it was all planned so the blame falls on me?'

'Well, it's a possibility, isn't it? I warned you she was trouble.'

'But she was the one who helped me get away from Pitmarsh.'

'So she arranged a getaway car, did she?'

'Horses, actually.'

'Horses, was it? Very fancy. Anyway, how did she know there was anything to get you away from? Sounds very dodgy to me. If I was you, Bernard, I would make it very clear to the world that you're nothing to do with the Primitive Front and your relationship with that woman is strictly *journalistic*.'

'But she's...'

'Yes, Bernard?'

'Forget it. I've had enough advice and theories for one day. Can we go to sleep, now?'

Bernard fell asleep quickly but he was soon woken from anxious dreams of troubled sandwich making and ghostly barbecues by Dillwyn's uninhibited snoring. As he lay on his bunk his thoughts kept returning to Animal and bombs and the Primitive Front. He had that familiar feeling of being sucked into something that had absolutely nothing to do with him. As much as he regretted admitting it, maybe Dillwyn had a point. Maybe Animal was bad news.

He got up and wandered downstairs into the front room where his father's rambling computer system was humming and glowing. He sat down by the keyboard and started to press the big clunky keys.

The Truth Behind The Primitive Front - My Adventures With The Terrorists...

An hour or two later Bernard had emailed it to his editor and crawled back into bed.

*

Breakfast was a mountain of things fried and buttered accompanied by milky instant coffee made in a percolator. Dillwyn chatted and ate simultaneously with great gusto while Bernard remained silent and pushed his food around on his plate with his fork.

When it came time to leave Bernard, with Dillwyn by his side, faced his parents on the doorstep. There was a moment of silence while each side searched for the fitting words to say good-bye. Bernard's father spoke first.

'Your mother and I... we worry about you sometimes, Bernie. It would be wonderful to see you settle down, wife and family, a job...'

'I've got a job.'

'He means a proper job,' said his mother.

'We always thought that Sarah girl was good for you. Do ever see her?'

'Yeah, I did actually, the other day...'

'Any chance of getting back together?' said his father, with a very obvious wink.

'I believe she's become a lesbian,' said Bernard.

'Oh Bernard, what a thing to say!' He shook his head and turned to his wife. 'He never did take rejection very well, did he?'

'Oh don't be so old fashioned, Arthur. Lots of intelligent women become lesbian. It's nice for them, of course - they don't have to worry about being pretty all the time, do they? And there's not so many diseases to catch.'

'Bye now,' said Bernard. Dillwyn shook hands and Bernard patted his father on the back and kissed his mother on the forehead, then they turned and walked towards the garden gate. Bernard's mother ran forward, pulled him back by his arm and whispered in his ear.

'So, Bernie, can I ask you something - just between you and me - that Dillwyn – is he your *special* friend?

'My what?'

'You know, you and him, do you, well, *room* together? You don't have to be ashamed, there's lots in the village now, but I try not the think about what they actually *do*. Vera across the road has got one. He's a fashion designer.'

Bernard's jaw dropped.

'No, suppose not,' she sighed, letting go of his arm. 'You'd be a bit nicer to your old mum if you were. And you wouldn't be seen dead in that awful old jacket. Just one more thing, Bernard...' she pulled something out of her pocket and pressed it into Bernard's hand, 'if things get too tough, try some of these.'

Bernard's mother smiled. He smiled back. She smiles a lot these days, he thought, then looked down from her soft wet eyes to the packet he was holding in his hand. It was a packet of pills with the brand name printed discreetly on the bottom – *BalZac*. She tapped the packet and leant forward to whisper in his ear again.

'They work wonders. Really they do.'

Nineteen

'Credibility and influence - two very different things'
                    - Inspector Frank Pitmarsh, Metropolitan Police

Bernard said good-bye to Dillwyn on the landing outside his flat.

'I've been thinking, Bernard, about you being innocent and that...'

'Well stop thinking. It's all over. I'm not a suspect any more. All I want now is to go inside my flat, bolt the door and be on my own. No more analysis and no more theories. Please.'

'Right you are, then. But keep vigilant – and knock on my door if there's anything you need, like.'

Dillwyn disappeared into his flat. Bernard turned the key to his own door which opened ominously easily. A curious scent of olive oil, garlic and continental cigarettes wafted out. As the door opened, he saw the source of the odour - a *Perdita's Scented Candle* glowing on the table, the same candle Animal had left behind. Animal? Could it be?

Bernard's heart beat faster as he stepped into the room. He heard a snuffling noise and caught the glint of a pair of green eyes under the table. The snuffling changed to a growling and, as his eyes became accustomed to the light, he saw a large, slavering dog and, just above it to the side, another pair of eyes. Slightly more human eyes.

'Bernard Hawks. How wonderful to see you again.' They were the unmistakable glutinous tones of Inspector Pitmarsh.

Bernard switched on the light to reveal Pitmarsh, slumped on the sofa holding the end of a taut lead. Straining on the other end of the lead was the dog, which looked exactly like a smaller, darker, more wrinkled version of Pitmarsh.

'Please get out of my flat. Haven't you heard the news? I'm innocent!'

'Oh no, you're not innocent, sunshine. You're more guilty than ever now. The charge sheet gets longer by the minute: disturbing the peace, resisting arrest, incitement to terrorism, conspiracy, possession of narcotics, arson...'

'That police station fire - the papers said it was nothing to do with me or that piece I wrote a year ago...'

The dog growled.

Pitmarsh laughed. 'I shouldn't have to tell you, of all people, that you can't believe everything you read in the papers.'

'All right, arrest me then.'

Pitmarsh sighed. 'The sad truth is, Bernard, I've had direct instructions from above not to pursue your case – just when I thought you and I were getting somewhere. The bastards told me they wanted to go softly softly because you're in the me-di-a...' The dog snarled as he heard this word. 'Seems they think you're more useful if we keep you running around free. Think you'll lead them to something.' Pitmarsh frowned and the dog growled again.

'But you haven't actually got anything on me, have you? It's all just coincidences.'

'Coincidence, Bernard? Call me old fashioned, but I never liked the idea of coincidence. I'm more of a traditional cause-and-effect man. Let's be scientific. You write about a bomb. A bomb goes off. You write about a fire. A fire happens. Now what happens if you write about a bomb going off again?'

'You tell me.'

Pitmarsh got up, reached out to Bernard, pulled him forward by the earlobe and whispered into his ear. 'Well, shall we find out?'

Pitmarsh slumped back on to the sofa. 'My professional intuition is telling me, Bernard, that if you write about a bomb, another bomb will go off. Perhaps you inspire those Primitive Front bastards. Or perhaps you're being used as a scapegoat...'

'Oh yeah? And how exactly is that supposed to work?'

'Can't you imagine the poor little wretches squealing in court about how the media corrupted their innocent minds? Oh no, they had no master plan, they read it all in the paper!'

'Well it's nice to know I'm useful to somebody but...'

'Shut up Bernard and listen carefully. I have a proposition: since I can't arrest you, I'm going to commission your creative services. You're going to write another story. Just for me. About planting a bomb.'

'I've stopped writing stories about planting bombs.'

'No you haven't. You'll write another story about planting a bomb and a bomb will go off. And you'll help me catch the bastards. My little coup.'

The dog barked excitedly.

'And what if I don't want to write about planting another bomb?'

'There are certain charges relating to fresh evidence, possession of certain chemicals, for instance,' he reached into the back of the sofa and pulled out a small plastic envelope with some whitish powder in it, 'which even my superiors will not be able to ignore. If, however, you co-operate with me, as I'm sure you will, this evidence will be our little secret.'

The dog sat up suddenly and began to sniff the powder.

'Whatever it is, it's not mine! My flat's completely clean!'

'Yes, spotless. Unfortunately. They had it thoroughly cleaned before I got a chance to do my inspection.'

'They? It was just the cleaner from next door...'

'On her own? I don't think so, Bernard. These agency bastards are always getting in my way. Now, as I was saying, I'm not one to let the lack of mere circumstantial evidence prevent me from getting to the deeper truth: you are a man who habitually breaks the law. It could be drugs, it could be explosives, it could be chemical weapons. I haven't actually decided yet.'

'You've planted that!'

'No, Bernard, but I shall.'

'But...'

'And when it's your word against mine, who do you think has the greater credibility? Does anybody believe anything you say or write?'

'If no one believes what I write, why do you want me to write something?'

'Credibility and influence, as you know, are two very different things. But now let's get back to my plan. You will write about a bomb and then your Primitive Front friends will get in touch with you...'

'How do you know? I'm not even sure that they exist?'

'Oh, Bernard, don't be difficult. When they contact you just find out their plans, where they're going to attack next, names of all those involved. Simple, really.'

'So, if I co-operate, how do I know you're not going to pull me in for incitement to terrorism or some other bogus crime? How do I know you're not just setting me up?'

'Because, Bernard, you are my inside man. A very valuable asset. One I want to protect.'

Bernard looked from Pitmarsh to the dog and back to Pitmarsh again. He heaved a sigh. 'There is this guy... says he's been planting bombs for me... I don't think he's anything to do with the Primitive Front, who I said probably don't exist anyway, more a sort of freelancer...'

'Oh really. You have a little friend who plants bombs for you?' Pitmarsh, or possibly the dog, emitted a low rumbling laugh.

'Not *for* me - he's just a blackmailer. If I find him for you, can we forget this-writing-about-bombs crap?'

'Trying to undermine my little scheme are you?' Pitmarsh narrowed his eyes, looked slowly up to the ceiling and down again. 'Very well. I'll give you a chance. If you've got someone I can arrest, well and good. But if he turns about to be your fantasy, I want that story and I want The Primitive Front. Especially that young woman, Animal.'

Pitmarsh got up and moved towards the door but the dog stayed where it was. Pitmarsh and dog both turned to face Bernard.

'The tide is turning, Bernard. People are beginning to appreciate old fashioned law and order.' He paused, as if this statement needed time to settle in Bernard's brain. 'One last thing - a little tip, picked it up on one of our training courses. I think your old patterns of behaviour have been getting you into trouble again. And do you know what you should do? Think of them as not being you, but belonging to a puppet. A puppet Bernard that controls the real Bernard. Then you can take that puppet and throw it away. I think you'll find that helpful.' Pitmarsh moved right up to Bernard, gripped him firmly by the shoulder and whispered in his ear again. 'Welcome to the force.'

The dog began to bark again excitedly, got up and pulled Pitmarsh forward and out of the door. Bernard jumped up to close the door and bolt it against any further intruders when he caught sight of a face lurking in the shadows on the landing.

'Dillwyn, is that you?'

Dillwyn stepped forward into the light. 'Everything all right, Bernard? I heard some barking and stuff and I wanted to make sure you were OK, like.'

'No, everything's fine. Just that copper again doing his routine harassment number...' Bernard hesitated for a moment, sighed and stepped out into the corridor. 'Actually, I could do with your help, Dillwyn.'

'You know me, always here to lend a helping hand. Not about that girl Animal, is it?'

'No, although... no, never mind. Talk about that later. I need to find out about the Primitive Front. Who they are, what they want. You had some theories...'

'Thought you had enough of my theories, Bernard?'

'All right, I've changed my mind. Just one will do.'

'Well, we were talking about all this the other day, weren't we. As I was telling you, now we're in the era of Post-Credibility...'

'I don't want a lecture, Dillwyn. I need to do this fast. I know there was some paranoid ideas about them on your disc, but now my Cydrax is wiped clean and I lost your disc when the computer was being repaired...'

'What disc is that, Bernard?'

'The CD Mel gave me. The one you left for me.'

'I didn't leave you any disc. Don't even have a computer. They're too dangerous.'

'And where's Mel?'

'Oh, she's gone now. They've given me a new, err, cleaner, see.'

'Who has?'

'The agency, like. Sending me another one.'

'I thought she was a friend?'

131

'Well, she was. You can get friendly with a cleaner, can't you?'

'I guess. Why would she have given me a disc and said it was from you?'

'Dunno, really. Told you to be vigilant, didn't I? That disk might explain a few things. You know, stuff disappearing, like, bits you've typed sent out all over the place?'

'So all that stuff that poured onto my screen... that was just *my* notes, not yours... oh shit.'

'You've gone pale, Bernard.'

'I lost everything on my computer. But not before it mailed out half my thoughts to the world.'

'Very nasty. Sounds like it got infected. Could be it was one of those *pande-mon-ium* discs, then.'

'Pandemonium discs?'

'Well, I thought they were all done with now. Legendary pioneering attempt at cyber anarchy.'

'By who?'

'Many theories. Could be some anarchist hackers, could be a software company creating demand for a new security product, could be part of a government surveillance strategy, maybe one of your friends did it as a joke.'

'But my computer – it's a Cydrax. They don't get viruses or spyware or anything like that.'

'All right then, you must be imagining it all. Or making it up. Have it your own way.'

'I was only saying...'

'Best thing for you, Bernard, is to dump that computer. It's infected. Rotten to the core, I reckon. Anyway, I'll see what I've got in my files and pop back in a tick.'

'One other thing, Dillwyn. You know that guy JJ who everyone talks about? I think I might have met him.'

A smile crept across Dillwyn's face. 'Well then. I've definitely got something for you to read. I'll slip it under your door soon as I lay my hands on it.'

When Bernard returned to his flat the phone was ringing. He stared at it for a few seconds, then an unfamiliar impulse, perhaps related to the memories stirred by the lingering scent of the candle, prompted him to pick it up. The caller spoke before Bernard had time to say a word.

'Bernard!'

'Not you...'

'You remember. We talked about the bombs we planted. We were going to come to some arrangement.'

'That's all history now. I'm off the hook. Reprieved.'

'"Reprieved" is not the right word. "Outbid" is how I would put it. That's what I wanted to tell you.'

'Yeah? Well tell me something that makes some kind of sense.'

'I offered you the rights to the bomb. With all the evidence. Then someone wanted to buy the attribution for the police station. So it's been transferred. Threw your ad agency one in too. All you owe me is the service charge, for my overheads, et cetera.'

'You're telling me terrorists don't plant their own bombs now?'

'Well, putting aside the suicide specialists – that's not a business I'd dabble in, 'cause of the risk factor - most would rather leave it to the pros. It's a specialised job. We used to only do them to order, but doing them on spec we get better prices. Particularly when there's some publicity around it. Shame, this one didn't work out 'cause I thought you and I had the potential for a nice little business together...'

'What if I wanted to, err... write again? About a bomb going off?'

'Having regrets now, are we? I'd love to help you but it might be tricky. Contractual obligations, you see...'

'Look, I need to talk to you...'

'There are just a few outstanding expenses to settle... 15% admin charge for the transfer to the new guy, then it's all over.'

'An admin charge... why am I not surprised. How much?'

There was a long pause as if the caller was working something out. 'Make it 300.'

'All right. If I settle that, can we talk? Like soon?'

There was no reply.

'Hello? You still there?'

'Yeah, I'm here. Day after tomorrow. Make it the evening.'

'Where?'

'I'll call you.' He hung up.

Bernard stared at the phone. His heart was pounding. He had just made a deal with an sinister extortionist who he was intending to betray to a vindictive, aberrant policeman. Had that really been a good move?

Bernard became aware of a flashing light emanating from just outside his vision. He turned round to find the Cydrax was pulsating in a rather self-satisfied rhythm, as if to remind him of its unassailable superiority. Then it began to chirrup in a way he had never heard before and a grinning face flickered on to the screen. The face spoke.

'Bernard, my friend. I thought it was time for a video chat.'

'My computer does video chats?'

'Of course it does. So what happened to you at the Retreat?'

'Casper, please fuck off out of my computer. It's infected enough already.'

'I heard you didn't complete. Ran away from yourself again.'

'I ran away from a pile of noxious crap. I don't know how or why you fell into it.'

'Oh Bernard, you really don't know what you are missing out on, do you? You could have joined us, but you missed your chance. Your could have discovered The Power of Attraction. Think success and you become successful. Feel good about yourself, you become healthy. Think bad thoughts and they will start to eat you away. You should know about that.'

'All I know is that you want to create a world of grinning smug bastards. Which is my idea of hell. What about the power of negative thinking? You know, rub our noses in the world as it really is?'

'This problem of yours, this pathological cynicism - it's not helping you one little bit. We were talking about you today and the consensus seems to be that the old cynical Bernard Hawks doesn't quite fit the *Glimmer* any more.'

'I was told that's exactly what they wanted. I wrote something nice and it got spiked'.

'New regime, Bernard.'

'Then fire me, I'd appreciate that. But you'll have to pay me off. I've got a contract, remember?'

'Oh we're not going to fire you. Just a slight shift of emphasis. We're giving you a new brief. From today you are The *Daily Glimmer*'s theatre reviewer.'

'The *Daily Glimmer* has a theatre reviewer?'

'It does now.'

'You bastard.'

'Think of it as a challenge - how did you describe theatre? *The most obsolete and lame of all art forms....* I'm lining up your first assignment now - it's with an outfit called The Human Company. Very famous once. And they've got your friends The Tranquility Foundation behind them. They're doing a special performance for Great Britain Day.'

Then Casper began to laugh. It was not a pleasant laugh, nor one that Bernard had heard before. In fact, it occurred to him that he had seen Casper grin and smirk and leer, he had heard him snigger and yawn and chuckle but he had never witnessed an actual laugh. It was a high pitched nasal whinnying, strangely unmasculine, in fact strangely inhuman. The cry of a little toy pony possessed by the devil.

Gradually Casper's laugh grew softer as his image faded on the screen until it almost, but not quite, disappeared. Bernard wrenched the power lead out of the Cydrax. It emitted a pathetic, bleating sound then shut down. He continued to stare at the screen for moment as an afterimage of Casper's insufferable grin, seemingly burnt into the tube, lingered on. Animal was right, even Dillwyn was right: that computer had to go.

There was a rustling sound and Bernard turned round to see a sheaf of paper sliding under his door - presumably Dillwyn had some more paranoid theories for him to study. He picked up the papers and read the title - *The Myth and Reality of Janek James*.

Twenty

Lecture to the Institute of Progressive Marketing,
Wormwood Hall, London, Christmas 2002.

The Myth and Reality of Janek James

Perhaps no other man in the history of our industry has been mythologised quite as much as Janek James, nor, perhaps, does any individual better personify the highest ambitions of your profession. In this talk I will attempt to deal with some of the speculation surrounding the man and his work and how it relates directly to the challenges that face us all in the 21st century.

Although known colloquially as 'The Man Who Turned Baseball Caps Round', it is clear that this was the least likely and, even if true, one of the least significant of his many achievements. The truth, if I may be permitted to use that word, is that, for the last three decades, all the activities of Janek James have been so cloaked in rumour, disinformation and outright fantasy that they are more part of folklore than the history of the science of Marketing and Public Relations. But then, for reasons that will become clear later, that is entirely to be expected. For authenticated documentation we have to go back to the late-1960's when a single research paper, apparently written by a postgraduate at Yale identified solely by the initials 'JJ', landed like a whale in a village pond. The waters have yet to stop rippling.

The projects outlined in the paper are well known: in particular we can all recall the anarchist guide to bomb making with recipes so distorted that anyone following them would have blown themselves up; the contamination of LSD with memory destroying agents to disempower radical dissenters; a covert campaign to discredit or even assassinate prominent celebrities and musicians if they became too influential; the formative experiments in mind control techniques by microwaves and underground cables; the trials of psychoactive agents in the water supply, and, on a global level, the interplanetary abductions and, of course, the early attempts to construct the New World Order.

As we know, none of these projects remained secret for long; all were common topics of discussion in underground circles. Very few of the strategies were ever actually implemented and JJ had nothing to do with their original conception – some, in fact, predated his adulthood by at least a decade. Nevertheless, it is JJ with whom we associate these initiatives.

JJ's breakthrough was simple but devastatingly effective. He realised how much more economical and effective it would be to spread theories of the projects rather than actually implement them. The more emphatically the authorities denied them, the more they would become part of urban legend. James was working with the intellectual equivalent of biological warfare on a battlefield where the blunderbuss was still the weapon of choice. From there it was only a small step forward from spreading rumours of covert operations that were planned but never implemented, to dedicating all available resources to inventing entirely fictional strategies. That step was taken, and those who followed would never forget the pioneering work of Janek James.

Perhaps the most notable achievement of that period was the Virtual Infiltrator. By implanting carefully constructed rumours of covert agents working within every radical pressure group at every major political demonstration, he watched the incipient revolutionary movement disintegrate through mistrust and suspicion, without needing to employ a single human operative. The dissemination of paranoia was so successful in the late 60's that a smoke screen of stultifying confusion descended upon most of society's dissenters. Of course, I don't need to tell you how, before very long, this technique moved away from the specialist area of dissident minority groups to become a crucial part of mainstream political strategy. The virtual 'enemy within' has become both the (physical) 'enemy without' and the even more potent combatant that lurks within our very consciousness.

Little is certain of James' activities in the 1970's. We know he embarked on a course of intense self-education, devoting himself to scientific research at an advanced level, probably including Non-Linear Studies, Complex Adaptive Systems and Analytic Philosophy. More exotic rumours suggest that he became a Zen master in Kyoto followed by a year of solitary contemplation in the Himalayas. Other sources suggest a direct involvement with (or even the instigation of) a Californian group therapy cult during this period. Some claim his studies encompassed an even wider field and that James became an adept in Method Acting, Psychoanalysis, Artificial Intelligence, Hypnotism, Juggling and Screenwriting Theory. I shall let you draw your own conclusions as to the validity of those latter claims.

It is in the 1990's that James' work began to surface again, and this time in a wholly commercial context. Starting, of course, with the Baseball Cap Reversal (now so much part of folklore that its authenticity is highly questionable), the Joke Broking ventures, the definition and refinement of the Cred Haven, and the pioneering work in Covert Rumour Operations which came to be known, rather crudely, as Viral Marketing. What is problematic about this very productive period is that, despite the certainty with which almost everyone attributes James' name to these projects, lifelong confidentiality agreements prohibit any of the corporations directly involved discussing James' work, or even to confirm or deny his involvement. This, of course, has only served to deepen his mystique even further.

It is not known when the concept of the Fourth Era, or Post-Credibility was first posited, but it is generally accepted that Janek James was responsible, if not for inventing the terms, for popularising their use. Despite, or maybe because of, some evidence to the contrary, JJ's name is inseparable from the concept of Post-Credibility and the strategies for influencing behaviour in a world where few appear to believe in anything. As to the recent obscurity of JJ himself, the enigma has propagated a number of fascinating theories.

The simplest is that JJ's work has been increasingly devoted to confidential matters of state security and it is therefore not surprising that a veil of secrecy surrounds him. Moreover, it has been suggested that an integral part of James' key strategy is to deliberately obfuscate his own contribution to the Fourth Era. This notion has a certain satisfactory resonance to those who have studied the theories of Post-Credibility at an elementary level. Others claim that the real Janek James actually retired in the 1980's, perhaps to his mountain in the Himalayas, and the difficulty of finding evidence of his involvement in more recent activities is simply down to the fact he had nothing to do with them.

A further, and perhaps more intriguing, theory is that JJ himself never existed and was purely a construction by the American intelligence agencies, originating out of the disinformation campaigns of the 1960's, and, perhaps, the first significant experiment with the self-replicating meme. If that was indeed the case, then we must say that the experiment was supremely successful.

Recently a revisionist version of the last theory has emerged, ostensibly from the U.S. intelligence agencies themselves. This accepts that JJ is a construction, but a construction not of the intelligence agencies but of the subversive elements themselves who needed a personification of state-sponsored conspiratorial forces and the devious machinations of advanced capitalism. A further spin is that this theory itself was part of another spurious campaign to discredit radical groups who had neither the interest or ability to create such a fiction. And so it goes on. Lastly of course, there are those who would maintain that *all* of the above theories were invented and disseminated by JJ himself.

What is particularly interesting to me is that all the theories, including the last, are entirely compatible with our current hypotheses of Post-Credibility, and thus there is no reason not to accept them all in their entirety. Within this context we can say that questions such as 'Who or what is the real Janek James?' are entirely specious. The existence or not of an individual human being, identified with actions assigned to 'JJ' is irrelevant. All that needs to be said is that the systems of the Fourth Era are now in place and only those ignorant of their supremely sophisticated mechanisms doubt their significance or efficacy. You may ask yourselves what has all of this to do with us? What is the role of Progressive Marketing in the Fourth Era? In the age of Post-Credibility, what is there left to believe? We shall address the questions, and more, after the break. Before you go I would like to leave you with these thoughts: I wrote this lecture with the sole purpose of illuminating the myth of Janek James. But I would like you to consider the notion that this entire lecture was written by Janek James himself to deepen his obscurity. Which is the more plausible thesis, or is there, in fact, no significant distinction between them?

Thank you.

Professor Rupert Kepler.

Twenty One

'People think that computers are becoming more like us, but it's the other way round – we're becoming more like them.'

- Animal

Around lunchtime the following day Bernard marched into the Dark Orchard. The man in black with the goatee beard was busy re-lighting a row of beeswax candles when Bernard placed his Cydrax on the oak counter.

'Please,' said Bernard, 'I'd like you to buy this back.'

The man in black smiled. 'That might not be easy. You see this is a Rev. C...'

'You said they were very rare.'

'Indeed they are. But that doesn't mean anybody actually wants one. Lovely machines, but they do have a reputation for being temperamental. Tough little creatures, though.'

'You charged me three hundred quid to fix it!'

'It involved a lot of specialist skills, and you have to admit she was working like a dream when she left.'

'Except that all my data's gone...'

'She'd suffered greatly. A *tabula rasa* was the only solution.'

'Yeah? And just who are you working for?'

'I beg your pardon?'

'Who made you wipe my computer?'

'Now please, sir. Our terms and conditions do not guarantee the integrity of any data on your drives. But I assume you did a back-up?'

'Yeah, well, fuck it - just give me my three hundred back and it's yours.'

The man smiled and shook his head.

'Two fifty,' pleaded Bernard.

The man shook his head again, raised his hands and leaned towards Bernard. His breath smelt strongly of camomile tea.

'I'll tell what I can do - purely as a favour, on the understanding you don't repeat this to anyone. I'll give you a hundred in part exchange for a new computer. A voucher to take to Vic's down the road. He'll give you a good deal on one of his nice beige boxes. One that works.'

'Vic? That old crook with junk shop?'

'Oh we're all the same company now. All part of the TF group. We have an arrangement, you see.'

Bernard's eyes narrowed. 'You bastard!'

The man shrugged. Bernard took hold of the Cydrax and stormed out of the shop.

Hailing a taxi is not easy when both of your arms are wrapped around a heavy computer, but, after fifteen minutes of vigourous nodding, one finally stopped.

'Just take me to wherever you get rid of these things!' he said to the cab driver.

'You what, mate?'

'You know, the tip, the dump, somewhere I can chuck this box of crap and never see it again.'

'Computer, is it? Have to take you across the river, mate. Only place I know that will take 'em. Full of toxics, they are. Can't just dump 'em in a skip.'

'All right, just do it.'

The taxi began its slow journey south.

'You'd be surprised how many people I've had in my cab who've got to where you've got. Want to do away with all this technology, get back to the simple life.'

'Oh yes?' sighed Bernard, knowing this was the beginning of yet another unwanted conversation. The cabbie needed no encouragement to continue.

'Like that lot who are planting the bombs. Maybe they've got a point!'

'You serious?'

'Why not? Maybe we should all get back to nature, get rid of all them machines! Can't go on for ever, can it?'

'What can't?'

'You know, using up the planet. All the waste. All these cars. Burning up all the air.'

'Aren't you arguing yourself out of a job?'

'Talking hypothetically, mate. Anyway, never saw much wrong with a horse and cart myself. By the way, you know there's a van that's been following us ever since I picked you up?'

Bernard turned round to look through the back window.

'Ah, too late, mate, it's gone,' said the cabbie. 'Must be getting paranoid in me old age.'

The taxi finally arrived at the fortified compound of Southside Recycling Solutions. It was mid-afternoon but storm clouds were forming a premature dusk. Bernard paid the cabbie and followed the signs pointing to 'computer disposal' until he reached a staircase built out of scaffolding. He struggled up the stairs to a platform that overlooked a vast steel tank and placed the Cydrax down. He stood up and clutched the handrail as an icy gust of wind buffeted him. The sky had become even darker. Then he heard a voice. A vaguely familiar male voice.

'Go, Bernie, push it over!'

He looked down into the tank. A chink in the clouds let a thin shaft of cold light fall on the splinters of a thousand trashed computers twenty feet below. He looked up and saw tall steel fences topped with razor wire and, higher still, observation towers. Then straight ahead on the opposite side he saw a figure silhouetted against the sky; a tall, scrawny young man holding a camera in his hand. Gabby, the guy who had driven Animal's van.

'What the hell are you doing here?' shouted Bernard.

'Been told to keep an eye on you. Animal's instructions.'

'Yeah, well, that's very nice of you, but can you fuck off and leave me alone now please?'

'Technology's the materialisation of Capitalism, right! So when we smash the last computer, Capitalism will fall!'

'Jolly good,' muttered Bernard. The camera flashed. 'So why are you taking my picture?'

'Just documenting the fall,' said Gabby. 'It's a good story - smart arse journalist joins our fight to destroy the machines.'

Bernard nodded, looked down into the skip below then up again. He hesitated for a moment, then let go of the Cydrax and watched it tumble down on to the pile below. He had expected, hoped in fact, it would explode dramatically but it landed intact with a dull thud. Any pleasure he might have got from the action was obliterated by the gloating presence of Gabby.

'The age of machines is over!' shouted Gabby, 'Welcome to the new age of pandemonium!'

Bernard stared at the Cydrax sitting proudly on top of the pile below. *Pandemonium?* The word seem to have a strange resonance... then he remembered where he'd heard it last. 'That disc... the one that fucked up my Cydrax and sent all my notes round the world. That was yours, wasn't it?'

'Come on Bernard, you know you didn't need it, all that crap was only clogging up your brain. I've got the van. I'll give you a lift home.'

'It was you and Animal - and I blamed the Cydrax...'

Bernard would never remember exactly why he decided to jump, or whether a decision was ever actually made, but jump, it seems, he did. In the rush of thoughts and feelings that followed Gabby's last remark one notion prevailed: he had made a lot of mistakes and the last and worst mistake was betraying the Cydrax. He had been wrong once again but the Cydrax was innocent. He wanted it back; the fall of Capitalism would have to be postponed.

Bernard's fall, however, was broken rather than postponed. His body crashed into a pile of a hundred cathode ray tubes that imploded dramatically on impact into a vast cloud of silvery dust. He lay still for a minute or two as the particles settled around him, shocked by his own calm and the fact he was not yet dead. A few yards away the unruffled Cydrax was rocking gently back and forth on a mound of disc drives. Bernard got up and made his way to a heap of boxes and, one by one, piled them up to make into a crude staircase leading to the top of the tank. It was only when this task was complete and he went to retrieve the Cydrax that he caught a glimpse of himself in its shiny surfaces. He was covered from head to foot in a layer of powdered glass and thin rivulets of blood had begun to flow from the top of his head and hands. Unperturbed, Bernard picked up the Cydrax and slowly made his way up the improvised stairway, cradling the computer in his arms as a father might hold his precious child, finally sleeping soundly after being lost all day.

When the floodlights were switched on the image of the scintillating Bernard rising from the abyss was really quite beautiful. It would have graced the climax of any mid-budget science fiction film; Bernard's overall demeanour was suitably other-worldly and the long red threads of blood running down him added a fashionably gothic touch. But the voice emerging from Southside Recycling Solutions' public address system offered a different narrative altogether.

'Could the gentleman in silver please make his way to the Security Office. You are under arrest.'

Bernard continued his way steadily down the scaffold staircase to the ground.

'Could you please make your way to the Security Office. Removing property from Southside Recycling Solutions is a punishable offence.'

Bernard paid no attention. He marched on forward, Cydrax in his arms, making his way with what he hoped might be dignity towards the gates of the compound.

'So where do you think you're going?'

As he heard these words Bernard felt something digging hard into his ankle. He looked down and saw the jaws of a small, rat-like dog clamped around the top of his shoe, whining as it slobbered over the leather. A leash from the dog's collar led to a thin, leathery faced man in a badly fitting uniform. He looked no happier than his dog and very ill at ease in his bright blue and gold braid outfit, which suggested circus band leader rather than security official.

'I'm going home,' said Bernard. 'Me and my computer have a lot of work to do.'

'That's not your computer, mate. It stopped being your computer the moment you dumped it in the skip. Therefore, what you have there in your arms is Southside Recycling Solutions' computer, so what you are doing now amounts to stealing their property.'

'And what are you going to do about it?' Bernard shook his leg but the dog stayed firmly clamped.

'I am going to ask you, as civilly as possible, to return that computer from where you got it, remind you that the security cameras have taken your picture and forwarded it to the central control centre of Southside Security Solutions, then go back into my hut and call the police.'

The two men stared at each other.

'Please,' said Bernard quietly.

The guard moved closer and lowered his voice. 'For a twenty quid administration fee I will carry out the last action with extreme thoroughness and as tardily as I dare; to whit, until you've scapa'd.'

Bernard continued to stare back at him. 'A tenner. And get that fucking mutt off my shoe.'

'Fifteen and he'll come off when he's ready.'

'All right. In my back pocket. You'll have to pull it out yourself. I'm not putting this machine down.' As the guard retrieved his payment Bernard turned his head to see Gabby beckoning him forward to his van. He began to make his way towards the exit with the dog still stuck to his foot.

'Best take it off. That shoe. Winston gets quite obsessed when he finds one he likes.'

Bernard struggled with the dog but the more he shook his foot, the more it clung, so he carried on walking with dog attached. The guard stood where he was, holding on to the dog's lead. After a few yards Bernard could feel the tension pulling dog and foot back. He made a final effort and, with a sudden burst of energy, ran towards the gates. The shoe with dog attached released itself from his foot and the run became a speedy hobble. As he neared Gabby his shoeless foot plunged into an icy puddle and Bernard and Cydrax fell hard into the back of the van.

'Oh, Bernard, why did you go and do that. You should have left that machine there where it belonged,' said a female voice from the shadows of the van.

'Animal...'

She pulled Bernard into the van and shut the doors.

'Yeah, what are you playing at, Bernard?' shouted Gabby as he started the engine. 'You should've left that box of crap in the skip! Dig the look though. Sort of retro-cyberpunk vibe.'

'I'm just giving it a second chance,' muttered Bernard. 'Like me, it's been through a lot.'

'Let's leave him alone, Gabby,' said Animal, 'you got your pictures.'

'Yeah, but I'm getting fucked off with this,' replied Gabby. 'I want to blow something up. When are we going to start smashing the machines? Shall we start with Bernie's?'

The van drove off. Animal nudged Bernard and laughed.

'Hey, Bernard! Aren't you pleased to see me again?'

'Well, yes, but... I don't know... I seem to get into trouble when I see you. You know, bombs go off, the police beat me up, buildings burn down... then last time I saw you...'

'You were going to the Retreat.'

'Yeah, and I reckon you really wanted me to go there, didn't you? What was all that about?'

'That's Animal's hang-up,' shouted Gabby, 'trying to sort out her fucked up childhood. Waste of time, if you ask me. Pond never wanted her to go back there. Ancient history. None of that old shit worked, the sixties, the seventies...'

'Shut the fuck up, Gabby. Just tell me what was going on there, Bernie.'

'Load of hippie bollocks with strings and puppets... fucking with my head so I'd admit to planting bombs.'

'The bastards... all that stuff was good, once, when we used to do it in The Hive. When I was a kid. Like, they strip all this shit away from you, so you just get back to your core... you can do it with acid too, some have done it with sex. Now it's turned into... don't know what you'd call it...'

'A factory making smug bastards who think they're in control but really do what they're told?'

'If you like.'

'I think I met JJ there.'

'You met JJ, did you? He's the one who's supposed to have taken all that shit and made it work the other way. What did he look like?'

'Very smooth - short white hair, ludicrously sharp suit, cufflinks with his initials on... said he was a consultant for the government.'

'Aren't they all,' she sighed. 'So Pond was right after all. JJ exists and The Hive has gone bad. Pond is always fucking right.'

'Who's Pond?'

'Shall I tell him?' shouted Gabby.

'No. He'll meet him soon enough.'

'You're pissed off with me, aren't you?' said Bernard. 'That piece I wrote...'

Animal shook her head. *'My days with the terrorists...* yeah, total crap. Still, it helped. Publicised the PF.'

'That's good, is it?'

'Sure. It's getting bigger every day. It's like a brand, you know, a franchise. Once it gets going there's no stopping it.'

'Yeah,' shouted Gabby, 'and like the more the state brings in laws to stop the Front, with surveillance and all that shit, the bigger the Front becomes. Then there's more cameras to smash and cars to burn!'

145

'Gabby sometimes misses the subtlety of our work. Do you know what I mean?'

'Actually, I don't what you mean. And, actually, I don't know what you lot want to do, or what you stand for, or anything. And I don't care, as this whole thing's over as far as I'm concerned. It's had its moments, but the story's coming to an end now. I'm meeting the guy who said he planted my bomb...'

'Oh yes?'

'...and I'm, well, sorting it all out.'

'You think it's that easy, do you?'

'I'm going to stick to what I'm good at. Sitting alone in my room writing crap that annoys everyone.'

'All right, Bernard. That's fine. But something tells me you're going to want to see me again.'

'Well of course I would, it's just...'

'We need you. Bombs need a narrative, don't they. You've got to write the story of Great Britain Day and how the Primitive Front are going to fuck it up.'

'Yeah, Great Britain Day, what's that all about? JJ said he was working on it. Said the government needed to - what was his phrase - something about evoking peril then showing how they can control it...'

'Well, he's going to get his fucking peril all right!' shouted Gabby, 'We've got these kids all over the city just waiting to burn something!'

'Just chill, Gabby, they'll get their chance. You know what's going to happen, don't you Bernard?'

'What?' said Bernard.

'The government are going to use this as some sort of military exercise. A show of strength when things start to go wrong. They'll fake some sort of disaster then save the day. That's your story!'

'But is that... true?'

'You, Bernard, you and us together. We're going to make it true.'

She smiled at him then turned away. Bernard lay back against the side of the van and closed his eyes.

Twenty Two

'Do I work digitally? I use as many fingers as necessary. Usually two will suffice.'

-Troy Sherman, in response to Arts Council Assessor.

Two days after Casper's face appeared on his computer screen, Bernard received a text message on his phone confirming his demotion to Theatre Critic was no idle threat: he had been assigned to interview Troy Sherman, Artistic Director of The Human Company, in his West End club.

At five o'clock a dread-filled Bernard hammered on a large brass knocker on the door of the Stylite Club. Under any other circumstances the Stylite Club was the last place in the world he would have visited without coercion. He made it a policy to boycott any club that had sent him an invitation to join, or refused him membership, or ever ignored him at the bar or forcibly ejected him from the premises. The Stylite fell into all four categories.

Bernard had once, briefly, been a member of one of the first clubs in Soho that catered specifically to those who hated clubs but needed somewhere to meet and drink, away from the hoi polloi. Its primary function was to enable people who believed they were celebrities to get outrageously drunk in front of other, similarly disposed, characters. The Stylite Club was in the second wave of clubs famous for the fact that nobody famous ever went there; ironically, they soon became retreats for anyone who had fears or fantasies of being recognised in public. No one else would have wanted to join for it was overpriced, dirty, the food and drink mediocre and the staff insolent. The Stylite was, above all, a place to hide. It was a labyrinth of dark, cramped spaces, the decor evidently designed by a depressed opium addict with a penchant for tapestry.

Bernard stumbled through several murky rooms until a voice boomed out from the shadows.

'Bernard Hawks. Britain's newly discovered theatre expert. How very wonderful to see you.'

Gradually Bernard's eyes adjusted to the gloom. In a watery trickle of sunlight seeping through a leaded window he caught a glint of eyes. Gradually, an image formed of very large bald man slumped on a pile of velvet cushions. Beside him was an open bottle of red wine and one glass. As far as he could make out, there was no one else in the room.

'You realise,' said Troy, 'this is the first time I've talked to the Press in over twenty years?'

Bernard gingerly sat down on what could have been an antique milking stool. 'Yeah, well, I feel appropriately humbled. I wanted to ask...'

'And do you know why I've agreed to talk to you?'

Bernard shook his head.

'I have been advised that the position you occupy as a widely loathed writer is strategically important for the promotion of my work. Does that strike you as strange?'

'Not particularly. Not compared to everything else that's been happening.'

Troy stared at him. Bernard squirmed on his stool and eventually broke the silence.

'I hear you've been in America for many years. What's it like to be back?'

Troy breathed in deeply then out again. 'I've been living in the land of illusions, where houses are built like film sets, where strangers smile at you and wish you happiness, where the sun always shines, where everything is attainable, everything is in abundance, anything can be bought. A land where all is fake. And do you know what I feel coming back?'

'Err - pleased to be home?'

Troy shook his head. 'Coming back to Britain, this is what I realise - it's just the fucking same. It's just another Disneyland, another Hollywood sound stage, but the sets are better built. The weight of history holds it all in place: the walls don't shake, the machinery is better concealed. We like to believe we've got mysteries buried in those walls, hidden profundities that foreigners will never understand, and for that we put up with the misery, the disgust, the understated arrogance, the obnoxious service and the endless fucking rain. We think we're above it all but we're not. It's just the same but the hamburgers are crap.'

Another period of silence followed. This was not going to be easy. 'OK,' said Bernard, 'can I start with simple question - what's this new show actually about?'

Troy smiled and leant forward as if Bernard was a small dog he was about to pat on the head. 'The rhythm of your life - how would you describe it?'

'Do you really want to know?' Bernard thought for a moment. 'Mostly relentless bewilderment and disorientation. Then long stretches of abject boredom sprinkled with brief moments of sheer panic.'

'Do you feel in control?'

'Is that a joke? Of course I don't.'

'Describe the feeling.'

Bernard heaved a sigh. 'All right, it's like...'

148

'Being part of somebody's master plan, but I having no idea what that plan is - or whether the somebody exists?'

'If you like... yeah, I suppose it is.'

'Very good. Take that scenario, Mr. Hawks, and consider it carefully. It is an important insight. You could say it is the basis for my performance.'

'I could say that, but I don't see where it would get me.' Bernard thumbed through his notes. 'Let me try again. What's the point of this show?'

'I want my audience to feel. I want them to experience emotions. I want to wake the bastards up from their apathy and to see the world as it is. To use the argot of another era, I would like to blow their minds.'

'O.K.... and then what? After you've blown their minds?'

Troy shrugged. 'It's the beginning of an adventure, or perhaps,' his eyes opened wide, 'the end of theatre!'

Bernard noted it all down. He felt he was being led down a very long and winding path that, quite possibly, would take him back to exactly where he started.

'And just how do your sponsors fit into all of this - the Tranquility Foundation? Doesn't seem like they want to wake people up. As far as I can make out, they just want to make people feel smug and forget the rest. Why would they want to sponsor you?'

Troy looked at Bernard and said nothing as a smile slowly spread across his face. 'That's the first intelligent question you've asked, Mr. Hawks.'

'And do I get an answer?'

'Shall we say they were advised, or possibly misadvised, that sponsoring the unexpected would enhance their reputation... or perhaps they desire a backdrop of disorder to exhibit their particular brand of tranquility...' Troy leant back in his chair and chuckled. 'Of course, it's not just us. You'll be amused to hear I am working alongside The Tranquility Campaign marchers, for instance. Famous for their giant puppets, I believe.'

'Oh shit. Not them.'

'Apparently they're under the illusion they're continuing my legacy of radical theatre.'

'Look, please give me a break. I'm supposed to be writing about this show but I haven't the slightest idea of what's actually going on.'

This seemed to anger Troy. 'That doesn't seem to have troubled you in the past. I'm sure you can make something up. You're a journalist, aren't you?'

What light there was in the room was fading fast and Troy was now reduced to a massive silhouette as the final rays of the sun reddened the wall behind him. He now seemed a rather pathetic character, a desperate fantasist from another era, a beached whale that would never be returned to the sea. Bernard began to warm to him.

'Perhaps you think I'm a madman,' continued Troy, 'or a confidence trickster. Perhaps you think our forthcoming performance is a phantom, my personal delusion. Would that make a good story for your paper, Mr. Hawks? The legend of a deluded and washed-up theatre revolutionary? Is that what you'd like to write?'

'A press release and some photos would do fine... to be honest, this is not a job I ever wanted to do. I don't even like theatre.'

'Nor do I,' said Troy, 'it's a loathsome institution. But there are no press releases and no photos. Let me ask you a question. Does the phrase Post-Credibility mean anything to you at all?'

Bernard heaved another deep sigh. 'Not that again. I first heard it from this guy Kepler. I went to a lecture of his once, then I keep reading articles by him that don't make any sense. Supposed to have been invented by a guy called JJ.'

'JJ's a genius. But he doesn't exist.'

'Oh yes?'

'JJ is a construct, a symbolic figure, a character of some significance in my work. A gift. But he's not a real person.'

'Are you sure about that?'

'I happen to know he's an invention of Professor Rupert Kepler himself. A character he created.'

'All invented by that old charlatan? Is he really a Professor or did he make that up too?'

'Kepler may be old, but to call him a charlatan is to grossly underestimate his talents. And yes, he is indeed a Professor.' Troy grunted then leaned forward in his chair and spoke quietly. 'I know him, you see.'

'Yeah. I heard he was one of your actors.'

'An actor, perhaps... but a little more than that. You could call him an ideas man. He was with us until the Asylum Show. That's when I asked him to leave. And that's all I have to say on the matter. If you want to find any more, ask Professor Kepler himself. Look him up in the entertainment listings - he's performing this weekend.'

Bernard stared at the scribbles on his pad. 'You see the problem is I've met him. I've met JJ. He said he was helping to plan Great Britain Day...'

'You think you've met him, do you? And what did he look like?'

'Late middle age, short white hair, lean, absurdly good suit, penetrating stare...'

There was no longer enough light left to discern Troy's expression but he seemed to be nodding. 'I think you are confused, Mr. Hawks. You're chasing your own shadow.'

'Well, thanks. Would you like to explain that?'

'To put no finer point on it, I suspect you have been a subject of an experiment, a victim if you like, or perhaps a scapegoat, manipulated by the very elements you think you are investigating. In other words...' Troy got up, walked over to Bernard and leant right into his face, '...you, Mr. Hawks, have been, and probably still are, a puppet!'

'A puppet?'

Troy sat down. When he spoke again, his voice was gentler. 'Perhaps, Mr. Hawks, I have been a little hard on you. There is a theme to my show, and I will reveal it to you and you alone. In return, I am going to ask you for your assistance.'

'My assistance? I know nothing about theatre.'

'Of course you don't. But I believe you have friends who know about planting bombs...'

'I've stopped writing about bombs and I never did know anything about them.'

'Of course not, Mr. Hawks. All an unfortunate coincidence. And the tunnels that run under the city. I'm sure as a journalist you can find something about them for me?'

'Look, you're asking the wrong guy.'

'Shush now! No pressure on you, but if you still have friends who like explosions, I'm sure we can be of mutual benefit. Here is a card with my private number on it.'

Bernard felt the card pressed into his hand.

'You said something about a theme...'

'Oh yes. My theme is the Plague!'

And then Troy began to laugh again. A terrifying, thunderous laugh that echoed round the walls of the now pitch-black room. Bernard felt some movement in the air and was aware that Troy's bulk was making its way out of the room. Troy's laughter receded into the unfathomable dark leaving Bernard alone.

Bernard moved over to the cushions where Troy had been sitting. He fumbled around until his hand fell on what seemed to be a table lamp, and after he few more fumbles he found a switch. A hammered metal lampshade, opaque but for a few small holes set with coloured glass, allowed just enough light to reveal the bottle of house claret that Troy had been drinking. He poured what remained into the glass and sank back on the cushions. Savouring the wine, he judged it to be a clever blend of blackcurrant juice, malt vinegar and rubbing alcohol.

'Doesn't give much away, does he?' said a voice from the shadows. 'Fat old bastard. That's what America's done to him. He used to be a skinny geezer. Didn't recognise him when he came back. Still the same awkward sod though.'

'Is that...'

'Mikey. From the pub. You asked me about Anton. Or Kepler to you.'

'Perhaps you could tell me something about the show I could actually use.'

'Well the Plague's one of the Elements - but he just told you that.'

'And what the hell has that got to do with Kepler and Post-Credibility?'

'That's just another of Troy's Elements. A bit of the zeitgeist, he says.'

'And just what is an Element?'

'I told you. That's what he calls the stuff he makes the shows out of. Takes the Elements then applies the Strategy.'

'So...'

'To be honest, he hasn't told me much more than he's told you. Except he wants to revive our biggest disaster. The Asylum Show. The one I told you about. Where we nearly all got arrested. But how he thinks he's going to do it in the streets, God only knows. I've just got a list of groups he wants to employ. Amateurs and volunteers - do you believe it? Likes to keep me in the dark, you see. So that I can improvise. Everyone else knows what they're doing but I'm the grit in the oyster, the fly in the ointment. I have to make it up as I go along. That, apparently, is part of The Strategy.'

'And you really have no idea what's going on?'

Mikey shook his head. 'Keeps me in the dark and feeds me shit. Feel like a mushroom.'

'Join the fucking club,' said Bernard taking a large gulp of wine.

Twenty Three

'That's the way to do it!'

- Anon

The first performance Bernard witnessed after becoming a theatre critic was as disturbing as it was unexpected. The cast and the stage were small, the acting wooden or hysterical and the content unremittingly brutal. The play started with casual domestic violence and the ritual abuse of a small baby then escalated into cannibalism and serial murder. The many attempts of the inarticulate, psychotic protagonist to cheat death culminated in a gruesome hanging scene where executioner became victim and evil triumphed. The fact that the story was devoid of hope or joy did not prevent every savage act being greeted with cheers and laughter.

It was mid afternoon when the show finished. Bernard waited until the unruly young audience dispersed, then he approached the striped canvas booth where the performance had been staged. The booth stood alone in the middle of the park and it was just large enough to hide one man. When that man finally stepped out to reveal himself, if he was surprised to see Bernard standing there, notebook in hand, he kept it well concealed.

'Professor Kepler...' Bernard began.

'You've caught me at my day job!'

'It wasn't easy. I spent a long time scouring the listings. This isn't what I was expecting.'

'Merely a little hobby really, but it's a fine tradition, don't you think? And isn't it curious how all of us who do this are called Professors? An excellent way to travel the country and observe. Would you like to examine the actors close up?'

'No.'

Ignoring Bernard's reply, Kepler thrust out Punch and Judy, still stuck on his hands, for Bernard to examine. Bernard recoiled in horror. The hideous varnished, carved faces were familiar but the costumes were distinctly weird. Judy was a slim figure in a red dress with bright blue eyes, Mr. Punch wore a finely tailored business suit in red and green with two initials embroidered on the top pocket.

'JJ!' exclaimed Bernard.

'My little joke,' replied Kepler, dangling the puppet's thin, pinstriped legs in front of Bernard's face.

'Your little invention - according to Troy Sherman. That's what I need to talk to you about. Everyone seems obsessed with this guy, then they tell me he doesn't exist. But I've met him. Maybe. So you've got some explaining to do.'

Kepler stared at the puppet with distaste. 'He's a difficult bastard this one, never quite does what he's supposed to.' He gave a weary sigh then looked up at Bernard. 'You're both right. I invented JJ. Then he became real.'

'What's that supposed to mean?'

'It all began when I was working with The Human Company. I was their writer, their poet, their ideas man. A formative experience...'

'Until Troy threw you out,' said Bernard, noticing that Kepler was beginning to look a little flustered and his hands, still puppeted, were flapping around as if propelled by forces of their own.

'That was a huge misunderstanding,' replied Kepler, 'and of course, all that stuff about me being some sort of government agent provocateur was arrant nonsense, as I'm sure you realise. An enormous shock at the time, I admit, but I have no bitterness, no resentment, not now. Perhaps these little shows help to compensate for the early demise of my theatrical career. But that may have been a good thing.... yes! The best thing that could have happened! It was only when I left the Company that I began to study and develop my theories. Would you like to sit down?'

Kepler pulled two wooden stools out of the booth and they sat down.

'My unfortunate exit from The Company gave me some invaluable insights into the power of the specious rumour, the insidious proliferation of suspicion and paranoia. I devoted myself to research into belief systems and Cred Havens – I devised that term, of course - those fragile zones where disbelief is put on hold. It became quite an obsession.'

The puppets on his hands had calmed down and began to move more deliberately, as if to illustrate Kepler's story.

'While developing the concept of the Virtual Infiltrator, I began to experiment with the covert distribution of rumours, the Universal Conspiracy Theory, the Principles of Post-Credibility - it was astonishing how powerful they could be. JJ emerged out of all of that research. Just a fictional character, a meme I created, a thought experiment. A personification of the techniques of manipulation.'

It seemed that as well as being a puppeteer Kepler had some basic conjuring skills as the puppets began to chase each other around his body, one second on his shoulder, the next peeping out of the bottom of his jacket.

'So Troy was right. You did invent JJ.'

'I'm afraid it gets a little more complicated. At the time it was a just a playful investigation, an amusement. But people really took to it. Initially it was quite exciting. I even attributed some of my own theories to him. Then I began to see posts on the internet from people who claimed to be JJ, they took up the idea and ran with it, positing

154

theories and counter theories, constructing myths then taking them apart, even claiming to *be* me - it was wonderful stuff, quite enthralling, actually. And the best thing of all, the mythical JJ became a Virtual Infiltrator! A man who didn't exist exploiting his own theories! Not that all the theories were mine... like all this rumination on post-chaos theory dialectical materialism...'

'Beg your pardon?'

'Fascinating, actually. How can the dialectic function in an unstable universe? Anyway, one individual seemed to take it a stage further. Having picked up on some of my writings and lectures he became JJ! Perhaps at first it was some sort of joke, or another marketing stunt for some new brand - like the way they copied my joke broking concept - but he furthered the myth until it reached the point...' Kepler hesitated.

'Yes?'

'It seemed he - whoever he was - found employment as JJ. Some rather lucrative contracts. Not just in commerce, but with government.'

'They fell for it?'

'Apparently.'

'Any idea who this JJ is?'

'No. There could, of course, be dozens of them. My instinct suggests to me, however, there is a singular entity behind most of the current excitement.'

'So that's the man I met – and he's a complete fraud?'

Kepler's face brightened and the puppets looked up. 'That's not quite how I would put it. To all intents and purposes he may indeed be JJ. In a way JJ, and by that I mean the nexus of memes that references JJ, is now, despite his fictional origins, as real as I am!' Kepler paused and gazed down at the ground for a moment, then continued. 'I've always thought it strange that Troy insisted I leave the Company. You see he told me I had this very special role; everyone else had a script, masterminded down to the last detail by Troy, but my role was different. It was my task to improvise, to make it all up as I went along! The grit in the oyster he called it, the Strategy! But then I always got the feeling he didn't like me very much, Strategy or no Strategy.'

Bernard was beginning to think he did not like this man either. He was amusing enough as an eccentric cabaret act but the notion that he might have some real power and influence was disturbing. Meanwhile, the puppets seemed to have reverted to type and Punch resumed the slow but relentless battering of Judy.

'Why should I believe a word you say?' said Bernard. 'Suppose I said there was a real JJ all along. What if none of the ideas are actually yours, you're just some sort of parasite? Suppose I said rather than inventing JJ, you've invented yourself?'

Kepler's eyes lit up. 'Well that's just it! Maybe JJ invented me! Or maybe I am the real JJ! Is there any difference? Yes, maybe it's my fantasy, maybe it's his! Don't you see? The ideas have lives of their own! We swim in an ocean of ideas, we drink them in and piss them out again, we think they're ours, but they're not, we just borrow them for a time...' Both puppets were now dancing wildly, causing the elated Kepler to get up off his stool and dance with them. He seemed remarkably agile for his age. 'Has it not occurred to you that your whole notion of individual consciousness is a construction, and hence your sense of free will, the uniqueness that you cling to so desperately is, in reality, a total illusion?'

'You know something? In the last few weeks, I've lost any sense that I was in control of anything, but I assumed that was just me going mad... stress or drugs or middle age or something.'

'Ah ha! There you have it! You have nothing left to believe! Welcome to the world of Post Credibility! You are well on your way to establishing the appropriate state of mind!'

'State of mind? Currently my state of mind seems about on the level of that thing stuck on your hand!'

'That's the way to do it!' squawked Punch as he lurched towards Bernard's face.

'Just fuck off!' said Bernard to the puppet.

*

When Bernard returned home he heard laughter coming from Dillwyn's flat. Female laughter. He knocked on the door and the laughter stopped. He knocked again and the door opened and he found himself staring straight into Sarah's face.

'Hello Bernard. I suppose you'd better come in.'

Bernard entered the flat. Mel was sitting on a sofa, Sarah went up and sat down beside her. They both leaned slightly towards each other so only their shoulders touched. Behind them, the bookshelves previously stacked with Dillwyn's carefully catalogued files were now completely bare. And there was no sign of Dillwyn.

'I don't know what you're doing here, either of you...'

'Don't worry,' said Sarah, 'we're just tying up a few loose ends. We'll be out of your way soon.'

He turned to Mel and stabbed his finger at her. 'Dillwyn said he got rid of you. He's got a new cleaner now. So you can fuck off for a start.'

'Cleaner? He told you I was his cleaner, did he?' said Mel, her huge head nodding from side to side as if her neck was struggling to support its weight.

'Well, yes. Cleaner and friend.'

'I was his *carer*, Bernard. I've was looking after him since he was released from hospital into the community.'

'Hospital? He didn't say he'd been in hospital.'

'It's not the sort of thing people like to talk about. And I couldn't say anything - patient confidentiality, you understand.' Her head began to nod faster as if she was she was trying to shake the last remaining expression out of an empty brain. She must have succeeded as her strangely inhospitable smile fell into place. 'I should thank you, really. It was very good for him to have someone who would listen... at first...'

'And then you encouraged him to leave the Tranquility Retreat,' added Sarah. 'That was a very bad move. It could cause permanent damage.'

'I did him a big favour. I broke him out of there - we were lucky to escape.'

'Escape?' said Sarah. 'The Retreat isn't a prison camp. Clients can leave any time they please.'

'But Dillwyn was a guard or steward there or something...' Bernard looked at Mel and Sarah's blank faces. 'Well, he said he was...'

'That course was the final part of his rehabilitation,' said Mel, 'but it's nothing to do with me any more. He's off the books.'

'Rehabilitation? I suppose just because he had, I mean has, a few eccentric, possibly subversive, insights you want to brand him insane? Throw him in the gulag or ram tranquillisers into his brain?'

Mel and Sarah shook their heads.

'Sometimes, you know,' continued Bernard, 'that crazy Welshman seems to make more sense than anybody else around. I'm beginning to think he's the only sane one among us.'

Sarah stared at Bernard intently for several seconds, then she lifted her index finger and wagged it slowly. 'All right, Bernard. I can see where you're going with this and I don't think it is going to work.'

'Work?'

'Don't play dumb, Bernard, I know you too well. You align yourself with Dillwyn to gain diminished responsibility for your crimes on the grounds of mental ill health.'

'What the fuck...'

'We could help you with this one if you insist, but it's a bit risky,' added Mel. 'There are substantial costs involved as well, of course... administration and paperwork... plus the electricity charges if they decide you need treatment...'

Mel and Sarah looked at each other and sighed.

'And where is Dillwyn, anyway?' shouted Bernard. 'Hey - if you weren't a cleaner, what were you doing cleaning up my room?'

Mel face froze for a moment. 'Just being neighbourly. And as a TF outreach worker, there are certain security responsibilities we have to maintain, particularly with a vulnerable client. Obligatory if there are any references to bombs.'

'You're a fucking spy!'

'Now don't get uppity, Bernard,' said Sarah, 'she was just doing her job. And it's not as if they ransacked the place. They left it very, very tidy. They have high quality standards.'

'Clean mind, clean house, clean planet,' said Mel, almost to herself.

Then, as if responding to a silent cue, Mel and Sarah both looked at Bernard and smiled. Their brightest, most repellent, Sunday school smiles.

'This is wrong. This is all so very wrong. It can't get more wrong than this,' muttered Bernard, as he got up to go back to his flat. He hesitated in the doorway and turned round. 'Hey, where is Dillwyn anyway? I need to talk to him.'

'Probably in the coffee shop. The new one in the high street. That's where he spends most of his afternoons now.'

*

As soon as Bernard stepped back into his flat his phone rang. He stared at it for a second then picked it up the receiver.

'Bernard...'

'Err, yeah, hello. It's you. My friendly blackmailer. We were going to meet up...'

'That's right. Matters outstanding. Meet me at seven o' clock tonight.'

'Where?'

The voice hesitated for a moment. *'Elysium Gardens. And bring the money.'*

'But what...' started Bernard, but the caller had hung up.

He thought for a moment, then took down Inspector Pitmarsh's business card that was pinned to the cork board Mel had installed.

He picked up the phone again and dialled.

Twenty Four

'It gets lonely in my job. People only ring me up when they want something.'

- Bob The Dealer

The small patch of municipal grass that made up Elysium Gardens was literally a stone's throw from Bernard's flat. In fact, many stones from Elysium Gardens had been thrown against Bernard's windows - the gravel path that ran its length was a handy source of missiles for the local youth. The Gardens were also becoming a sort of Bermuda Triangle of hope for Bernard. This was where he had gone to meet Animal and found Dillwyn instead, and on the evening he entered the park to rendezvous with his bomb-planting blackmailer he was greeted with the sight of Bob the Dealer, slouched against the gates of the Gardens, his long, sad head hung low. It was an unmistakable silhouette, despite the addition of a large, unfamiliar, battered leather cowboy hat. As Bernard approached the hat and head rose.

'Hello, Bernard. Have you come to give me my money?'

'Bob, this is a very bad time...'

'Saw you go to the cash machine on the way here. Seems you took some cash out.'

'I can't explain now, but really, you shouldn't hang around. I've got a feeling the police might turn up any minute.'

'The police?' Bob nodded his head slowly. 'You'd better give it to me now, then.'

'I can't give it to you. I need if for...'

'The expenses. For transfer of the rights. To the bomb.'

'Bob, how did you know... what the fuck... you're not... you are... you're my fucking blackmailer!'

Bob took off his hat in a vague and unnecessary gesture of revelation. 'I'm sorry, Bernard, but I had to get my money out of you one way or another. Thought I'd try out a new strategy.'

'So all that stuff about planting a bomb, and evidence I did it...'

'Just a marketing gambit. They call it virtual entrepreneurship. Didn't have to do anything, really. Just made a couple of phone calls. Better than standing out in the cold on street corners.'

'But when you called the other day... when you said you wanted a mention in my column... what the fuck was that all about?'

Bob shrugged his big sloping shoulders. 'I don't know, Bernard, I like to think it's not all about money. Just like some recognition - it just gets lonely in my job. People only ring me up when they want something...'

159

'But you're a fucking dealer!'

'...they never ring me up just to say hello.' Bob stared at Bernard and blinked. 'So you going to give me my money? Three hundred we said, didn't we?'

Bernard pondered for a minute or two wondering how to get his revenge on Bob for causing him such grief. At the same time, he felt an enormous sense of relief that this was only Bob, and adversaries don't come much less threatening than him.

'I thought it was two sixty.'

'Overheads, Bernard. Telephone calls. Marketing expenses...' he breathed in, looked up to the sky and down to Bernard again. 'All right, seeing as it's you, two sixty.'

'Come on, let's get this over quick. Before the pigs arrive.'

Bernard counted the notes into the large, grimy palm spread before him, but he was surprised to find Bob wasn't looking at him or the money. His eyes were narrowing and focused on something behind Bernard's shoulder. Before Bernard had a chance to turn round he heard a familiar voice.

'Hello Bernard. And Bob - didn't expect to find you here... oh no, surely not. This isn't your bomber, is it?'

'Hello Inspector Pitmarsh,' said Bob, slowly counting his money and stuffing it into his pocket.

'Bernard,' sighed Pitmarsh, 'couldn't you do better than this?'

'But... I thought he was... how was I to know... and why aren't you running away, Bob? And why aren't you trying to arrest him?'

'Bob and I go back a long way. One of my main sources of information, aren't you Bob?'

'Ear to the ground, eyes to heaven, that's me.'

Pitmarsh walked over to Bob, patted him on the small of his back and pointed at Bernard. 'This piece of shit here thinks he's delivered me a dangerous terrorist.'

'Huh,' said Bob, making a noise somewhere between a laugh and a cough. 'That's the thing with old Bernard. He's always getting the wrong end of the stick. Anyway, I'd better be on my way. See you both soon.'

As Bob ambled off, Bernard, restrained by Pitmarsh's familiar grip on his shoulder, shouted after him.

'You're crap, Bob, do you know that? You're a crap dealer, a crap businessman, a crap human being. I bet you're a crap informer, too!'

'Where's your compassion, Bernard?' sighed Pitmarsh. 'Bob does his best. It if wasn't for Bob, I might never have known about you and that girl Animal.'

As Bernard stood there contemplating this information, Pitmarsh's hand still clamped tightly on his shoulder, he became aware of a rustling in the bushes and glimpses of dark blue uniforms behind them.

'Nothing more to do here, you can all go back to base now,' shouted Pitmarsh, 'just leave me alone with this cretin for a few more minutes.'

There was more rustling, followed by the slamming of van doors and the sound of vehicles starting up and driving away, then all was quiet.

'Just you and me, Bernard. You and me together against the world.'

'Not quite how I see it, but thanks for the thought.'

'So it looks like you'll be writing that piece for me after all. Time to get those metaphorical bombs planted.'

'I'm just a theatre reviewer now...'

'Not my problem, sunshine. Write that story and bring me that girl Animal and I think you'll find your life will suddenly become much easier.'

'If I write that story...'

'When you write that story.'

'...suppose nothing happens? Suppose there is no Primitive Front?'

'I think you underestimate the creative power of writing, Bernard. You do your job and I'll do mine.'

'All right, just tell me what you want me to do.'

'Follow her, Bernard. Be her best friend, be her lover, fuck her senseless for all I care. I want to know their plans. I want to know how many of them there are. I want to know where they are going. You're going to be my mole. My snivelling little inside man.'

Twenty Five

'Computer viruses are just information that knows how to reproduce.
Some mutate into ideas.'

- Animal

As Bernard approached the coffee shop he could see Dillwyn sitting at
the counter looking out over the street. He seemed thin and pale
against the black and white photograph that filled the wall behind of
wrinkled, dark-skinned men letting coffee beans fall joyfully through
their fingers. Dillwyn waved as he saw Bernard approach.

'So, Dillwyn,' said Bernard, as he sat down on the stool next to
him, 'this is where you spend your time now?'

Dillwyn turned to Bernard and nodded, then looked back to the
street outside. 'I sit here and watch the world go by. I can do my
researches from here, see. Don't need to travel much. Like being at the
pictures. Look at her!'

Dillwyn pointed to a small girl in a pink tracksuit, staring
through the window at them as she chewed her gum. 'The thing is,
Bernard, are we the audience, or are we the show?'

A bubble grew from the child's mouth until it obscured her face
completely, then burst leaving a residue of gluey pink strands on the
plate glass. She laughed silently then floated away horizontally as if
she was standing on a raft. Or a conveyor belt.

'What the fuck...' said Bernard.

'They have wheels on their shoes now. That's how they do it.
The little rascals!'

'Listen to me, Dillwyn, I need your help. There's a lot of stuff
I've got to sort out.'

'What stuff is that, then?'

'Where do I begin... for a start there's Mel. You told me she's
a cleaner, but she claims she's some sort of nurse...'

'Well, all the same thing, really. Tidy house, tidy mind, isn't
it?'

Bernard stared at Dillwyn. He looked no tidier than usual, but
he seemed uncharacteristically calm. And happy.

'What the hell did she do to you? She and those Tranquility
shysters?'

'Nothing, really. Got past all that. Never did need her really,
you see. Just played along with her, let her think I was a bit doolally
and she was being useful, got more information that way. You know
what I mean?'

'Look, I think… maybe I'm on to something. That guy JJ, you gave me all that stuff about? The one they say came up with the idea of Post-Credibility?'

'Oh yes? JJ. I used to read his stuff a lot.'

'I met him, Dillwyn. *I met JJ.* Had a whole conversation with the guy. He says he's behind Great Britain Day. But then I met Kepler again - he happens to be a fucking Punch & Judy man by the way, did you know that? - and he claims he invented JJ… Dillwyn, why are you grinning like that?'

'Grinning, am I? Well, you just seem to take all this stuff so seriously. Relax, like. I wonder if they do those shoes in adult size?'

'Concentrate, Dillwyn. Sadly, I don't know who else I can to talk to about this. I was being blackmailed for evidence that didn't exist for a bomb I didn't plant by a blackmailer who turns out to be my dealer who is, in fact, a police informer. Then this copper Pitmarsh wants me to write about another bomb that doesn't exist so he can arrest a terrorist organisation that doesn't exist, but I can't write about bombs anyway because I'm only a fucking theatre critic…'

'Take it easy, Bernard, you're getting all hot and bothered. Can I get you a iced coffee? They got liquorice flavour on special today. Lovely, it is.'

'Dillwyn, what's going on? Have those Tranquility bastards done something to your brain?'

'No one's done anything to me. And per'aps those Tranquility people aren't as bad as all that, really.'

'But they're fucking spies… they did over my apartment…'

'Well, I think it's just their contractual obligations, like. Everyone has to do that now. Particularly if bombs are mentioned in the presence of 'vulnerable people'. Like me, see.' Dillwyn chuckled.

'For fuck's sake… all that brainwashing stuff, and the surveillance and all the security shit you warned me about… like I used to think you were a paranoid nut but now I think you might have been right all along.'

'I've stopped worrying about all that now. All gets a bit tiring, don't it?' Dillwyn pointed to the street outside where some men in fluorescent waistcoats were putting up barriers along the pavement. 'I see they're putting up the barriers, then.'

'Yeah, I'm sure that's really interesting, but I need to find…'

'They're getting prepared for Great Britain Day, see…'

'Fuck Great Britain Day and look at me! What's Mel been doing to you? All your shelves are empty - where there used to be all those files. Did Mel throw them out? Have they been getting to you?'

'No, that was me. Just been doing a bit of tidying up. Decided to simplify things. Got it all down to one notebook. More of a diary, really. Very focussed, like.' He held up to a large black notebook. 'Those pills helped in the end, you see.'

'Pills?'

'The ones your Mother gave me.'

'Not the BalZac? She gave you some too?'

'That's right. Did you take yours?'

'Of course I bloody didn't. And looking at you, it's the only good decision I've made in months.'

'Never thought you had anything against self-medication, Bernard.'

'I do when it has a brand name on it. I always thought those pills were a sort of municipal version of ecstasy, like a party drug for a very, very dull party.'

'Here you go - it's all written it down in there, see.'

Dillwyn passed the notebook to Bernard. The first half dozen pages were packed with Dillwyn's surprisingly neat handwriting, but the writing became sparser on the pages that followed. On the tenth page Dillwyn had changed from brown ink to green and had written these lines:

`Wednesday started taking the BalZac. Had no effect.`

Bernard turned a few pages forward.

`Saturday to Sunday. Pills still don't work, but I've stopped worrying about it.`

Bernard turned the page again.

`Wednesday. Stopped worrying about everything.`

Bernard looked at Dillwyn, smiling and rocking back and forth very gently on his stool, and sighed.

'Dillwyn, this is tragic. I was coming to this bizarre conclusion that you might actually have some idea about what was going on...'

Dillwyn's smile diminished and he began to speak softly in a slow, flat voice, still staring straight ahead through the window. 'Viruses, Bernard. Computer viruses mutating into human viruses. Maybe we're all infected. Sometimes things don't make sense. Not in that way. You have to break those simple chains of cause and effect.'

'That's what Animal said and I never did know what the fuck she meant.'

'Maybe there wasn't a bomb. Maybe there was never a bomb at all.'

'What the hell are you talking about? I was there. It knocked me to the ground.'

'There was an explosion, all right. But maybe it was just an accident.'

'What do you mean?'

'A gas pipe or something. That's what's they're saying.'

'But...'

'Per'aps the agency wanted some sympathy. Per'aps the government needed a bomb scare. People like to have reasons, don't they? They're funny like that. Cause and effect. Good guys and bad guys. The ones that make you feel everything's all right, the ones that make you think everything's wrong... sure you're not going to have a coffee with me?'

Bernard closed the book and shook his head. 'Yeah, I'll have a coffee.'

'And there's was something I've been meaning to tell you. About that girl Animal. Something important. Only I can't remember what it was.'

'Thanks, Dillwyn. That's really helpful.'

Bernard drank the soapy coffee and they watched the world go by the window, a world that every day made a little less sense than the day before. He wondered if he was becoming as mad as Dillwyn. What was it like to lose your mind? Would it be an sudden shock, or a subtle process, like weakening eyesight or a stiffening limb, day by day everything becoming a little stranger? Or would he remain blissfully unaware of the whole process, becoming an oblivious senile curmudgeon or an amiable holy fool?

'You've gone all quiet, Bernard. What are you thinking about?'

'I was thinking about my uncle. My uncle who went deaf...' Bernard looked down into his coffee and gave the froth a stir. 'He told me once how he had quite looked forward to going deaf, you know, it might be nice for the world to be a little quieter... but when it actually happened it was like the volume stayed the same but every sound became blurred. It was like he could still hear but nothing made any sense. Made him shout a lot.'

'And, Bernard?'

'Yeah, that's it - what if it's already happening? Maybe I am going mad, or deaf or blind, or all three, and I just don't know anything about it. I'm stranded inside my head and I can't see out.'

'Like what I said with the brainwashing. If they do it properly, you know nothing about it. You don't feel a thing.'

'Thanks again, Dillwyn. That's very reassuring.'

'You know what I think? I think you should give some of those pills a try.'

It was a full minute before Bernard replied. 'It's not the pills I need. I've got to find Animal.'

Twenty Six

'You see they killed the cats when they should have killed the rats, the cats killed the rats, the rats that spread the disease…' - *Andrew Pond*

It was very early in the morning when Bernard woke up for the fourth time. He wasn't sleeping well these days; two desperate feelings were competing in his head. The first was the need to see Animal again. It was she who'd got him into this mess, it was she who seemed to have some sense what the fuck was going on, and it was she who made him feel... the startling novelty of the phrase tumbling through his brain had wrecked his sleep - *good to be alive*.

The other sensation, burning inside him like a fever, was that he could never see her again. Of course, it could never work out with Animal, but worse, much worse than that, if he saw again he was destined to betray her to Pitmarsh.

His dreams about Animal had hardly faded when he opened his eyes. He could still see her. He blinked hard to clear his vision. He blinked again but an afterimage remained. Then it spoke.

'It's weird watching you sleep. Not very good at staying still, are you?'

He sat up. 'Animal? How the fuck…?'

She was sitting cross-legged on the end of his bed. There was just enough light to see her smile. He could have reached out and touched her, but he didn't.

'Good paranoid piece you wrote about the Front and the government's real plan for Great Britain Day threatening to ruin the theatre show.'

'Why are you here… and don't tell me you're really going to blow up it all up, are you?'

'Do you want to know how?'

'No, I don't want to know how. Please don't tell me… and how did you get in?'

She leaned forward. Her eyes caught a glint of light. They were blueish grey.

'What's the matter, Bernard?'

'It's just... the less I know about what you're doing the better. Really.'

Animal sighed. Bernard listened to the tick of his alarm clock as he waited for her to say something. After a few seconds she spoke but her voice betrayed little emotion.

'Is someone leaning on you?'

Bernard breathed in deep then out again. 'It's fucking Pitmarsh… he wants me to rat on you. Like he's blackmailing me…

he's fucking mad. He thought if I wrote about you or the Primitive Front or whoever the fuck you are planting a bomb, you'll do it. That's why I wrote...'

'That's great, Bernard.'

'How can that be great? How does it even make any sense? He's going to frame me and he's going to frame you and we'll all end up in some high security dungeon with electrodes in our skulls. Anyway, if they believe a word of it they're just going to double the security forces or cancel the whole thing.'

'Well, either way the PF wins doesn't it? You know, basic Post Credibility tactic - the more people think The Front exists, the more it will exist, the more will join it?' She leaned back against the end of the bed. 'But they're not going to cancel it. The government needs its enemies, just like Pitmarsh needs you.'

The sky was brightening through the thin blue curtain behind Animal, turning her from dim mirage to silhouette. Outside the odd vagrant bird had begun to sing.

'So...' muttered Bernard, 'it doesn't matter if what I write is true or not, as long as it builds up the idea the Primitive Front exists...'

'That's right, Bernard. You're beginning to get it.'

'Am I? I really wish that made me feel better.'

'Get dressed. Gabby's waiting with the van. We're going to take you to see Pond.'

*

Outside the first hints of colour were trickling into the dull grey of the morning. The van's engine was already running. Gabby opened the door for Bernard to get in the back. Animal climbed into the front passenger seat and they drove away towards the city centre.

'Something I need to know,' said Bernard. 'The bomb - the one in the ad agency, when I first met you - was that really a bomb? Dillwyn reckoned...'

'Does it matter?' replied Animal, turning round to face him. 'You said there was going to be a bomb. Everybody thought it was a bomb. It looked like a bomb. It felt like a bomb. What's the difference?'

'It makes a fuck of a lot of difference if people think I planted it.'

'Of course you didn't, Bernard. But say you did, then maybe it helped the government, maybe it helped those who want to bring it down... who knows... don't get tied up in the chains of cause and effect...'

'And I never got this 'hung up on cause and effect' stuff...'

'Cause and effect, Bernard... like once there was time when no-one made a connection between sex and having babies... did you know that? People fucked when they felt like it and babies just happened... no worrying about the consequences... no ownership crap...'

A sudden, icy sensation shot through Bernard's body. 'You're not trying to tell me... you're not...'

'Not what?' Animal looked puzzled. She paused for a second then burst out laughing. 'Don't be dumb, Bernard, we're not in a soap opera. I was just... hey Gabby, Bernard wants to know about cause and effect. You tell him.'

'It's like, buy this/you'll look younger, buy this/you'll be beautiful, buy this/you'll be cool, need this/buy that, destroy this/win that... break those chains, you break the system.'

'That...' said Bernard, 'that's like saying what you do doesn't have any effect. So what's the point...'

'All actions have effects,' Animal replied, 'but usually we don't know what they are.'

'Live by accident and necessity, Bernie. Like the animals. Stuff that happens by chance, stuff we have to do to survive. That's it. Like you're always saying, the world's fucked. We're still savages, but, like, with technology we can kill thousands at a time. What's so good about that?'

'He's right,' said Animal. 'What's there that's worth keeping?'

Bernard shrugged and lay back against the side of the van. He began to go through a list of things he liked about Western civilisation. He thought of pain killers, the sprung mattress, cigarette lighters, cash machines, trains... but it began to feel too much like a Christmas song from an old Hollywood musical.

'I just preferred it when it was simpler. You know, when terrorists planted real bombs and peace protesters weren't sponsored by ad agencies and drug dealers sold drugs without going on training courses and everything you touched and heard wasn't part of some elaborate fucking PR operation... when the world wasn't divided into those who don't give a fuck about anything and smug bastards who think they're in control...'

'Stop getting romantic, Bernard. Pond will explain it all to you. We'll be there soon.'

He looked up through the windows in the back of the van as they drove through the West End. There wasn't much to see but the tops of the buildings. At ground level he knew they were all the same, the flat shiny surfaces of shopping, but at the top the world was different. Bursting out of girdles of plate glass and chrome were gothic mansions, cupolas, palladium columns, garrets, spires, statues, sooty palaces and crumbling cathedrals. Monuments to forgotten

168

entrepreneurs and lost religions, follies and fantasies, the frozen music of a cacophonous past. He wondered what it would be like to see it all fall down. To start again.

The van came to a stop by a building site on the outskirts of the City.

'We've got to put on these,' said Animal, taking three yellow fluorescent waistcoats out of a bag.

'Do we have to? I was told yellow wasn't my colour.'

'It's to make us invisible. And you need the hat too.' She threw him a white plastic hard hat. Gabby got out and opened two large chipboard gates, then got back into the van and drove onto the site. It was a patch of wasteland, surrounded by new office blocks and cranes, with scattered piles of bricks and timber and a shabby green caravan in the corner. Three battered plastic chairs were set in a semi-circle around a glowing brazier. Gabby sat down in the middle one, Animal and Bernard took the others.

'So what is all this?' said Bernard to Animal.

'It's just a camp. We keep moving. There's always a building site where no one will notice us. You've probably seen us hundreds of times.'

'And do you dig up the roads too?'

'Oh yeah. Of course. That's how we control the traffic.'

By the look on her face it didn't seem like a joke.

'So what do we do now?' asked Bernard.

Before Gabby or Animal could answer, a door opened in the caravan in the corner of the site. A tall man, also wearing a fluorescent waistcoat and hard hat strode slowly towards them.

'This is Pond,' whispered Gabby as he got up from his chair and ran over to the other side of the site.

Beneath the waistcoat Pond wore a spotless white boiler suit. He had long, flowing black hair and a full beard. His age could have been anywhere between 40 and 60.

Pond stood still, his large, gleaming eyes fixed on Bernard. Gabby came back carrying a fourth chair which he placed just behind Pond. Still keeping his gaze on Bernard, Pond sat down and Gabby returned to his seat.

'Hey, Bernard, how are you doing?'

The voice was warm and confident but edged with a little too much enthusiasm for Bernard's comfort. And he didn't trust the smile; it reminded him of a youth worker. Or a hippie evangelist.

'As well as can be expected,' answered Bernard.

Pond continued to stare at him. He looked across to Animal sitting on the other side of the brazier. She was smiling at Pond but her face was rippled by the rising currents of hot air and Bernard couldn't tell whether she was in awe or bemused. Finally Pond spoke again.

'So, Bernard, what do you know about chaos theory?'

'Umm - saw a TV programme once...'

'It's a wonderful thing. A very, very important phenomenon. Chaos occurs when opposing forces within a system, instead of balancing each other out, instead of reaching a point of equilibrium or a regular rhythm, tip the system into the unpredictable.'

'Yeah, chaos Bernie! That's what we want, isn't it?' shouted Gabby. 'Stop pretending we're in control so we can we be free! Smash it all up!'

'Quiet now, Gabriel. Let me explain to Bernard. Those old dialectics, the struggles between the classes, the good and the bad, the left and the right... all that is history. None of that is relevant in the era of Post-Credibility. Do you understand?'

'Yeah, well, all very interesting, but I don't see it's got anything to do with me.'

'Animal, tell Bernard why we need him. He was your idea, after all.'

Animal turned to face Bernard, but he had the sense she was talking to Pond, not him. 'You were, like, somebody on the inside. You were part of the mainstream, but had a glimpse of how everything is fucked. Then you started planting your virtual bombs... all in the right place, like you'd seen the future...' She turned back to Pond who continued.

'You see, any act of resistance means nothing without a story around it. We all need our stories, Bernard. You've helped write some of them. The Primitive Front needs to be seen to be a threat, so that society can respond and show its true face, reveal its brutality, its desperation.'

A large rat ran across in front of them and for a moment stood still, staring straight at Pond. Pond looked back and nodded slowly, then the rat disappeared into a pile of rubble.

'I lived among the rats. In a manner of speaking,' continued Pond. He laughed, then picked up a brick and threw it with great force at the rat's hiding place. There was a loud crash and three rats shot out and ran into the shadows.

'That must have been very... interesting.'

'That was when I bought and sold the future, Bernard!'

Oh Jesus, thought Bernard, *another madman*. He smiled and nodded.

'The rats had a time machine,' continued Pond, sounding like he was beginning a well rehearsed confession. 'It sucked money back into the present, so we could spend tomorrow's money today. Rivers of money. The rats swam with the tide... always with the tide... rats are lazy, you see. Greed made them buy when prices rose, fear made them sell when prices dropped.'

A small, low value coin dropped into place in the back of Bernard's brain. 'What... you were like some sort of city trader or something?'

Pond kept his eyes locked on Bernard, then he beckoned to Animal who walked over and sat down on the ground beside him. 'For a while all I did was watch how it flowed...' He nodded his head as he spoke, as if to affirm the importance of this statement. 'I studied the form, the dance of rat desire, rising in five steps and falling in three, a fandango of persuasion and surrender. The rats chased each others tails, round and round in circles. At first it was like belonging to a cult. Then I realised it was much more than that: it was a disease. The rats were sick. I saw the signs; the red eyes and the runny noses, the shouts and the tantrums... ' Pond's voice began to falter as if he was losing control of what he was saying. 'But I didn't join in the dance, right? I just watched how the money moved, how it formed eddies and currents, and waited for the turbulence. That's where I dipped my hand into the stream and played. While the rats swam around in circles. I made money, Bernard. Oceans of money.'

A rich city fucker gone mad, thought Bernard. *Probably too much Charlie. Now it's beginning to make some sense.* 'So if you were doing so well, why did you stop?'

'I saw through it. I saw it for what it was - a collective hallucination, a fantasy played out on the screens of their computers. You see nothing real ever moved - no ingots or coins, not even pieces of paper, just infinitesimal pulses of electricity, symbols of symbols of money. Atoms of belief. Without the faith, bank notes are just slips of coloured paper... and these were the people who thought they were in control of the world, the people who thought they were steering our fate. But they weren't, you see. It was the machines. The machines had taken over. The machines did the buying and selling, they had the power, but they fought amongst themselves... a war of machines. That's when I realised it all had to go. This delusion, this pantomime they call civilisation...' Pond released a barely audible laugh, and his voice began to dwindle away again. 'Once I studied the flow of money, now I study the flow of ideas. If systems of money can crash, then systems of ideas can crash too, if currency can lose its value, so can ideas...' He paused again and his composure returned. 'Have you heard of a man called JJ?'

Bernard looked at Animal for a cue, but none was forthcoming. 'Yeah, I've heard of him.'

'A great inspiration - even if though he would abhor everything we're doing. How do you operate in a world where there is no longer any belief? I realised I could apply my knowledge to the flow of anything... money, traffic, ideas, beliefs...' Pond paused once more, as though he was trying very hard not to be diverted again into another

171

train of thought. 'A chaotic system is not random, Bernard, but the exact outcomes are impossible to predict. If we can tell when systems are moving into a chaos, maybe we can tip them in that direction, then we can invest... '

'I still don't see how I fit in to all of this.'

'You've helped a little, Bernard. You've helped construct our opposing forces. To create turbulence. To create the unpredictable.'

Pond touched Animal gently on her arm. It seemed to be a cue for her to speak.

'Bernard,' said Animal softly, 'are you going to help us again... against all those people celebrating in the streets and telling us everything is all right? Against all those fucked up politicians and stupid fat policemen and fascist farmers and shrinks who are trying to control your brain? Are you, Bernard?'

'What do you want me to do?'

Animal looked straight at Bernard and smiled. But it was Pond who spoke.

'Animal thinks you can get us into Great Britain Day. Behind the lines. Into the show. Can you, Bernard?'

Bernard thought for a moment or two. *Is this going to a good thing or a bad thing? Does anybody know? Does anybody care?* He looked into Animal's blue-grey eyes; she nodded encouragement, he nodded back. Before Bernard had time to make a decision he heard himself speak.

'There is this... this guy I met. Runs a theatre company. They're doing a big thing on Great Britain Day. Says he wants some people to cause trouble. Who know about bombs and tunnels and stuff...'

'That sounds perfect,' said Pond.

'You see,' said Animal, still smiling at Bernard, 'I said he was a genius!'

Bernard reached into his back pocket and pulled out Troy's card. 'But Pitmarsh...' he mumbled, 'this copper's on my trail... wants me to write about Great Britain Day, about bombs again...'

'As you suggested in your last piece, we believe the government's going to stage a demonstration of a terrorist incident, which they'll want us to take for real, and then they'll deal with it calmly and efficiently. What we're going to do is to make sure those incidents will be far more than they can control.'

'But what do I tell Pitmarsh?'

'Tell him everything, Bernard. Tell the people how the ground is about to open up under their feet.'

Bernard looked from Pond to Animal and back to Pond again. 'The weird thing is, no one believes anything I write. But they still seem to want me to write it.'

'That's right, Bernard,' said Animal.

She was still looking at Bernard and smiling sweetly, but her head was now leaning against Pond's knee. Pond began to stroke her hair gently with the tips of his fingers.

Twenty Seven

'No one complains about BalZac as its side effect is to stop you complaining.'

- Bernard Hawks, The Indicator - 'Notes From The Shadows'

Bernard was woken early by a distant chorus of car horns and shouting followed by the slamming of doors. But now all was quiet, deathly quiet. He opened the window. The background screech and rumble of traffic had gone. An ominous start to Great Britain Day.

He knocked on Dillwyn's door. Dillwyn opened the door and grinned.

'Oh God, Dillwyn, you're not still on those pills are you?'

'Well, I think they're wearing off a bit. Things are sort of coming back to me now. You know there was something I was meaning to tell you about Animal?'

'That she's working for the state? That I should keep well away from her?'

'Not that...' Dillwyn screwed up his face. 'No... it's gone again.' His grin returned.

'Thanks Dillwyn. You know I think I preferred it when you were paranoid and dodging the security cameras. Just wondered if you wanted to come into town with me - you know, witness this Great Britain Day crap? I'm supposed to be writing about it.'

'I'll catch up with you later, Bernard, if that's all right. Got a bit of work to do first.'

'Please yourself. And I'd appreciate if you cut down on the grinning a bit. It doesn't suit you.'

As Bernard shut the front door behind him all he heard was the clunk of the lock echoing down an empty street. Why so quiet? Where were all the cars? Just another everyday weirdness. Traffic had become like Weather, an envoy of chaos prone to histrionic mood changes, running free one moment and struck rigid the next.

The morning was dull and cold, the sky was a flat yellowed grey. To his left the end of his street was blocked by a row of silent, stationary cars. He wandered around for a few minutes and found that all the roads north, west and east of his flat were barricaded by cars, bumper to bumper, all abandoned by their drivers and passengers.

He turned the corner into the high street. The only vehicle in sight was a milk float parked on the pavement. A steady stream of children were removing the last remaining bottles from the crates in the back. The milkman was sitting on the ground beside his vehicle, intermittently whistling as he rolled a cigarette.

'Funny old morning,' said the milkman as Bernard approached. 'Can't do my round, can't go back to the depot, so I thought I'd make the most of it.'

'What's happened?'

'Gridlock, mate. All the traffic around the outside of the city seems to have tied itself up in knots. Sit back and enjoy the show! Go on, treat yourself to a Gold Top!'

It was still cold enough to see your breath but the sun had begun to break through the clouds. The air glittered as if the light was shining through a tinsel curtain. On the other side of the road a small crowd clustered around a bus stop. Apparently resigned to the absence of buses, they had started an impromptu picnic and were passing round sandwiches and Thermos flasks. A little further on, thirty or more people were queuing outside a bread shop, laughing and exchanging pleasantries as they stamped their feet and hugged themselves in the cold. Bernard looked back to the whistling milkman. Something very odd was going on; he had not heard a milkman whistle for twenty years. They all used to do it: milkmen, postmen, chippies and brickies, men of all trades would whistle - it was considered part of the job. Then, some time in the 1980's, it all stopped. Maybe Thatcher eliminated it along with the trade unions. But it was not just the whistling that was disturbing - everyone was far too happy.

Then it hit him. *Good God*, thought Bernard, *I wrote about this!* He had experienced it twice in his life, once when his street was flooded, once when he was snowbound for days in a small Welsh village, an event that left a lasting and deadly impression. Yes, there was no doubt, here it was again, stronger than ever.

'It's the fucking War Time Spirit!' he said out loud.

The milkman stopped whistling and gave him a knowing wink.

'Nice to have it back, mate, don't you reckon?' shouted the milkman. 'Didn't you hear the tanks in the night? Good thing they moved 'em in before all the roads got blocked.'

'Tanks?'

'Security preparations. Rumours there's going to be a bit of trouble on the streets today. Nice and quiet now, though - make the most of it while you can, it won't last long.'

Oh yes, this is what he had written about all right.

The War Time Spirit waits patiently, deep in the most ancient part of the British psyche, primed to kick in on those once or twice in a lifetime moments when centuries of cynicism and reticence can be swept aside by the blissful knowledge that today all action is futile, that the absurdity of existence is not a writer's conceit but a spectacle manifest for all to see, and that they and every other bastard are going nowhere. On

175

these rare occasions the British are briefly, magically transformed. Intoxicated by a common burden of doom, the liberating joy of collective stasis, all barriers of class, status and colour collapse; they will talk and laugh and joke with strangers, they will share tea and cake with rivals, they will drink and dance in the streets. A ritual re-enactment of a pre-capitalist Eden, the good old days before the Fall, when you never had to lock the door and everyone knew your name and the kids still played in the street. Yes, in a hour or two you expect the music hall spivs to emerge and, with a nudge and a wink, fulfil your orders from crates stacked in lock-ups and lean-to's...

Bernard winked back at the milkman - it seemed like the right thing to do - then walked on. As he drew closer to the city centre thin streams of people flowed into the main road from the side streets. Cheerful strangers walked past exchanging biscuits for smiles and joked about the weather. But he knew it wouldn't last for long - it never did. Just as the snow would melt or the waters drain or the final all-clear sound they would wake from a dream, the chatter would cease and normal life would be resumed as rapidly as possible.

As he carried on down the road The War Time Spirit already seemed to be retreating. The mass stroll was beginning to take on the quality of a march, the light hearted banter diminished and the friendly smiles interspersed with familiar scowls and sighs. The sky had clouded over again and Bernard felt some half-hearted rain. He sheltered in a doorway and watched a couple of dozen people go past holding furled banners and placards. The placards were not yet raised and all Bernard could recognise was the familiar red logo of the *Daily Glimmer*. Many of them looked like family groups, equipped for a long day out at the seaside, grimly determined to complete their outing whatever the weather.

He turned off the main road into the back streets where shops hiding in the shadows of tower blocks offered forlorn displays of plastic buckets, tired vegetables and obscure detergents. The area had the abandoned quality of a decaying studio back lot and the few people he passed looked bewildered and out of place. Some were wearing strange clothing, as if they had started to dress for a fancy dress party and then forgotten the theme and location.

Outside a silent betting shop four men stood wearing a curious selection of rags and blankets. One of them was holding a large red and while golfing umbrella over their heads. The rain had begun to show a little more determination.

'Which way is Hyde Park mate?' said the man holding the umbrella. 'We're here to do the riot.'

'The riot?' said Bernard.

'Yeah, we're 1855. What year are you? 1968?'

'What year?'

'Never mind, just thought you might be Grosvenor Square '68. Must be the jacket. It was Grosvenor what started ours, of course. Didn't want us to shop on Sundays.'

'The park's about a mile and a half that way. You do a lot of rioting?'

'Not really - and we're about 20,000 short to do this job justice. Mostly it's battles, civil war, jousting, that sort of thing. But you have to be prepared to diversify these days, don't you?'

'And who hired you - it hasn't got anything to do with The Human Company, has it?'

'The what? Who hired us, Dave?'

'Dunno. Just came through the agency.'

'There you go. Just an agency booking. Probably some pop star's party. All right then, best be on our way, never looks good to be late for a riot. Ta-ra!'

Bernard carried on through the back streets. The closer he was to the heart of the city, the more ominous the feeling in the air. The skies had darkened and the occasional gust of cold wind buffeted him if he dared stand still for a moment, as if Weather had taken it upon itself to harass loiterers. A small group of policemen walked past. They appeared good humoured and relaxed, as if they were gathering for a social event rather than maintaining law and order.

Turning the corner Bernard found his path was blocked by a group of half a dozen elderly men in a motley collection of army uniforms. Two of them had rifles, the others what looked liked pikes and, in one case, simply a large wooden stick.

'Excuse me sir, may we see your identity card, please?'

'And who the hell are you?'

'We're the Home Guard. Sir!' said the eldest of the group, as he clicked his heels together. Judging by his uniform, he had attained the rank of Corporal.

'Yeah, yeah, of course. I should have guessed - you're another lot of re-enactors. I've just met your mates doing civil disturbances...'

'Oh no sir, we're not actors,' said the Corporal sharply, 'we really are the Home Guard!'

'I thought...'

'No, no, we never went away. We've just been waiting and training until the right occasion arises. Identity Card, please sir!'

Bernard flashed his press pass. This seemed to satisfy the Corporal who gave a nod of approval and a salute.

'And what is the right occasion?'

'Well I'm not really supposed to tell you this, but since you look like a decent sort of chap I'll let you into a little secret. We're here for the Exercise. Preparation for the Emergency, God forbid, should one ever arise.'

'So whose exercise do you think this is?'

'It's the Government's, of course, sir. Testing out the Emergency Procedures.'

'So why today of all days, surrounded by all the crap of this wretched Great Britain Day?'

'Funny you should say that. I asked myself the very same question. Why would they want to practise on a day when everyone is out on the streets celebrating?'

He glanced from side to side, then narrowed his eyes and wagged his finger at Bernard conspiratorially. 'And do you know what I've worked out? It's because they'll have an audience! They want to show just how well prepared we are to tackle the very worst! Which, God forbid of course, we hope will never happen.'

'And if the worst should happen, God forbid, what do you suggest?'

He leaned forward and whispered loudly. 'Failing the availability of the full protective suits, which, for logistical reasons, have been delayed, we recommend a tea towel. A tea towel soaked in water tied tightly around the mouth and nose. That'll keep most of the poisons out. For a while!' He winked and tapped his nose. Somewhere in the distance there was the sound of marching feet. 'I see your lot has done us proud.' He pointed over Bernard's shoulder.

Bernard turned around and saw that down the high street the marchers were holding their banners and placards aloft, all graced with the red logo of the *Daily Glimmer*, and the slogan, *We're Here To Keep Britain Great.*

'Good to see some old fashioned patriotism, isn't it!'

'Yeah. Terrific.'

In smaller letters on the placards he noticed the words:
Serenity With Security - Free DVD in this issue!

Twenty Eight

'If this is civilisation, then bring on the savages' - *Bernard Hawks*

The closer Bernard got to the city centre, the busier the streets. Ahead of him barriers set along the pavement separated the swarming mass into spectators and participants. At the side of the road hawkers were selling small paper flags on sticks and dubious plastic objects that glowed, flashed and spun. He pushed sideways through the throng and sheltered in a shop doorway. The Tranquility Campaign marchers went past in silent, orderly formation, holding up banners emblazoned with the pastel yin-yang symbol of the Tranquility Foundation - *Peace in Our Minds! Peace in Our Street! Peace In Our World!* Then he heard a familiar voice behind him.

'Hello Bernard.'

It sounded like Bob, but when he turned round he found himself staring at a stranger in a suit.

'I've been following you, Bernard. You didn't seem to notice me.'

Bernard blinked. It was Bob all right, but something was very wrong. His hair and beard were trimmed but what was more shocking was the suit; it was a wrinkled linen suit, the colour of faded denim, but it was a suit nevertheless.

'Bob...'

'I've got some new drugs.'

'I don't do that stuff any more...' He looked into Bob's mournful eyes, then to the street where the The Tranquility Campaign Marchers were followed by a military band and then a parade of men and women on horseback in full hunting pink. 'But, now you've mentioned it, if it carries on like this I might need something for later. Looks like it's going to be a long day.'

Bob's eyes opened very slightly wider. 'You're in luck, Bernard. I've got a new commission. Doing some special promotional work. Big money behind it. They say drugs are the future of the entertainment and travel industries - no pirating hassles, no pollution, carbon neutral, excellent customer loyalty... I'm supposed to ask you where you'd like to go for the next twelve hours...'

'I don't mind where I go. Just make sure the journey's pleasant. Nothing to make me too stupid. Or stupidly happy...' He was interrupted by the sound of hunting horns and enthusiastic cheering. 'Bob, you get around - do you have any idea of what the fuck's really going on today?'

Bob shrugged and fumbled in his pockets. 'If you ask me, it's the end of the world, Bernard. I suppose that'll be good for business, though. Here you go...' Bob pulled out a small vial containing a crystalline powder. 'This is supposed to make everything burn a little brighter, very clear...'

The cheering of the crowd was turning into rousing, patriotic singing.

'No, no, I don't want too much clarity, not with this going on. I've tried clarity and it doesn't help at all. Nor empathy - too much of that's no good either. Ideally, I'd like to sit watch the world go by. Safe, involved, but a little distant.'

'All right. I've got just the thing. Just out.' Bob took a small, polished white plastic box out of another pocket. 'Engineered in California. They say it turns the whole world into a movie.'

'What sort of movie?'

'Don't ask me, Bernard. My job's just to dish 'em out, I don't write the copy. I'll have a look...' Bob peered into the box. 'Ah! Colour or black and white?'

'You're taking the piss!'

Bob shrugged. 'See for yourself...'

He held out two small, rectangular pills with rounded edges. One was speckled and multicoloured, the other split diagonally into black and white. The sounds in the street were getting louder and more aggressive.

'Better have them both,' said Bernard.

'Very wise. List price is fifty quid, and, from what I've been told, worth every penny. But since this is a Special Promotion, you can have them for free. Just give them a nice write-up if you enjoy the show.'

'You want me to review your drugs?'

Bob nodded and dropped the two pills on to Bernard's palm. Bernard stared at them, turning them over in his hand, as he pondered Bob's career development.

'So, Bernard, I expect you've got one of those Back Stage Passes. You'll be able to sip champagne in the Green Room. That'll be nice for you.'

'Err - I guess. I suppose I should pick my pass up...'

'From Tranquility Tower - the TF headquarters. That place over there.' Bob gestured towards an imposing tower block wrapped in dark green glass with a pink neon sign on the top. The glass had a mirrored surface, like some starlet's sunglasses, glinting gold in the last rays of the sun.

'Yeah, of course.'

Bob's eyes began to twitch. 'So, Bernard, are we friends now?'

'I wouldn't go as far as to say that.'

'But no hard feelings, over the blackmailing stuff?'

'Yeah, well, forget it, you bastard. It's the least of my troubles now.'

'And the police station fire...' Bob's eyes were twitching rapidly now and there was a definite tremble in his voice.

'The what?'

'Sorry about that. I could see it might have given you a bit of grief.'

'Oh, for fuck's sake, Bob... what in the name of God made you...'

'It was Pitmarsh. He made me do it. Said he'd lock me up forever if I didn't. Said I had to fulfil your prophecy.'

Bob stared at Bernard wide-eyed, as if he had just startled himself with his own revelation, then he threw both hands into the air, spun round and ran off into the crowd. Bernard looked down to the pills in his hand, hesitated for a moment, then dropped them into his pocket.

The crowds on the pavement were getting thicker and it took some effort to push against tide of people towards the Tranquility Foundation headquarters. There was a drumming in his head that sounded like a distant samba band and his feelings of unease were aggravated by the groups of smug policemen standing on every street corner.

When he finally reached the marble steps of the Tranquility Tower he was greeted by a uniformed security man. Bernard nodded, flashed his press pass and walked towards the double glass doors that led to the Press Room.

'Sorry sir, I can't let you in,' said another security man, holding out an arm to block Bernard's way.

'What are you talking about?

'Strict instructions. Invited journalists only.'

Bernard peered over the outstretched arm through the glass doors behind. Striding through a room full of telephones, computers and journalists was Casper.

'Ask him - he's a friend, well, colleague of mine... he'll vouch for me... CASPER!' Bernard pushed past the guard to bang on the door. Casper turned round and strolled over, giving a discreet nod to the guard who immediately moved aside.

'I'll give you five minutes, Bernard,' said Casper as he pulled Bernard forward into the room.

'That guy was outrageous - he wouldn't let me in to get my Back Stage Pass.'

'And what makes you think you're entitled to one of those?'

'I'm supposed to be reviewing this show for a start.'

'You clearly don't read the papers.'

'Of course I don't. I write for them.'

'Not any more, you don't.'

Casper picked up a newspaper from the table and passed it to Bernard. It was a copy of *The Indicator*. Under the headline:

DAILY GLIMMER REPORTER UNMASKED AS NEO-LUDDITE ACTIVIST!

was a picture of Bernard, his hair blowing in the wind, tossing his computer into the skip.

'And this one's even better...' Casper passed him another paper.

THE ENEMY IN OUR MIDST!
Discredited journalist scavenges refuse skip to raise cash to buy drugs.
Security cameras catch disguised Daily Glimmer reporter bribing security employee to steal computer...

'You know that's all bullshit,' said Bernard, throwing the papers back onto the table, 'and, anyway, I've still got a contract...'

'Which, of course, you broke by committing acts of gross impropriety likely to bring the paper into disrepute. You had your chance, Bernard. You could have been part of the New Great Britain. Listen to them cheering outside, don't you wish you were sharing all those positive feelings, helping to put confidence back in the nation?'

'Sounds like a cross between a fascist rally and a carol service to me and I don't like it one bit.'

'Parades, processions, pageants - everyone is joining in, celebrating our heritage with pride, looking with confidence towards the future...'

'Fuck it, Casper, something very bad is going to happen today and somehow I'm right in the thick of it.'

'You're suffering from delusions of self-importance. Nothing that happens today has got anything to do with you. No one gives a toss what you write any more, haven't you got that?'

'Haven't you got it that this whole ludicrous event is just crying out to be sabotaged?'

'We've all had enough of your paranoid, negative thinking. I'm sure the police and security forces have everything under control.'

'What about the traffic? That was fucking weird! Doesn't that suggest that someone's out to sabotage this whole event?'

'I heard there were some congestion problems this morning, but I'm sure that's not going to spoil a good day out for everyone. Now look, Bernard, just to show there's no ill feeling between us I can let you have a regular pass. See the show from the ground, even take part in it...' He smirked and pinned a small tin badge printed with the word 'Press' and the TF logo to the lapel of Bernard's jacket. 'Make sure you leave that on or you'll miss out on the fun. Now I think you'd better go. There's someone outside waiting for you.'

'Don't worry, I'm off. And who exactly is waiting for me?'

Casper smiled but said no more. Bernard turned round and walked out of the press room into the foyer where, standing in front of him with his arms crossed, was Inspector Pitmarsh and, beside him, two burly uniformed policemen wearing bullet-proof vests.

At the sight of the policemen Bernard's body went into panic mode; his hand plunged into his pocket, pulled out Bob's two pills and threw them into his mouth. He gulped them down.

'Hello, Bernard,' said Pitmarsh. 'Good of Bob to send you to me.'

'Sodding Bob, when will I learn...'

'But you do look tired. You need a holiday.'

'Yeah, well, thanks for your concern but today I'm just going to take it easy and enjoy the show.'

'No, Bernard, I know what's best for you and it's time for a little journey.'

The two uniformed policemen frog-marched Bernard into a waiting lift and Pitmarsh pressed the button for the top floor. The lift was mirrored on all four walls, creating a disturbing myriad of amber-toned policemen and Bernards as they rocketed upwards. Within seconds the lift reached the top and the doors opened.

'So, was that the journey?' asked Bernard.

'Oh no,' said Pitmarsh, 'it's barely begun.'

They stepped out on to the roof. Daylight was beginning to fade and, below them, the gaudy coloured lights of fairgrounds were flickering into life across the city.

'Magnificent view, Bernard. So, shall we go on a cruise? Or, even better, how about a gondola ride? Very romantic!'

The policemen picked up Bernard, dragged him forward to the edge of the roof and pushed his head down towards the street below. A few feet beneath, suspended from an overhanging rail, was a window cleaner's gondola. The policemen gave Bernard a shove and he fell down onto it. The platform shuddered and banged against the side of the building. Pitmarsh clambered down and sat beside him.

'Bernard, please put this on...' Pitmarsh passed him a canvas harness connected to a long chain.

'What the fuck...'

'Health and Safety, you understand.'

'That's very thoughtful.'

'Insurance, Bernard. Liabilities and all of that. Mustn't be sued for negligence.'

Bernard put on the harness and Pitmarsh clamped the end of a chain to the handrail of the gondola.

'Sitting comfortably? Then we'll begin.'

With a sudden, violent movement, Pitmarsh pushed Bernard under the safety rail then kicked at his buttocks and ankles until he was completely over the side. Bernard screamed as he tumbled through the air until, about five foot below the gondola, the safety chain jerked taut and he was left suspended face down, his head rather lower than his feet.

'Oh Jesus, you're not going to do that puppet number on me, are you?'

'The puppet number?' shouted Pitmarsh, as his colleagues hauled him back onto the roof.

'You know, wanting me to cut my strings and all that shit?'

'No, Bernard, I'm just trying to scare the living daylights out of you, that's all. To focus your mind.'

There was a creaking of pulleys and the gondola began to move jerkily around the building, causing the suspended Bernard to sway erratically from side to side. Pitmarsh strolled casually on the roof above and shouted down to Bernard.

'You know, Bernard, there was a time when I was proud of my job. More than that, it was a great privilege. I was respected. But now... who are the bad guys? Who are the good guys? You and I, Bernard, we're part of the past.'

'What the fuck do you want?' screamed Bernard.

Pitmarsh knelt down on the roof. His voice became softer. 'This is our last chance. I want the villains. You're going to tell me what the Primitive Front are planning.'

'Fuck knows what they are going to do... fuck knows what they want... fuck knows who the hell they are, really...' Bernard stared down into the streets below. If he told them all he knew would that be betraying Animal, or would it be betraying Animal if he didn't?

'Where have they planted their bombs?'

The edge of Bernard's vision was tinged with a pink glow from the Tranquility Foundation's neon yin-yang symbol just above his head. It was almost dusk and below him streams of people with lanterns and torches were converging on Trafalgar Square then flowing down towards the river. Tears welled up in his eyes as he felt himself taken back to the top of the hill at night when Dillwyn showed him the city, the city that made nothing but ideas. There it was, stretched out before him as one glittering machine... except now it didn't seem like a smooth working mechanism at all, it was a swirling mass, a slow turning maelstrom sucking everything and everyone into its centre.

'I don't even know... maybe everywhere...' *Pond said the ground would open up under their feet...* 'Tunnels... like tube stations, subways, sewers...'

'Very good, Bernard. Now concentrate: how many in the group?' Pitmarsh tugged the ropes of the gondola and Bernard began to swing out in a circle.

'How many? I've only met three...' *should I tell him it's more like a franchise, and every who wants to join can? No, that sounds too weak...* 'you know, they all work in separate cells, no one knows who the others are...'

'Standard practice, my friend. So who are the three you know?'

'There's Animal. You know her. Then this guy Gabriel who drives the van...'

'Oh God, give me strength... and the third?'

Pitmarsh pulled the ropes again and Bernard swung in and hit his head hard against the windows of the building. He had to tell him something. *Pond! Give him Pond. He didn't like Pond anyway. Pond was bad for Animal.* 'There's a creepy older guy called Pond. Looks like a hippie, but seems to be some sort of city trader gone native...'

There was a pause before Pitmarsh spoke again. 'Andrew Pond?'

'Don't ask me. He kept going on about chaos theory. And rats.'

'Well of course, I should have guessed. They're back together again.'

'Who the fuck's Andrew Pond?'

'Thank you, Bernard,' shouted Pitmarsh, 'that will be all for now.'

'You're not going to leave me here, are you?'

'Of course we are.'

'I know about the police station fire. I know it was you! You did it just so you could bust me!'

'You do make me laugh sometimes. As if I'd do a thing like that.'

'But...'

'Try some good old fashioned evidence. The testimony of a known drug dealer and self-confessed extremist against an officer of the law? I don't think so, Bernard.'

Pitmarsh gave the ropes a last hefty tug and Bernard swung violently towards the windows of the building. The room behind it was empty and dark but for the glow from dozens of unattended computer screens. On the first swing, Bernard's head smashed into the window full on and he bounced off. The second time he was prepared enough to stretch out his palms and cushion the blow. As he swung towards it he saw the room was not, in fact, empty; there was a man working among the computers, an overweight young man wearing a black T-shirt decorated with skulls and demons. When Bernard crashed into the window for the third time the man looked up and waved as though he knew him. Bernard recognised him too: he was the IT guy from the offices of *The Indicator* who had claimed to be his editor, now gesturing enthusiastically behind the double glazing. He grinned at Bernard, pointed upwards and left the room.

The radius of Bernard's pendulum swings began to diminish. After a few minutes, the gondola shook and began to descend. Below him was a terrace, formed from the flat roof of the wider, second storey of the building. The terrace seemed to be moving towards him at alarming speed. He closed his eyes until the movement stopped. When he opened them he saw he was swinging about six feet above a cement floor. A couple of minutes later the IT guy appeared.

'All right there?'

'Never been better,' muttered Bernard.

'What you lot get up to!'

'So what the hell are *you* doing here?' asked Bernard.

'Could ask the same of you. What was it, some sort of stag night gag?'

'Yeah, something like that... I guess you're not working for *The Indicator* any more either?'

'Nah, mate, when the paper got bought out by the TF they moved me here. In charge of their dealing room.'

'Dealing room?'

'Well, all these companies now, they like to do a bit of trading with their surplus funds. That's where the real money is. I'm just running the back end of it. Futures, securities, gilts, stuff like that. Yeah, a bit dull I guess, but pays better than journalism.'

'Don't supposed you've heard of a guy called Pond? Andrew Pond?'

'Too right I have. That wanker's always causing problems here. Still hasn't got over his missis chucking him out. Thinks she's got all his money, of course.'

'Am I supposed to know who that is?'

'Jesus, I thought you guys did research. You know, Perdita thingie? Famous for her candles? Runs the whole shebang? Yeah, all the Tranquility bollocks? Married rich city wanker Pond - made a fortune using chaos theory on the markets, then flips out completely and becomes a sort of mad hippy. Which apparently is what he was in the first place. Everyone knows that, don't they?'

'They probably do. Except me.'

'Been in all the papers. But I bet you don't read them, do you?'

'Don't write for them either, now.'

'Yeah, heard you got the shove from the *Glimmer*. Shame. That new guy, Casper, doesn't like you much, does he?'

'You could say that. Look, is there any chance of you unstrapping me from this thing? This is getting a bit boring swinging around on this chain.'

'My pleasure, mate.'

He undid Bernard's harness and Bernard fell on top of him. They both tumbled to the floor. The IT guy giggled.

'Thanks,' said Bernard, as he picked himself up and tried to flex his aching muscles.

Above them rockets were plastering the skies with glittering gold canopies as barrages of explosions ricocheted between the buildings. The air was thick with smoke coloured red and green by the lights and fireworks.

'Have you got any idea what's going on today?' said Bernard. 'I mean, what are they actually celebrating?'

'Beats me... 'doing it cause they've been told to, I suppose. Saves them having to think up there own reasons for a party.'

'Never did like parties...'

'Funny you should mention that Pond geezer. Saw him lurking round here yesterday. Shame he didn't bring his daughter with him.'

'His daughter?'

'Yeah, tasty little thing. A bit wild, lots of hair, skinny, weird coloured eyes...'

'Yes,' said Bernard, 'her. Of course.' *Of course.* He watched as shimmering gold spirals fell from the sky. 'I don't suppose you know where... the people who are doing the performance... you don't know where I might find them?'

'Performance? Not really my area, mate. But there's some tents set up in the square there, couple of blocks away. Dressing rooms or something. They might have something to do with it.'

Twenty Nine

'Cut the strings! Throw away your puppet!'

© The Tranquility Foundation

When Bernard left the TF headquarters he sat down, still shaking, on the cold marble steps outside and tried to work out what to do next. Go back home? Find Animal and warn her that Pitmarsh was on her trail? Or at least, Pond's trail. And Pond was her *father...*

His back was aching again and he wondered when Bob's pills were going to kick in. So far, they seemed to be having no effect whatsoever. *Sod Bob. Sod his corporate packaged useless drugs. Sodding end of the sodding world.* He watched the end of a long procession go past, or what he could see of it over the heads of the crowd. He caught glimpses of fish-shaped lanterns on poles, the heads of huge illuminated sea serpents, sinister deep sea monsters and a Neptune and a Britannia who strode above the crowd on stilts. They were followed by a series of bands - brass bands, steel bands, pipe bands - all playing, as far as he could make out, entirely different tunes. The atmosphere was getting a little edgy; there were occasional impatient jeers and some scuffles were breaking out at the fringes. When a beer can hit him on the head he knew it was time to move on.

He got up and, pushing his way along the edge of the crowd, managed to slip into an alleyway. Ahead of him he could see what could be the tents the IT guy had referred to, but before he reached them, a weary and vaguely familiar voice stopped him in his tracks.

'Hello again, mate.'

He turned to see a group of dishevelled men lying on the ground, some groaning with pain.

'Remember us? The Sunday Bill rioters?' said a man winding a dirty bandage around a wounded knee.

'Right. Of course. So how did the riot go?' asked Bernard.

'We never made it to Hyde Park, to be honest. All over before we got there. It was going fine until the blokes playing the police started to get a bit carried away. Rode their bloody horses straight into our lot! So we stopped the show...'

'Sorry to hear that.'

'...but then some others picked it up again. That's the thing with these young ones, they got no sense of self-control, don't pace themselves.'

'Maybe they were real police?'

'You could have a point there. You'd be surprised how many off-duty coppers we've got in our little group.'

'Not quite what I meant, but never mind.'

'Don't wander off too far, though. Particularly if you're Catholic. Could be dangerous. The guys doing the Gordon Riots will be opening up the prisons soon.'

'Of course,' said Bernard, none the wiser, as he headed towards the square.

It looked like nothing so much as the preparations for an ambitious village fete. There were khaki marquees festooned with bunting and union jacks, brass band music playing over a Tannoy system and long trestle tables stacked with cups and saucers. All it was lacking was people - there was no one in sight apart from a large, jovial woman, standing by the tables, clutching a huge enamel teapot.

'Hello, dear,' said the woman. 'Make-up...' the hand not holding the teapot flapped to the left towards a large tent behind her, 'or shower?' To the right were several long lines of cubicles made up of plastic sheeting strung to metal poles.

'Don't think I need either just at the moment.'

'Oh I think you do, dearie. Do you have a number? Everyone has a number. You're either a zombie or a survivor.'

'No, I'm just sort of... Press.' He pointed to the small tin badge Casper had fixed to him.

'Oh well, you're not supposed to be here yet. It's all meant to be a bit of surprise, so I'm told.'

'Who's in charge? I've really got to find someone who actually has some idea what's going on.'

'All right, don't get shirty. You could try in that pub,' she pointed across the road. 'There's some people in there who seem to think they know what's happening.'

As Bernard walked towards the pub he realised he *was* now beginning to feel a little strange - perhaps Bob's pills were finally working. His limbs felt longer and distinctly rubbery, like a character in an early cartoon film.

The pub declared itself to be a 'Sports Bar'. The windows were plastered with flyers offering bargain pints and sporting attractions and neon signs celebrating the size of its television screens. Inside it was bright and noisy, packed with football fans clustered around vast flat screens hanging from the ceiling. He noticed the pile of headgear and bats in the corner and realised they were players rather than fans, some sort of American baseball team.

'Hi, Bernard. Enjoying the show?'

He turned round to see a mountain of a man with wild ginger hair leaning against the bar.

'Mikey... I need your help. Animal and her Primitive Front mob - they're working with you, right? I thought I might find them backstage - in the Green Room or something?'

'Backstage? Someone's been pulling your pisser, mate. Since there's no stage, they're can't be any backstage, can there? But your mates turned up trumps. That trick with the traffic this morning was impressive.'

'So that *was* them...'

The TV screens were now showing live news reports of Great Britain Day. About half dozen men and women on horseback dressed in hunting outfits were confronting groups of Tranquility Campaign marchers who were shaking their giant puppets angrily.

'That geezer Pond,' continued Mikey, 'weird fucker... specialises in the flow of stuff, move a few bollards here, dig up a bit of road there...'

'I think he might be in trouble.'

'Yeah? Don't surprise me. They got maps of all the tunnels, which is just what was needed. They liked that idea of a military exercise, you know, see what would it would be like if some terrorist did plant a bomb, and I said go ahead...'

The cheers and shouts of the demonstrators outside the pub echoed the sounds coming from the screens.

'Troy must be loving this,' continued Mikey.

'So where is Troy?'

'Don't know, mate. Haven't seen head nor tail of the bastard all day. Probably hiding somewhere, watching it all happen. This is what he always wanted, you know, get rid of the line between theatre and the world...'

'Isn't he supposed to be running the show?'

'Nah, it's always me what does the real work. I got the rioters, then ordered up some actors, all amateurs - that's what he asked for - and let them get on with it. Not like the old days, now you just go on-line and find a few agencies. Yeah, and your mates got me a gang of kids on some sort of youth opportunity scheme, and they're up for anything. That's the beauty of the Strategy, I can do what the fuck I like, unlike everybody else...'

The sounds in the street outside were getting louder. Bernard had to shout to continue the conversation. 'You know he said that to Kepler too?'

'He what, mate?' shouted Mikey.

'The Strategy - that he was the only one who could improvise and everyone else were told what they were doing. I reckon he tells everyone that...'

Bernard wasn't sure whether Mikey had registered what he said as at that moment a large object outside smashed against the windows of the bar. On the television screens it looked like a full riot was underway.

'What the hell's going on out there?' shouted Bernard.

'I wouldn't worry your head about it,' said Mikey, his eyes gleaming, 'just a bit of theatre.'

'So, Animal - any idea where she is?'

'Got the hots for her, have you?'

'No, well, no... I need to warn her...'

'Can't help you there, mate. I reckon you'll have to wait for her to find you. Anyway I gotta go. Sort out some more pyros and find out what the hell's happened to Troy.' Mikey downed the rest of his pint in one gulp and made his way towards the door.

It was just after Mikey left the bar that the giant bird appeared. Silhouetted in the doorway, it was the most frightening creature Bernard had ever seen. The size of a man, it had a long, curved white beak emerging seamlessly from a white, boney face and, below it, a vast, brown featherless body. It lumbered over to him and leant down until its beak almost touched his nose.

'Oh fuck,' said Bernard.

'Don't worry, it's just me, Gabby, Animal's mate. Remember?'

'What the...'

'Just a costume. I'm the plague doctor.' He removed the mask and grinned.

'You bastard.'

'Sorry, Bernie, didn't mean to upset you.'

On the television screens the giant puppets had been set alight.

'It's not the mask,' said Bernard, raising his voice above the noise of the disturbances outside, 'it's you. Those photos you took - they ended up losing me my job...'

'Yeah, well, I thought *you* were the problem. Now I know it's Pond.'

Something smashed through a window and landed on the floor close to him. It was the flaming hand of a giant puppet, long scaly fingers emerging from a burning sleeve.

'Pond - where is he? I've got to find him. And Animal.'

'You won't find them together. Not any more. Think they've fallen out.'

A series of explosions shattered the remaining windows of the pub.

'What the fuck...'

Gabby laughed. 'Don't panic, Bernard.'

'Don't panic? How can I not panic? That sounded like a fucking bomb!'

'Nah. Just some firecrackers. All part of the show.'

'How do you know?'

'We put 'em there. Anyway, there were never any bombs. Sadly.'

'What, none?'

'The bombs were your idea, remember?'

'My idea…'

The baseball players were beginning to leave the pub. One by one they picked up their armour, headgear and bats from the pile in the corner and put them on. The outfits looked surprisingly sombre for a sporting event - they were all dark navy blue. One of the men turned to face Bernard and a chill shot through him. He was staring at a policeman fitted with full riot gear, a shield in one hand and a baton in the other. The policeman grinned and waved his baton at him in a friendly manner, then followed his colleagues out through the door.

'Yeah,' shouted Gabby, 'you're the one who wrote about the bombs. You started the story. And it worked, didn't it? The riot squads are out to protect the nation.'

'The police - I gave them Pond's name… I think they're going after him.'

Gabby didn't seem at all put out by this news. 'I never liked the bastard anyway. He's just been using me and Animal.'

'Animal… do you know where is she?'

'I can take you to her, if you like. We're going to the party.'

'Not another fucking party.'

'In the park. Everyone's going there.'

'Are we going to make it through the crowds? Doesn't look very safe outside.'

'Come with me. I've got to take the stiffs to the plague pit with the cart. Weird how everyone gets out of my way when I'm wearing this mask.'

Gabby pulled the long-beaked mask back into position and led Bernard to the back door of the pub and out into a small yard. Sitting in the corner was a hand cart, a basic wooden affair which looked like it had seen long service as a fruit and veg stall. A tarpaulin covered its lumpy load.

'You can walk beside me and ring the bell.' He handed Bernard a mask with a slightly smaller beak and a well-worn hand bell. Bernard put on the mask and followed close behind as Gabby pushed the cart out into the street.

The parade was still in progress but the streets seemed calmer now as lines of police were keeping the rival factions apart. A military marching band in bright red Victorian uniforms went past followed by a group brandishing 'Ban The Bomb' placards, whose beards and woolly jumpers seemed just a little too self-consciously 1950's. It occurred to Bernard it was impossible to tell who were actual demonstrators and who were part of the pageant. He wasn't too sure about the authenticity of the police, either.

Bernard stopped ringing his bell and turned to Gabby. 'All this stuff about the government staging some fake attack and then sending the troops in to save the day...'

'You mean the story Animal told you to write?'

'Yeah. Is there any truth in it or is it all some sort of fucked up theatre show?'

'It'll be true sooner or later, Bernie, won't it? And keep ringing that bell - you're slowing down.'

'And what did you mean earlier about Pond not me being the problem?'

'Like, Animal stopped wanting to blow things up. I thought that was your fault. Then I realised it was Pond, fucking her mind with all this virtual JJ stuff. All those theories.'

'And Pond's her father, right?'

'Stepfather. From that hippie commune she came from. He turned up again a couple of months ago and fucked everything up. If I find the bastard, I'll mark him out, all right?'

When they reached the park they pushed their way through the crowds to a gate labelled 'Artists Entrance'. Gabby, Bernard and the cart were waved through and they made their way towards a large scaffolding structure. The park had become one giant party; the trees were festooned with coloured lights and towering loudspeakers were booming out music.

'Sorry, Bernie. Got to leave you here now. Got work to do.'

'Animal?' said Bernard, shouting above the noise.

'Don't fret, she'll turn up.'

Bernard took off his mask and realised the mass of scaffolding he was standing next to was a staircase at the back of the stage on which a rock band was playing. He climbed to the top of the stairs and found he was looking out over a large backstage enclosure separated from the revellers by a steel barrier. Giant video screens in each corner of the park were displaying the events of the day across the city.

It was when the flickering started he knew the drugs were definitely working. He noticed it first in the lights as they shone through the smoke-filled air. Then he caught the reflection of the moon in a puddle and saw it was pulsating quite fast. Somewhere in the back of his head a whirring sound began, like an old home movie projector dragging the world, frame by frame, past his eyes.

Something strange was happening on the screens. It looked like some sort of science fiction film set in a riot-torn future where men in giant green space suits were herding earthlings into small groups. A mass ritual baptism was taking place in portable showers, the converted emerging wet and confused in bright orange capes, perhaps the vestments of a bizarre alien religion.

As Bernard walked back down to the ground his path was blocked by a figure slumped on the bottom step. It was only when he got closer he realised it was an abandoned ventriloquist dummy. Of all puppets, the ones that could speak and roll their dead eyes as if possessed were the worst, but this was a particularly horrific example: huge and ugly, a ghostly white face covered with red blotches and grey, string-like hair. Then the devil-doll rose up and spoke.

'Hello Bernard.'

The dummy was speaking but there was no ventriloquist in sight. Perhaps now they had some digital gadget to make the bastards work by remote.

'Don't look so terrified. It's only me, Dillwyn. Just got a bit of make-up for the final scene. I always liked amateur dramatics - lovely to be offered a part, it was. I'm supposed to look a bit poorly, like. One of the plague victims, see.'

Bernard's relief was tempered by the fact that, make-up or no make-up, Dillwyn didn't really look quite right. His head seemed a little large and his eyes were swivelling in a very disturbing way.

'Jesus, Dillwyn, this is all getting very confusing.'

'Well they want you to be confused, don't they?'

'I don't know anything any more. There's police and soldiers everywhere and it's making me nervous. And all this stuff on the screens - it's like they've got the whole city covered...'

'The security cameras - they've connected them all together into the screens. Had to happen, really - it's the telly of the future, isn't it?' Dillwyn reached out and grasped Bernard's wrist. 'Were you watching the decontamination event?'

'So that's what it was...'

'Emergency exercise - rehearsal for what we'd have to do if there was a bio-chemical attack, see. Classic post-credibility strategy. Perfect cover for state forces to plant their own real bombs, isn't it?'

'But that wasn't real, was it? I thought the Primitive Front were faking a bomb attack to bring the police out on to the streets, or maybe it was The Human Company... '

'Don't really matter any more 'cause the exercises will become real enough soon, won't they? Typical JJ, Bernard, just like I was saying... Oh, I remember what I was going to tell now you about that girl Animal - she's the daughter of...'

'Andrew Pond. City trader gone native.'

'You knew that, did you? And that Pond and his wife set up the Tranquility Foundation?'

'Yeah, that too.'

'And that Pond and his wife are back together again?'

'No, you got that wrong. They hate each other.'

'But I've seen them. I've seen them together.'

'Where?'

Dillwyn got up, lunged towards Bernard and whispered loudly in his ear. 'They're behind the hedges, Bernard.'

'They're what?'

Dillwyn winked. 'Sorry, can't tell you any more now. Not just yet.' Then he walked off into the distance. Except he didn't walk, he glided away, as if there were wheels on the bottom of his shoes.

If anything was clear to Bernard it was that Dillwyn had finally flipped, but he still went over to the hedge that ran along the side of the park to see if there actually was anyone behind it. There was no sign of Pond or his wife or anyone else who might be connected with the Tranquility Foundation, just thick electrical cables that snaked into the distance and a few frantic technicians communicating to each other via headsets and hand gestures.

Bernard's brain was now feeling very strange indeed. The video screens seemed to have grown larger and were now completely dominating his field of vision. He felt an urgent need to lie down. He lowered himself carefully to the ground and stretched out behind one of the screens still displaying the chaotic events across the city.

The images above him became blurred and a figure strolled into the foreground of the picture. At first it was a silhouette, then a light faded up and his features were revealed. He had short white hair, an immaculate suit and gold initial cufflinks. Bernard could not be sure whether the man was a projected image or actually standing right in front of him.

'Mr. Hawks!'

'Do I know you?'

'We have met.'

'You're JJ... all this stuff that's going on now - you planned it, didn't you?'

'As I mentioned before, I advised the government on some strategies. But I can't take credit for everything that's happening today. I must say you seem a little confused, Mr. Hawks.'

'People keep telling me you don't exist.'

'And yet here I am, larger than life!'

'You're supposed to be a figment of Rupert Kepler's imagination. He said he invented you, then you became real.'

'Ah, he conjured me up, did he? How amusing. I created a career for the dear man. You could even say I created Kepler! If you like, he is my puppet. I gave him a fantasy and he has profited from it ever since.'

'And the Theory of Post-Credibility?'

'Have you not learnt by now, Mr. Hawks, it is not so much a theory? Rather, shall we say, a series of conundrums and parables.' JJ's voice sounded remote, like he was speaking to an empty auditorium and Bernard was somewhere behind him backstage. 'Kepler mythologised me and I encouraged it. He has helped turn me back into a fictional character. Since I don't exist I can be infinitely more powerful. A little like God.'

'But I don't understand...'

'At least you must accept it's an intriguing idea - a non-existent character offering imaginary solutions for a government that no one believes in?'

'Is *anything* I've heard about you true?'

'Many, many initiatives have been attributed to me, much more than one man could possibly achieve. But the reputation can be advantageous - sometimes all I need to provide is a fantasy of control, a placebo of power.' JJ's cold grey eyes shimmered as if lit from behind.

'You mean... it's all in the mind of your clients?'

'The thing you must remember about placebos is that they're cheap and they work. They work very well indeed.'

'I don't know if you should be telling me all this. I used to be a very influential journalist. This could make a great story...' As Bernard spoke these words they no longer seemed to belong to him, his voice had left his body and joined JJ on a distant stage.

'Write a story about me if you like, Mr. Hawks, but, as I said before, no one will believe you. I suggest you relax now until the day is over.'

The screen got brighter until it became one vast blinding white light and another silhouette appeared, the silhouette of a woman, hands on hips. A volley of fireworks filled the sky above with shimmering silver rain.

'Animal,' shouted Bernard, 'is that you? I thought... I thought this was all leading somewhere... I thought today something was going to make sense...'

She turned towards him. 'We're not living in a movie, Bernard.'

'Not living in a movie...' She seemed to be moving towards him, but her voice was coming from elsewhere, from all around.

'Walking off into the sunsets, that old shit.' Animal's face grew bigger until it seemed to fill the screen. Or maybe she was just leaning over him.

'You see I took these pills... and they're supposed to turn the world into...'

'I told you Bernard, drugs don't help any more, they don't cut through the crap like they used to, they just add to it...'

'... into a movie. You see, I thought Pond was...'

'He's my stepfather.'

'Yeah, I know now. But...' Something very weird was happening. When he spoke he saw his own face staring back at him. And when Animal spoke he saw her face.

'I hadn't seen him for years 'til he joined up with us a few months ago. He used all these theories to make a killing on the stock markets... till the machines took over... that's why he hates machines...'

'You told me theories were another kind of drug, once...' Again, his own face replaced Animal's when he spoke. *Fuck, this drug... I'm cutting between close-ups...* He looked back to the screens which were switching between cameras right across the city. The genre had shifted from science fiction to horror as hundreds of people emerged from every tube station, subway and underpass. Pale figures with tattered clothing and faces scarred with red sores walking haphazardly forward, arms outstretched.

'Zombies... fucking zombies...'

'Nah, that's the Human Company's plague victims, coming out of the pits. Not very good, are they? Troy's fault - that's what you get when you employ amateurs.'

'Troy? Where is Troy? Isn't he supposed to be in charge?'

'You were talking to him just now.'

'No, that wasn't....'

'Troy threw Kepler out of the Company, Kepler created JJ, Troy became JJ... '

'Are you serious? Like one was a thin guy and one was a fat guy...'

'They're actors, Bernard, they pretend they're someone else, that's what they do.'

'But Troy was the director, wasn't he?'

'There's a lot of people who think they're in control, who think they're directors when really they're just actors. Who knows? Maybe JJ created Troy. Maybe Troy created JJ. Maybe they're all the same. We don't need any of them now. We're on our own.'

Bernard continued to stare at the events on the screens. Some of the spectators were laughing and throwing bottles at the plague victims, others seemed to be running away in panic. The police were beating truncheons against raised riot shields and advancing into the crowd. Other teams of police were rounding up those who were trying to flee, forcing them together into small groups. In the distance there were sounds of gunfire. A stream of bewildered looking men and women wrapped in blankets wandered across the screen.

'Who are all those sick-looking people? More actors?'

'Could be real - they're throwing out the non-critical patients out of the hospitals to make room for the casualties. They'll be blocking the mobile phones next. That's when the real panic starts.'

197

'Jesus! People are getting hurt... this is... this is chaos... this is hell...'

'You started the story Bernard. What do you expect? A nice resolution? A happy ending?'

He looked out across the park. Everyone now seemed to be fighting. Bernard's head was churning with fragments of memories: the IT guy in the TF dealing room trading in gilts, securities and futures, Dillwyn saying they were hiding behind the hedges, Pond and his desire to create chaos. He saw himself back dangling from the top of Tranquility Tower, looking down over the city that had become a monstrous creature sucking everything deep into its guts.

'Fuck - I'm getting flashbacks already, while I'm still taking the drug... like a fucking trailer... something's gone very wrong, hasn't it? Maybe I shouldn't have taken them both...'

He looked up to the screens again and saw Tranquility Tower, its pastel yin-yang symbol glowing bright. The cameras zoomed in and there below, swinging on a window cleaner's gondola, was a creature with a long white beak, a paintbrush in his hand, painting a large red cross on the side of the building.

Bernard knew this was a sign, the building was rotten with death... and Gabby had promised he would mark out where Pond was.

And then it all came together in his head. *Guilt not gilts, security not securities, the future not futures...*

Abruptly, with a gesture that amazed even himself, he grabbed Animal by the arm. 'You've got to come with me...'

She laughed, but followed him effortlessly as he ran back up the steps at the back of the stage, her arm feeling weightless in his grip.

Bernard was surprised to find there was no band, just a DJ in the corner and an unattended microphone on a stand downstage. He went up to the mike, grasped it in both hands and yelled, his words booming thunderously in his head. He looked down - the barrier between the stage and the audience had been broken down and there was now a writhing mass of people below him right up to the edge of the stage, fighting.

'Listen everyone, listen... you gotta stop fighting... don't you realise, the bastards have set all this up, everything's going to fucking pieces...' Bernard listened to the echoes of his own voice. It sounded at once alien and horribly close, as if the words were tunnelling up from somewhere deep inside. 'The Tranquility Foundation, all that peace and love stuff, they were hedging their bets, making money when people felt good, making more when people felt bad... gambling on the Future... why can't you fuckers hear me? Don't you know how to get angry any more? And a guy called Pond, he's there now, in Tranquility Tower, burning up all your money...'

'They can't hear you because the mike's not turned on, Bernard,' said Animal, now standing close beside him. 'In fact, it's not even plugged in.'

Bernard looked down at the cable running out of the microphone and saw it ended it a small spiral heap on the stage. 'But it sounds loud to me... I just want to stop everyone fighting...'

'They're not fighting, Bernard,' Animal stretched out her hand to Bernard as she seemed to sink down into the crowd below, 'they're dancing.'

He took her hand and followed her down. He stood there still for a moment, surrounded by the pervasive tang of sweat, buffeted by joyful heaving bodies. The music was so loud that it was just a pressure pulsing in his brain. Too loud to hear himself think, but the beat kept banging in his head, as if it had climbed right inside him, pushing and cajoling every organ to join in. Rhythms within rhythms colliding against each other and spinning off into more, but beneath it all a relentless primal throb, always the same and yet always building, higher and higher, to the point of climax, then further still. Animal was now dancing with total abandon, the locks of her hair swinging wildly to the beat. He caught her eyes; she smiled and her lips mouthed something he couldn't hear. The bass pumped harder and then strobe lights beamed down, freezing time, making snapshots of Animal and all the dancers around them.

He looked up and saw the pale hands of the DJ, delicate fingers flying between faders, one ear to a headphone, spinning the discs back and forth, a seamless mix where no tune started or ended, great tides of noise breaking then retreating. As he watched an idea trembled in Bernard's mind, an echo of something Animal once said; this man was not making the sound, he was just a channel for the beat, the waves that flowed straight through him. His fingers flipped the faders back and forth and in an instant Bernard knew what Animal meant. The guy in control was not in control; the beat was moving him, the faders rose and fell and his fingers followed. Driven by the beat, slaved to the machines. And then Bernard found himself dancing.

That was the night Bernard escaped from time. Time had been shattered into fragments and flung into the shadows. There were no great times in the past for looking back, no great times in the future for looking forward, no times and no time, no past and no future, there was only now. Out of his head and into the world, Bernard danced till dawn, it could have been an hour or two or it could have been forever. He had found his beat. And all those thoughts, the maelstrom of ideas that swirled through Bernard's head were not Bernard, they were not part of him any more than the shirt on his back was part of his flesh. The thoughts were thinking Bernard, not Bernard thinking the thoughts and anyway, they weren't part of the real Bernard, they belonged to

the puppet Bernard, the puppet he had created, the puppet that had
been ripped away and thrown on to the fires that were burning bright
across the city.

Thirty

'My type? I've been out with lot of very sane and attractive women'
- Bernard Hawks

'How are you feeling?'

Bernard sat up in bed. He was at home and the morning sun was streaming through the window. It would have been a pleasant morning if not for the long, pale face looming over him and the disconcerting voice that emerged from it. He had been woken up by Bob the sodding Dealer.

Bernard glanced around the room and then looked back to Bob. It occurred to him he was feeling much better than he deserved to.

'Well,' said Bernard, reluctantly, 'all things considered, not bad at all.'

'Modern technology. They say they've engineered the pain and guilt factor out of the pills. No after effects. This is supposed to be the future.'

Was it his imagination, or was Bob looking a little healthier? His face muscles had relaxed into a shape that was the closest Bernard had ever seen them get to a smile. His watery eyes had the merest suggestion of a gleam, like a dusty light bulb reflected in the dregs of a coffee cup.

'Mind you,' continued Bob, 'they could have been placebos. Market research. They have to do that sort of thing.'

'Bob, you're a complete bastard. You conned me, blackmailed me then betrayed me to Pitmarsh *three fucking times*.'

'I'm a only a drug dealer, Bernard. What do you expect?'

The door to the flat opened and a familiar bespectacled face appeared.

'Back in the land of the living, is it, Bernard? Is he all right, then Bob?'

'Seems OK to me, Dillwyn. I'll be off in a minute. Let you look after him.'

'So what why are you hanging around here anyway, Bob?' said Bernard. 'You've got your money now.'

'Pitmarsh asked me to help you back home. Make sure you were all right. I'll go now your Welsh mate's turned up.'

'Pitmarsh? What the fuck does he want now?'

'He wants me to look after you,' said Bob. 'He likes you now he's got his villain. That's all he wanted. He arrested Pond.'

'He did? How the hell...'

'Insider trading in Peace Derivatives, isn't it?' said Dillwyn as he pulled up a chair and sat down by Bernard's bed. 'Hedging their bets, just like I told you. But I'm proud of you, Bernard, for telling everyone up on the stage. I'm a bit shy for that, see.'

'The stage, yeah... but hang on... no one could hear me... the mike wasn't even plugged in...'

'Pitmarsh heard you,' said Bob as he walked to the door with an unlikely suggestion of a spring in his step. 'He bugged you. Didn't you know that?'

'Pitmarsh bugged me?'

'I think your friend Casper did it for him. Inside that little tin press badge. Picked up everything you said.' Bob opened the door. 'I'm off now. Got business to do. Made a few useful connections yesterday. See you.'

Bernard gave a cursory wave good-bye then turned to Dillwyn. 'Who can you trust these days? Once upon a time the dealers were the good guys. And that bastard Casper! Seems he was working for the police all along.'

'Not really, Bernard. Some of the time he was working for Pond, I reckon.'

'What do you mean?'

'Well, just a theory. You see Casper got you into the Retreat, Casper introduced you to Troy, maybe Casper got you to meet Animal in the first place. Not that Casper knew he was doing all this, of course. But then none of us really knows who we are working for, do we? Don't suppose you thought you'd end up working for the police, did you?'

'Dillwyn, I can't take any more theories...' Bernard breathed in deep then out again and laid back. 'Just get me a cup of coffee. Please.'

'She's making you one. She couldn't find any coffee here so she's gone into my kitchen.'

'She... don't tell me that wretched Mel's still around. Don't think I could cope with her right now.'

'No, not her. She got caught up with the other Tranquility Foundation rioters. Probably spent the night in the cells with all the others.'

'Rioting? You're joking - I thought the nearest those fuckers got to revolt was holding hands and humming out of tune.'

'Have a look at the TV, Bernard. I put it on for you specially. You don't really know what's happened till you see it on the telly these days, do you?'

Bernard sat up and turned towards the small, battered portable television that was playing in the corner with the sound turned down. The news was showing Tranquility Tower, now covered in large red painted crosses, surrounded by well dressed people waving their fists and hurling missiles.

'They'd put all their money into the TF, you see,' continued Dillwyn. 'Must have seemed a good idea at the time. When news got out last night that the stock had crashed they all went a bit crazy, like. They went and stormed Tranquility Tower.'

'Why don't I remember this?'

'Because you were dancing, Bernard,' said Dillwyn as he got up and made his way out of the room.

'Dancing? Me? Oh, yeah... dancing...'

Bernard lay back on his bed again. He had been dancing. Dancing with Animal. She had come back with him. Here. Last night.

Then there, silhouetted in front of him in the doorway holding two mugs of coffee was Animal herself. She was wearing just a large, pale blue T-shirt. The sun behind her was strong enough to reveal the outline of the top of her thighs through the fabric.

'Hey, Bernard. So you got some sleep, then?'

'Yeah, I guess... been dreaming...' he stopped before he got to the words *about you*.

Animal walked towards Bernard, sat down on the edge of the bed and passed him a coffee. 'You heard they arrested Pond?'

Bernard took the cup in both hands and nodded. 'How long have you known?'

'That Pond never believed in the Front? That he set us all up?'

Bernard nodded again.

'Dunno, not long. It was sort of creeping up on me he was using us, just hadn't worked out how.'

'And all that stuff about Kepler and JJ and the retreat?'

'Just trying to work it all out. In the end I thought I'd wait for his plan, whatever it was, to peak. Like I had this feeling he'd get sucked down with it, deep down into all the shit.'

'So what really happened last night?'

'Last night?'

'Yeah.'

She shrugged. 'A couple of months ago Pond saw the TF was doing so well, then he sussed he could make even more by selling short if the stocks were going down. Raise the price by making people feel good, then let it all collapse. He used all that JJ Virtual Infiltration stuff - just plant the idea of bombs, then let everyone else do the work. Start the rumours, wait for the turbulence, then let it tip over into chaos. Make money by letting it all go out of control.

'So that's what happened last night. The credibility systems broke. Some thought there was a real enemy attack, others thought it'd been faked by the government to scare them into submission. Those who weren't frightened went wild. Imagine it, trying to escape a poisoned city in flames and the forces of the state are holding you back. Wind you up a bit, wouldn't it? And even the Tranquility mob -

lost their money then got beaten up by the police - that will have focussed their minds. It's a start.'

'No, I meant you and me. Did we have sex?'

'Like you don't remember?'

'I remember you getting into bed with me... I think... then I remember you coming in just now with a cup of coffee, but the bit in between...'

'It's been cut out?'

'More sort of a dissolve. You know, like in a movie...'

'You'd better cut down on the drugs, Bernard. They're not helping you. There's work to do now.'

'Work?'

'Yeah! Now this world's crumbling, time to start on the new one...' her voice became a whisper. 'Close your eyes - I've got a surprise for you.'

Bernard did as he was told. A few moments later he felt something unbelievably delicate brush his ankles, a wisp of silken feathers accompanied by a gentle vibrating sound. He knew something very special was about to happen. He kept his eyes tight shut, savouring the moment. A tingling sensation moved slowly up his body and he felt a faint warm breath on his cheek.

Bernard slowly opened his eyes. Animal was nowhere to be seen. He turned on his side and saw two liquid green ovals in a sea of darkness. Staring up at him with an expression he knew so well, a look of infinite longing with just an edge of suspicion, was the cat. She'd returned.

The End

www.ingramcontent.com/pod-product-compliance
Lightning Source LLC
Chambersburg PA
CBHW031336170626
46807CB00002B/730